3 8002 021 515

D0314924

CITY OF COVENTRY LIBRARIES
WITHDRAWN
FOR SALE

Debra Webb, born in Alabama, w[...] nine and her first romance at th[...] spent three years working for th[...] Curt[...] [...]ve year stint wit[...] her true calling. A collision course between suspense and romance was set. Since then she has penned nearly a hundred novels. The *Faces of Evil* is her debut thriller series. Visit Debra at www.debrawebb.com

Praise for Debra Webb:

'Webb keeps the suspense teasingly taut, dropping clues and red herrings one after another on her way to a chilling conclusion' *Publishers Weekly*

'Fast-paced, action-packed suspense, the way romantic suspense is supposed to be. Webb crafts a tight plot, a kick-butt heroine, a sexy hero with a past and a mystery as dark as the black water at night' *Romantic Times*

'Romantic suspense at its best' *New York Times* bestselling author Erica Spindler

'Compelling main characters and chilling villains elevate Debra Webb's *Faces of Evil* series into the realm of high-intensity thrillers that readers won't be able to resist' *New York Times* bestselling author C. J. Lyons

'Bestselling author Debra Webb intrigues and tantalizes her readers from the first word' www.singletitles.com

'Masterful edge-of-your-seat suspense' www.aromancereview.com

By Debra Webb and available from Headline

RUTHLESS

DEBRA WEBB

headline

Copyright © 2012 Debra Webb
Excerpt from *Obsession* copyright © 2011 Debra Webb

The right of Debra Webb to be identified as the Author of
the Work has been asserted by her in accordance with the
Copyright, Designs and Patents Act 1988.

Published by Forever Yours in 2012, an imprint of Grand Central Publishing,
part of Hachette Book Group, Inc.

First published in Great Britain in 2013 by
HEADLINE PUBLISHING GROUP

1

Apart from any use permitted under UK copyright law, this publication may
only be reproduced, stored, or transmitted, in any form, or by any means,
with prior permission in writing of the publishers or, in the case of
reprographic production, in accordance with the terms of licences issued by
the Copyright Licensing Agency.

All characters in this publication are fictitious and any resemblance to real
persons, living or dead, is purely coincidental.

Cataloguing in Publication Data is available from the British Library

ISBN 978 1 4722 0702 9

Typeset in Palatino by Avon DataSet Ltd, Bidford-on-Avon, Warwickshire

Pri   plc

Headline's   papers that are natural, renewable and recyclable
        pro   cts and made from wood grown in sustainable forests.
The loggi   nufacturing processes are expected to conform to the

Coventry City Council	
TIL*	
3 8002 02110 515 2	
Askews & Holts	Sep-2013
	£7.99

The saying 'it takes a village' is so true when it comes to our children. From the folks sitting on their front porch in your neighborhood to the clerk behind the counter at the market on the street corner, it takes all of us to look out for the safety of our children. There is nothing more terrifying than when a child goes missing. For all those who pay attention and act when a child is in peril, you are my heroes. You are the people who make the difference. Don't ever stop.

Acknowledgments

Creating a compelling story and bringing a book to life is a considerable and sometimes uphill journey. It takes a number of folks to make the magic happen. From my awesome support team of friends (you know who you are) on the writing end to the fantastic vision of the cover artist (thank you, Kendel Flaum) to my incredible agent (Stephanie Kip Rostan), it takes hard work, dedication, and undying determination. But, along the way, there is one person who literally makes all the difference between a good story and a great one. One person who sees beyond where the story is to where the story could be, and that leap is the most pivotal of all. That one person is a good editor. My heartfelt thanks and immense respect goes to Amy Pierpont, a truly amazing editor.

*I recognize in thieves, traitors, and murderers,
in the ruthless and the cunning, a deep
beauty – a sunken beauty.*

– Jean Genet

Prologue

Birmingham, Monday, August 16, 10.45 P.M.

He waited until well after dark before setting out to do his work. It wasn't a task to be done in the light of day.

No, this rotten burden was best carried out in the dark to hide his shame.

Yet nothing was hidden from God.

He raised his face heavenward. 'I have no choice, Lord. Forgive me.'

He dropped to his knees beneath the burying tree. Thousands of trees stood all around him, but he knew this was the one. He had not visited this secret place in many years, but he knew it by heart. He skimmed the beam of his flashlight over the towering, gnarled Live Oak. Excitement pumped through his veins, and he cursed himself for allowing the vile reaction.

'Satan!' he growled. 'Get thee behind me!'

He ripped open his shirt and reached for the obedience belt he wore. Gritting his teeth, he tightened the wide leather to the next notch. He screamed as the nails dug deeper into his flesh. With small, shallow breaths, he forced his body to relax and savor the agony of his failure.

Hands shaking, he fastened the buttons of his shirt. The sooner he was done with this, the better for all concerned.

He clicked off the light and set it aside. No need for light. The map of his treasures was emblazoned across his soul. He was as familiar with the texture and terrain of this place as he was with his own body.

He swept aside nature's blanket. The heat of dog days had caused the leaves to start to fall earlier than usual, but that was no hindrance. His fingers roved and caressed until he found the spot where he wanted to begin. He lifted the portable spade from his backpack and began the slow, tedious work of moving the rain-softened soil.

'Bless me, Father,' he implored, his teeth clenched against the searing pain of his every move, 'for I have sinned.'

The shaking that had started in his hands traveled throughout his body as his pleading words grew more fervent. *Thirteen years*. Thirteen long years he had abstained from the sweet allure of his one true weakness. No matter how intense the urge, he had remained stoic. His life had changed, and with that change came the

2

necessity to turn aside from the sinful lusting that had haunted him all his days.

Finally, he put the spade aside and closed his eyes. The rest he must do with his bare hands. A renewed thrill dared to trickle through him as the memories of the night he had tucked his prize in this place whispered through his mind. He prayed harder, fought the carnal sensations. He worked his fingers through the earth until he found her. His heart thundered so frantically he wondered if he would survive the coming moments.

He begged for death . . . but it did not come.

There was no choice but to continue.

He lifted the bundle from its earthen cradle, and his chest ached with the sheer effort of breathing. 'Hello, precious one.' Scorching tears flowed down his cheeks as that old craving howled in the deepest recesses of his soul. 'I've missed you so.'

Chapter One

Birmingham Police Department,
Tuesday, August 17, 10.00 A.M.

Her chest too tight for a decent breath, Jess Harris stared at the television mounted on the wall. The images of three young women, brunette and beautiful, remained frozen on the screen. The scroll beneath those bright, smiling faces urged anyone who recognized one or all to contact the FBI's hotline.

Every news channel, website, and newspaper in the state was running the photos. The story, a tragic true-life reality show guaranteed to boost ratings, had been picked up by the national news. Fox, CNN, they all posed to the world the single question that burned in Jess's brain:

Have you seen these women?

The Player had started a new game. And Jess was caught in the middle.

The Bureau was in charge of the case, since it involved their ongoing investigation into the serial killer known as the Player, a sadist who was suspected of having murdered countless young women already. Not to mention the two federal agents he and his protégé, Matthew Reed, had murdered last month.

Damn you, Spears . . . I will get you somehow.

This time the tables were turned. They knew the perpetrator, but they couldn't identify the victims . . . and there was no way to predict when the crime would occur. The Bureau and every law enforcement agency in the state were on alert for a crime that hadn't happened yet.

Jess glanced at her cell phone that lay, oddly silent, on the conference table. Spears had repeatedly turned her life upside down, starting with the demise of her career at the Bureau. And now, the bastard had sent the photos of those three women with a warning that one was about to become his first victim in a new game. Then he'd shut Jess out. She hadn't heard a word from him since the package containing the photos arrived nearly forty-eight hours ago.

Eric Spears, aka the Player. She squared her shoulders and tried to clear the lump from her throat. No one, not even the Bureau, was denying that Spears was the Player now. Didn't matter that Jess had told them weeks ago. She hadn't been able to prove it. So here they were more than a month later, and Spears was out there, free to torture and murder whomever he pleased.

Starting with one of these young women.

Wherever Spears was, rather than communicating with her, he had one of his friends or a hired lackey watching Jess. The texts he'd sent last week proved that much. How else would he know to send *Cheers* when she was having a glass of wine? Or *Bang* right after some creep in a dark Infiniti sedan pretended to take a shot at her? And she couldn't forget the fishing worms someone stashed in the fridge at her apartment. *Are you going to fish or cut bait?*

Spears had gone fishing all right. Jess had to find him . . . before anyone else died.

'Damn it!' She shoved back her chair and stood. She couldn't just sit here.

From his desk, Chief of Police Dan Burnett swung his attention toward her. 'What's wrong?'

God, didn't he get it? Everything was wrong. 'You mean besides the fact that you won't let me out of your sight even to do my job?'

His need to protect her had gone from excessive to completely unreasonable, numerous long and heartfelt talks be damned. No matter how Dan claimed to trust her abilities and instincts, no matter that she had warned him this incessant hovering was making them both look bad to the rest of the department, Spears had made a move and all that had gone out the window.

For the past hour Dan had been going over updates on open cases while she sat here at his conference table pretending to review reports from her detectives on cases she couldn't investigate. She'd closed out the Five investigation yesterday with a full confession from the perpetrators of that travesty. This morning she'd pretty much been twiddling her damned thumbs.

Visibly resigned to a battle, Dan set aside the report he'd been reviewing and pushed back his chair. Those same grim lines he'd been wearing since Sunday were etched even deeper in his face.

Before she could outmaneuver him he stood in front of her, his strong hands curled around her upper arms, making her long to fall against his chest. *Get a grip, Jess.* Just went to show how crazy not being able to do something about Spears or anything else was making her.

'You're worried sick,' he said softly. 'I get that.'

Why the hell did he have to treat her as if she were made of glass? 'No.' Tears stung her eyes, making her all the angrier. 'You do not *get it*. At least one of those girls will die.'

Fear and anger tore at her heart, stealing her voice for a moment. 'She'll be tortured for days . . . until he grows weary of her and then she'll die an ugly, brutal death.' A sharp breath stabbed through Jess. 'And it's all because of me.' Her hand went to her throat as if she could somehow hold back the hurt rising there. '*I* started this.'

She wished his blue eyes didn't reflect so very accurately the fear and pain torturing her. This was ripping him apart, too. 'Gant and his team are doing everything possible to identify and locate those women. They *will* find Spears.'

Jess choked out a laugh. She couldn't help herself; the anguish was giving way to hysteria. 'They won't find him, much less stop him, Dan, you know that.'

This time he looked away. He couldn't deny the truth any more than she could. Her lips started that confounded trembling again, and she couldn't manage to summon the proper words to explain the rest of what needed to be said.

Someone would die *soon* . . . because of her.

Her heart pounded in her ears, ticking off the silent seconds. If he would just back off . . . give her some space . . . so she could do what needed to be done.

'All right.' He exhaled a heavy breath. 'But you will not make a move without Sergeant Harper or Detective Wells right beside you. You will not go home or anywhere else without one of them or without me. Understood?' He shook his head, the look on his face dead serious. 'No exceptions, Jess. No pretending this time that the danger isn't real and imminent.'

Relief rushed through her so hard her knees almost gave way. 'You have my word. You can put a tracking device in my bag. Whatever makes you feel comfortable.' Truth was, that wasn't a bad idea. As desperately as she wanted to do something besides sit here, she understood the danger was all too real. And definitely imminent. As badly as she wanted to stop Spears, she didn't want anyone to die in the process – including her.

The MO he was using this time around was similar to the games he'd played before; he'd simply taken a different and startling new strategy to get from selecting his victim to abducting her. Spears wasn't playing with her this time. Jess sensed that cold, hard fact to the very core of her being. What did a killer who sat at the very top of the most evil scale do for a finale?

'I'm glad you feel that way,' Dan said, hauling her back to the here and now. 'I'm assigning a surveillance detail to you 24/7.'

Daniel Burnett, her friend, lover, and boss – not necessarily in that order – wasn't going to take any chances this go-around. He knew her a little too well. Jess had a habit of going rogue when the need arose.

'Whatever it takes. Cooperation will be my middle name,' she promised. As long as she got to get back to work and out from under his thumb.

He assessed her a moment longer before heading for his desk to put his warning into action. 'You'll keep me apprised of your every move.'

'Absolutely.' She felt like a bird just let out of its cage as she gathered her bag and files. 'I'll head on down to SPU now and let you get back to your work.' The Special Problems Unit and her office was just a short flight of stairs or a brief elevator ride away – the latter being her preferred method of getting from here to there. Four-inch heels and stairs just didn't go well together.

Dan shook his head. 'I'll have Harper come get you.'

Her jaw dropped. She couldn't move about inside the building, for heaven's sake, without an escort? Before she could demand an answer to that question, Burnett – she was too mad now to keep calling him Dan, even in her mind – made the call.

Opting to choose her battles, she snapped her mouth shut and decided that getting her way with Harper would be a whole lot easier than trying to get anything over on Daniel T. Burnett. He was far too hardheaded and impossible to persuade into seeing things her way when any measure of risk was involved.

'Harper's on his way.' He tossed his cell phone back on his desk. 'Don't make me regret this decision, Jess. I'm counting on you not to let me down.'

'I gave you my word.' If her record didn't show otherwise she might be offended. But she had a well-documented history of doing things her own way regardless of instructions from her superiors. 'Besides,' she added with a shrug, 'I've never once disobeyed orders unless it was best for the victim or the case. You can't say otherwise.'

That part was the irrefutable truth.

Even her former employer, the Federal Bureau of

DEBRA WEBB

Investigation, couldn't claim she'd bent – or broken, more often than not – the rules without the best interest of the case at heart. There were some evils out there that simply couldn't be stopped by the book. The Player was one of those.

Fortunately, a rap at the door prevented Dan's pursuit of that topic.

Thank God.

'You wanted to see me, sir?' Harper glanced from Burnett to Jess.

She gave her detective a nod sans the victorious smile now tugging at her lips and waited quietly, obediently, as Dan laid down the law. Her frustration dissipated faster than fog clearing beneath the rising sun as the reality that she was really getting out of this office-turned-prison seeped fully into her veins.

I will get you, Spears.

When Harper had been fully informed of his grave duty, he gave a nod without so much as another glance at Jess. 'I understand, sir.'

Jess was out of the chief of police's office and heading for freedom before Harper could turn around. She bypassed the elevator, since it was monitored by security, and she needed a word with her detective in private. She waited until she and Harper were in the stairwell headed down to SPU before voicing her request.

'I need a disposable phone, Sergeant.'

12

'Something wrong with your phone, ma'am?'

At the door to their floor she gave him a skeptical look. 'You don't want to know the answer to that. Just get me one I can use without anyone tracking it.'

'I'll send Cook to Walmart.'

'Thank you.' She finally let that triumphant smile she'd been holding back make an appearance. 'We have work to do.'

He gave her a nod. 'Yes, ma'am.'

A kind of calm descended and Jess's pulse rate steadied as she entered her own domain. Her small staff waited for her. SPU's team consisted of her and only three others, and the floor space allotted for their offices was just one big room, but it was her unit and she couldn't be happier for some sense of normalcy. The past forty or so hours had been unbearable.

'Good morning, Chief.' Detective Lori Wells looked as relieved to have her back as Jess felt at being here.

More so than anyone else at the BPD, Lori had as much reason as Jess to want Spears caught. His protégé, Reed, had kidnapped and tortured her just to lure Jess into a trap that mercifully fell apart, but not before people died.

'Good morning, Lori.' Jess gave her and then Officer Chad Cook, the youngest of their team, a nod. 'Cook.'

'Ma'am,' Cook greeted. 'We've missed you.'

A statement as simple as that shouldn't have had her struggling to hold a fresh rush of emotion back, but it did.

This was her new home and it felt exactly like that. A mere six months ago she wouldn't have believed she would ever be back in Birmingham feeling like she belonged. But here she was and it felt right.

The television mounted on the wall opposite their case board was running the same news coverage as the one in Burnett's office. Jess hoped someone out there would recognize those three women and call in. Soon. There was no way to know if one or all three were already missing or even where they lived. For now, the Bureau was focused on the state of Alabama, since the package containing the photos had been mailed from Montgomery. But the truth was they had no clue who or where these women were – they had nothing except the photos and the promise of bad things to come.

Spears was too smart to get caught easily. He had no doubt selected very carefully for this pivotal game. Women who were loners, maybe had no families. Women who wouldn't be missed right away. That strategy would buy him the time he wanted to draw out the game.

Every step he took was judiciously calculated for optimal gain and leverage.

While Harper pulled Cook aside to give him his task, Jess parked her stuff on her desk and headed for the case board. Lori, with a manila folder in hand, joined her there.

'I was waiting until you got here to start.' Lori opened the folder and revealed copies of the photos of the unidentified women and a photo of Spears.

The unsavory combo of anxiety, fear, and frustration almost got the better of Jess again. 'Thank you.' She was extremely lucky to have Lori and Harper on her team. Cook, too. The vacant desk reminded her that SPU was a member short since Valerie Prescott had moved on to the Gang Task Force.

A sense of foreboding churned in Jess's belly. Captain Ted Allen, head of Birmingham's Gang Task Force, was still missing. More than a week now. Whatever else she knew, Jess understood with complete certainty that his disappearance had something to do with her. Yet she couldn't connect Allen's disappearance with Spears and his game. Had to be the high-profile Lopez drug case she and Allen had repeatedly butted heads over. Although there was plenty of gossip floating around the station that she'd had something to do with Allen's disappearance. She didn't like the captain, and liked the fact that he may very well have planted a bomb in her car even less, but there was only one man she wanted dead enough to do the deed herself.

Eric Spears.

If she let herself contemplate all that had happened in the last six weeks or so, she might just lose it. After all, what forty-two-year-old woman wouldn't want a serial killer kidnapping innocent women to get her attention and a cop who hated her going missing – after possibly planting a bomb in her department vehicle? Gave new meaning to the term midlife crisis.

'I was thinking about a replacement for Prescott,' Lori said, evidently noting Jess's lingering attention on the vacant desk.

Thankful for the reprieve from the other thoughts, Jess set the self-pity party aside for now. 'I doubt we'll get any cases thrown our way until this –' she blew out a big blast of frustration '– is over, but we do need to fill that vacancy. Who'd you have in mind?'

'Lieutenant Clint Hayes. He's over in Admin right now, but he's been looking for an opportunity to get in the field.'

Jess placed the photo of Spears on the case board. She hated those pale blue eyes of his. Not the same deep, true blue of Dan's. Spears's were that pale, ghostly color that warned pure evil thrived beneath them. 'Give me some stats on Hayes.'

'Thirty-four. Single. Went to Samford. Finished law school with high honors but opted not to go that route. Instead he hired on with the BPD.'

Jess stalled before getting the final photo on the board. 'Decided he'd rather be one of the good guys, is that it?'

Lori gave a halfhearted shrug. 'Something like that.'

There was more to this story. 'Something like what . . . exactly?'

'There was a morals issue in the background check,' Harper chimed in from his desk.

With the last photo in place Jess turned to her senior detective. 'What kind of morals issue?'

'The state bar association discovered he had worked his way through college' – Harper strolled up, hands in pockets and wearing a smirk – 'as a gigolo. They refused to certify his character.'

A frown puckered her eyebrows. Jess rubbed at what would end up another wrinkle if she didn't stop the habit. A *gigolo*? Do tell. 'Evidently he was never arrested for solicitation.' That kind of mark on his record would have kept him off the force as well.

'Never,' Lori confirmed. 'Character references killed his chances with the state bar association – a couple of his own friends ratted him out. Cost him his chosen career and the city one hell of a sharp attorney.'

'Good Lord.' Jess looked from one detective to the other, certain she had misheard. 'You're telling me the bar association ignored his superior academic prowess and refused to admit him because he'd worked as a man-whore?' She could think of far worse things lawyers did every day, and it rarely got them disbarred.

'I'm telling you' – Harper chuckled – 'that the BPD hired him *because* he was a manwhore.'

Now Jess was really confused.

'It was the mayor's idea,' Lori interjected, wearing her own smirk now. 'Rumor was that Clint's little black book included Mayor Pratt's wife's name.'

17

In spite of the insanity going on around her, Jess had to laugh. Seemed like for all their old money and power the mayor's family and friends just couldn't resist dancing around the dark side. And in the South, even in a city the size of Birmingham, everyone who was anyone knew everyone else. 'Don't you just love small-town justice?'

Harper leaned in closer. 'You think he called up Mayor Pratt and asked for a favor, or do you think the mayor's wife took care of it for him?'

'Good question.' Jess cleared her throat. 'If the two of you think Hayes would prove an asset to our cozy little group, I'm fine with a probationary period.' She wouldn't mention the idea that having a little dirt on the mayor would make her immensely happy. 'Talk to him,' she said to Lori. 'If he's agreeable and Burnett approves it, we'll bring him over as soon as possible.'

Before Jess turned her attention back to the case board she wanted one more administrative issue out of the way, since their youngest member was out of the room. 'We need to start grooming Cook for the detectives' exam.'

'I can handle that,' Harper offered.

'Excellent.' Whether or not Cook got a promotion wasn't such a priority right now, but Jess needed to hang on to a few threads of normalcy. Spears was doing all within his power to take that from her.

Ruthless, that was what he was. Ruthless and pure evil. If she had her way he would die screaming.

Satisfaction warmed her heart. *Oh yes. I will get you this time.*

'Your realtor called.' Lori hitched her head toward Jess's desk. 'There's a message. Something about the last week of September for the closing date on your house.'

There was another normalcy Jess had been hoping for. It also meant she only had to pay one more house payment before that burden was lifted. There would be some fees involved with the sell, but her equity in the house would take care of that.

'I'll give her a call back later today.' Jess realized then that both detectives were staring at her. 'Oh, sorry. With all that happened, I forgot to tell you. My house in Virginia finally sold. Full asking price.' Thank God for that last part. 'The call came Sunday afternoon just before' – she gestured to the board – 'this happened.' A splinter of fear needled its way back into her chest.

You have to do something, Jessie Lee. Something that will stop him in his tracks. Fast.

'So.' She walked to her desk to prowl for her glasses. 'The hotlines have no confirmed leads on the identities of these women.'

'A few callers,' Harper said, 'insist they've seen one or the other around their hometown but they don't know their names. Most of the calls are coming from the Montgomery and Mobile areas.'

'The FBI's adding an additional layer to the searches in

those towns, but it's like the proverbial needle in the haystack,' Lori added.

'No matches to Alabama driver's licenses?' Glasses in place, Jess moved back to the case board.

Harper hummed a note of regret. 'Nothing yet.'

There was no way to know how much time they had before Spears took the next step, but Jess suspected it wouldn't be enough. 'These women are the right age to be college students. Maybe students from other states. That could explain why we didn't get a hit with the DMV.' Damn it. Or new residents of Alabama who hadn't had time to make all the documentation changes.

'The FBI is checking all databases at their disposal,' Lori mentioned.

That was something. But unless these women had passports or had committed a felony, they wouldn't likely be in any of those databases.

Across the room Jess's cell clanged. Wouldn't be Dan. If there was a new development he would just appear at the door. Maybe Lily had news. Her sister was pretty frustrated with the inability of her doctors to figure out what was going on with all these crazy symptoms plaguing her. Jess was damned frustrated herself. Her sister had always been as healthy as a horse. The concept of a serious health issue just didn't seem possible.

'Carry on,' Jess suggested to her detectives, as she hurried back to her desk.

Lori created the time line and added the notes Harper recommended. The two had been dating for a few weeks now, and thankfully so far the fledgling relationship hadn't affected their work in any way. Jess hoped it stayed that way. She knew from experience it wasn't an easy balancing act to sustain.

At her desk she picked up her cell and frowned at the screen. Why would Gina Coleman be calling her? Jess had nothing on the Spears case to give Birmingham's favorite reporter. As far as Jess was concerned, after the business with the Five case the two of them were even on who owed whom what.

'Harris.'

'You need to get over here, Harris. *Now.*'

Adrenaline kicked Jess's heart back into that same frantic pace she'd been suffering most waking hours since Sunday afternoon. 'What's going on?'

'A package was left with the receptionist at the studio. It's addressed to me but there's a message on the inside flap that says I should give it to *you*. I don't know what it is, but it smells dead.'

Chapter Two

Channel Six Studios, 12.45 P.M.

The fact that he was the chief of police with a job to do gave Dan no comfort when what he wanted right now more than anything in this world was to protect Jess from opening that damned bundle.

Every part of him howled with the need to do this himself, but Jess would never stand for it and with a unit from the Bomb Squad as well as a dozen other cops including evidence techs standing by, he couldn't exactly argue with his newest deputy chief.

Deputy Chief Jess Harris had a job to do, too.

The building had been evacuated of Channel Six personnel, including Gina Coleman, who had argued the edict all the way out the door. The experts had examined the box intended for Jess and pronounced it free of incendiary materials and other destructive substances.

That assessment made the package's contents no less explosive.

Bones.

After a thorough analyzing, including digital X-rays and probing, the contents were deemed skeletal remains wrapped in disintegrating burlap and plastic.

Once placed on a trace sheet to ensure no evidence was lost, the bundle had been removed from the cardboard shipping box. With Harper standing on one side and an evidence tech on the other, Jess carefully opened the bundle of fabric. Dan and the rest of those gathered stayed back. The fewer bodies crammed around that table, the less likelihood of contaminating whatever evidence the package contained or represented.

The Channel Six security video showed the delivery was made to the station via UPS just after ten that morning. Detective Wells and Officer Cook had interviewed the clerks at the originating UPS Store. One clerk remembered the guy, who'd given his name as Smith Johnson. Johnson was old with thick-lensed glasses, thin gray hair, and a walking cane. His long sleeves and gloves despite the August heatwave hadn't triggered the usual alarms. The clerk figured he was just an old man trying to avoid sun exposure.

The return address Johnson gave was just as bogus as the name he'd used.

Detective Wells was standing by at the UPS Store for a copy of the video footage from the security system.

A new rush of frustration rammed Dan. What the hell was Spears up to now? Had he dared to disguise himself and waltz into that store right here in Birmingham so he could personally mail this package to Jess? Wasn't it enough that he was torturing her with potential victims?

More outrage threatened to consume Dan whenever he thought of the SOB, and it had to be wrestled back. If he was going to be any good to Jess or this department, he had to keep his emotions in check.

Harper and Jess exchanged a look, and Dan's attention zeroed back in on the here and now. 'Chief,' Harper said with a grim look in Dan's direction, 'you should call Deputy Chief Black.'

Black? Why would they need another cop on the scene? To hell with it. Dan strode to the table. Harper pointed to the newspaper article preserved in a small plastic sleeve that he had placed on the trace sheet next to pieces of crumpled newspaper and ragged burlap along with the first of several small human bones.

SEARCH CONTINUES FOR MISSING CHILD.

Recognition slammed Dan in the gut, and the blood in his veins went cold. *Dorie Myers.* 'Jesus Christ.'

Jess stared up at him, her face showing the same shock and confusion he felt. 'Do you know the name?'

The dread resonating in her voice made what he had to

say all the more difficult. 'A third grader who went missing twelve . . .' he shook his head '. . . no, thirteen years ago.'

'The Man in the Moon,' Harper said quietly.

God Almighty, this would rip open old wounds in this community that went back decades.

Jess's breath caught. 'Oh my God. I remember that case.'

Though she hadn't lived here for the past twenty years she would remember the case from before . . . when she was a kid. Just as Dan did. Like anyone who had resided in or around Birmingham in those days would. He'd been almost ten when the first little girl went missing. His heart felt like a massive rock in his chest.

Twenty little girls had gone missing and were dubbed victims of the so-called Man in the Moon. For two decades he had struck every fall on the night of the harvest moon, like clockwork, and then, thirteen years ago, he suddenly stopped . . . with Dorie Myers.

This wasn't Spears's kind of evil, but it was the work of an equally ruthless monster.

BPD Conference Room, 4.00 P.M.

Mayor Joseph Pratt and all the division deputy chiefs lined the long table in the center of the room. The somber sound of Black's voice filled the heavy air. Dan's mind still reeled with this latest turn of events.

Deputy Chief Harold Black headed up Crimes Against Persons. Kidnappings and murders fell under his domain. For nine years after making detective with the Birmingham Police Department, Black had worked the Man in the Moon case. He knew the case. Knew the families involved. Had suffered as much as anyone when the monster couldn't be found.

Dan stretched his neck and attempted to stay focused on Harold's briefing. The man was not going to like it when he got the news that this case would not be his this time.

But the cold, hard truth was that all of Harold's experience with the case couldn't trump Jess's uncanny instincts when it came to hunting down killers like the Man in the Moon. This killer or someone who knew him had reached out to Jess, so assigning SPU to handle the investigation was the only reasonable move. SPU had been created for precisely this sort of case. Equally important was the fact that Dan needed Harold working with the FBI on the Spears case as well as leading the investigation on Ted Allen's disappearance. Harold couldn't argue that rationale.

But he would.

'Why "Man in the Moon"?' Wells asked. 'Was it because the missing children attributed to him all disappeared during a full moon?'

'That was part of it.' Harold stood in front of an elaborate case board he had put together in record time for this briefing. Photos of all twenty children suspected to be related to the case lined the board.

'Each year for approximately two decades a female child between the ages of seven and nine went missing on the night of the harvest or hunter's moon, the full moon nearest the autumnal equinox,' he explained. 'That particular full moon always seems closer to the earth. At some point there was a comment in the media about how it was almost as if the moon got so close to the earth that the man living there reached down and snatched a human child so he wouldn't have to live alone.' Harold shrugged. 'The legend stuck and the unknown perpetrator has been referred to in that way since.'

'Has this sudden delivery after all these years,' Mayor Pratt spoke up, 'given us new evidence as to the identity of the monster we're looking for?'

'Not yet, sir,' Harold admitted, 'but our forensics personnel are still analyzing evidence. We hope to have something soon.'

Pratt grunted. 'What do you propose to announce to the press?' he inquired with blatant skepticism. 'This won't stay under wraps long, I can guarantee you that. People have waited a very long time to know what happened to these children.' He surveyed the table, his attention landing lastly on Dan. 'This department has enjoyed a lengthy reprieve from this monster but the people, particularly the families still seeking closure for their immense losses, will demand action. How do you intend to handle that, Chief Burnett?'

'This department,' Dan said emphatically, 'will do what it always does – everything possible to find the person or persons responsible for these despicable acts. As soon as the remains are officially identified, the family will be contacted and we'll make an announcement to the press. I hope to do that by six this evening.'

Pratt gave him a look that suggested he wasn't convinced, then he shifted his holier-than-thou regard to the next unexpected aspect of this development. 'Why was this package sent to Harris?' he asked, as if she weren't in the room and he wasn't looking straight at her. 'She had nothing to do with this case. She wasn't even here for the better part of the time frame we're looking at.'

Before Dan could suggest there was rarely any logic to the acts of a deranged killer, Harold interjected, 'I'm certain Chief Harris's recent notoriety has garnered his attention. Sociopaths and psychopaths often crave that sort of attention. He most likely feels a connection of sorts with Chief Harris.' Harold presented an indulgent smile to Jess. 'No offense intended, of course.'

'None taken,' Jess assured him. 'I'm sure you'll have your own fan club one day.'

Dan scrubbed a hand over his jaw, mostly to cover

the smile her comeback aroused but also to prevent telling Harold to sit down and shut up. 'Considering his probable age' – Dan directed this at Harold – 'it's possible he's suffering health issues and has decided to reveal himself through the highest-profile deputy chief in the department.'

Harold's posture stiffened. One day the man would learn to play nice with Jess.

'I hate to disagree with the two of you,' Jess said, as she divided her attention between them, 'but I sincerely doubt either of those scenarios.'

Silence expanded in the room. Just like old times. What was a briefing without a standoff between Jess and Harold? Or Jess and everyone else in the room, for that matter? How that made him love her all the more was a mystery.

'Well,' Harold said, waving his hand in invitation, 'I'm quite certain we'd all like to hear your analysis, Chief Harris.'

'Since I had little time to review the case, my impressions are based primarily on what I've heard here today.' Jess adjusted her glasses and surveyed the case board. 'If these abductions, only one each year over a two-decade span, are indeed the work of a single perpetrator, then he is incredibly disciplined. He has likely led a normal life within the community. Married with kids and grandchildren.' She shrugged. 'He has shown no desire to draw attention to his work in the past. If all the cases are indeed connected to him and he's still alive—'

'They are all connected to him,' Harold interrupted.

'By date alone?' Jess challenged. 'How many other children went missing during those same years? Children of the same age group,' she pressed, 'and with no clues left behind as to why they were taken? Timing alone is a skimpy link, Chief.'

'Your points carry merit,' Harold agreed, his back still ramrod straight and his expression no less skeptical of Jess's opinion.

Dan waited for the other shoe to drop.

'But only one child in a one-hundred-mile radius around this city went missing precisely on the night of the harvest moon each and every one of those years. Coincidence?' He held his hands out, palms up. 'Perhaps.'

Jess acknowledged his move with a dip of her head. 'Then again, after the third or fourth year, the media made a big to-do about the harvest moon connection. Copycats love to capitalize on that kind of attention.' She looked around the table, confident in her assessment. 'Whatever we think we know, it's our job to dig deeper and find the elements that connect the victims to the person or persons who chose that date to do his dirty little deeds. Bottom line, we need a motive. Was he lonely? Satisfying sadistic sexual urges? Are we dealing with one perpetrator or several? Can we adequately connect all of those cases?

We have a lot of questions and not nearly enough answers.'

While Jess and Harold continued their debate, Harper slipped out of the room. Dan's instincts went on point. He hoped the detective was seeking privacy for an update from the forensic techs. They could damn sure use a break about now. So far they had three decades of nothing except missing little girls and no clues.

'Who's lead on this case?' Pratt demanded, evidently weary of the back-and-forth between the deputy chiefs. He glared at Dan. 'We need forward momentum, not this pointless rehashing and butting of heads.'

'I couldn't agree more.' Dan had intended to discuss this with Harold in private. So much for keeping the peace in the department. Since all eyes shifted to Dan, there was no getting around making that announcement here and now.

The door opened and Harper returned. He walked straight to Dan and passed a note before taking his seat.

As he read the words Harper had scrawled on the page, Dan's throat went dry.

He'd read the words twice before the silence in the room dragged him from the haze of disbelief. 'The forensic techs have been analyzing and dissecting the packaging used for delivering the remains to Channel Six. The perp left us a note by circling letters and words on the pages of the newspapers.'

31

Reluctance and more of that frustration coiled deep in his gut. *'Hello, Jess.'* Dan's gaze connected with hers. *'We're all waiting for you to find us.'*

The pain on Jess's face ripped open his chest a little wider. How the hell could this happen? Another killer wanted to play games with her?

'How do you intend to proceed, Chief Harris?' Pratt demanded. 'Obviously the decision as to who will be lead on this case has been made. This monster wants *you* to find him and his victims.'

'This year's harvest moon will be on September nineteenth,' Detective Wells offered when no one else in the room seemed able to find their voice.

Before Jess could answer, Tara Morgan cracked the door open and stuck her head in the room. Dan motioned for her to come on in as the debate between Harold and Jess reignited, a little hotter this time. Tara lingered near the door rather than coming to the table, the signal loud and clear. She had news to relay that she didn't want the others to hear. Dan didn't bother excusing himself from the table. He doubted anyone would notice.

As soon as he reached her, Tara leaned close and whispered, 'Chief, there are . . .' she chewed her lip a second before she said the rest '. . . *people* in the lobby demanding to see you. I told them you were in a briefing, but they won't take no for an answer.'

'People?' Confusion jumped into the mix of frustration

and worry churning inside him. 'Reporters?'

Tara shook her head. 'Parents of some of the –' she nodded toward the case board '– children.'

A press briefing was tentatively scheduled for six. Nothing about this investigation was supposed to be released to the public until then. A wave of fury gave his gut a twist. 'How many, Tara? How many parents are we talking about?'

'Four.' She gave him the names.

'Okay. Show them to my office.' His cell vibrated. Bloody hell. If there was more news like this he could do without it. 'I'll be there as soon as I can,' he assured her.

To tell them what?

The cell phone in his pocket started that damned vibrating again. He checked the screen. *Gina*. She'd better have one hell of an excuse for this breach of trust.

It was one thing to hold a press briefing to inform the public that remains from a cold case had been discovered and to assure the citizens that the BPD was on top of the matter. It was entirely another to inform the parents of victims before remains were properly identified. Gina had given her word that she wouldn't release a word until he gave her the go-ahead.

Now he would have to deliver the heartbreaking news that they had nothing . . . except the promise of more anguish to come.

Chapter Three

City Records, 5.30 P.M.

'Here we go.' Lori rolled the library-style ladder to the row of upper shelves where she'd spotted the boxes marked with the case number corresponding to the Man in the Moon investigation.

Jess counted off the number of boxes involved. *Holy cow!* 'We may need a truck or at least a couple more strong backs.' Since the case was officially hers, she wanted all the background material she could get her hands on.

Lori lowered the first box to her. 'Only twenty more to go.'

Jess started a stack on the floor. 'Do you remember watching these cases play out in the media?' Jess vividly recalled the disappearances that happened while she was in grade school and junior high. She didn't remember the first one at all. Her parents had just died in a car crash and she and Lil were stuck living with their Aunt Wanda. Between grieving for their parents, the men coming and going at all hours, and finding Wanda passed out on the floor every morning when they readied for school, it wasn't exactly a charmed childhood.

Later Jess had wondered if the little girls who went away with the Man in the Moon were happy. Sometimes, during their stay at one foster home or another, she'd wished she and Lily could just disappear like that. She shuddered. Those little girls needed to be found. A big breath filled her lungs. *We're all waiting for you to find us.* She could not let them down.

'I remember my mom being terrified whenever September rolled around,' Lori said, 'especially after my dad died. She didn't let me and my sister out of her sight. The disappearances stopped when I was twelve. Eventually, it seemed everyone forgot about the Man in the Moon.'

Except the parents of the missing children. Poor Dan was dealing with some of them right now. That was the hardest part of a case like this.

'Are you worried he'll try to get close to you? Like Spears?' Lori asked, her voice heavy with concern.

Jess had thought about that the past couple of hours. 'I suppose he already has, in a way. He's been watching me, apparently.'

One of the things she tried to do, for her own sanity,

was to avoid thinking about how the evil out there looked at her. 'He can watch me all he wants and get as close as he dares, as long as he doesn't start obsessing on little girls again.'

That was the critical aspect of this new case. The Man in the Moon hadn't suddenly reemerged for no reason. He had an agenda. It was the prospect of where that agenda went from here that scared her to death.

A few more boxes made their way to the stack on the floor before Lori asked the question Jess had been expecting for the past two days.

'Do you think Spears is here?'

That was another million-dollar question. Despite having considered that scenario at length, thinking about it now had knots twisting in her belly. 'I can't say for sure.' She settled another box on the floor. 'What I can say with absolute certainty is that he has someone watching me and the people closest to me.' She held Lori's gaze as she reached for the next box. 'Don't let your guard down, Lori. Not for a minute.'

'Don't worry,' she promised. 'I have no intention of letting that bastard or one of his followers get close to me again. Once was more than enough.'

With the final box on the floor, Lori climbed down the ladder. Jess surveyed the stack. 'We need Cook and Harper and a hand truck to get these over to SPU.'

Lori slid her phone from her pocket. 'I'll tell them

to grab any warm bodies they can find and get over here.'

Jess searched for the boxes containing the most recent files. The perp had started with the last case. She lifted the lid from the Dorie Myers investigation.

'The guys are heading this way.'

'Great. Thanks.' Jess thumbed through the reports. The Bureau had provided a profile on the unknown subject. That should be interesting. The official BPD reports were signed off on by Deputy Chief Black. Some were completed by . . . *Buddy Corlew*, former BPD detective.

'Well, well,' Jess noted, mostly to herself. 'My old friend Corlew was involved in this case.' The guy who tried to use her to get back at Dan back then and who had just recently stuck his nose into the Five case. The same old friend who, since his fall from grace with the Birmingham Police Department, appeared determined to make the BPD look bad. Or maybe he just wanted to annoy Dan now that Jess was back in town.

'That should make things interesting,' Lori stated.

Just last week Corlew had insisted BPD had fallen down on the job twelve years ago when investigating the death of a young man named Lenny Porter. The idea that the truth Jess uncovered had lent some credibility to Corlew's charges had done nothing but inflate his already oversized ego.

If he got wind of the reopening of this case, and he

would, he'd be right back on that anti-BPD bandwagon again.

'Let's just hope no one has to die before he cooperates with us this time.'

9911 Conroy Road, 11.05 P.M.

Two boxes emptied of their contents sat on the floor in front of the sofa. A few feet away piles of timeworn folders surrounded Jess. Her legs ached from sitting cross-legged for better than two hours, and she was far from finished.

She hadn't brought all the files from the Man in the Moon investigation home, just the meat from the most recent cases. Interviews with family and friends. Forensic reports. Photos of the children and their bedrooms, which was the last place each little girl was seen the night they disappeared. Exterior photos of the bedroom windows and other access points for each family home.

If one perpetrator was indeed responsible for the twenty abductions attributed to the Man in the Moon, he hadn't screwed up even once, it seemed. Each child was taken in the middle of the night. For those who had them, family dogs never sounded an alarm. Neighbors hadn't witnessed a single thing. No sign of forced entry.

'Just like Peter Pan.' The visitor came, and the children appeared to have left with him of their own free will. Just unlocked the window and flew off with the Man in the Moon. The way she and Lil as kids had dreamed of escaping.

Only those sweet little girls hadn't escaped . . . they had been taken by an evil not a soul had seen coming.

She needed more coffee.

Groaning, Jess pushed her aching body off the floor. There was a time when her body wouldn't have grumbled so at being abused this way. Evidently that time had passed. These days she felt every ache and pain of getting the job done. She cut herself some slack – she'd had almost no sleep in the past forty-eight hours. She and Lori had hefted old case file boxes until they were ready to drop. Mainly . . . she was just weary of running in circles to stop Spears, and now this case that had baffled BPD for three decades was active again.

No use whining. What she needed was coffee. At the counter she twirled the nifty display rack until she decided on a blend of coffee, then she popped it into her single-cup brewer. She stretched her back and shoulders and promptly changed her mind. What she really needed was a long, hot bath and then a serious massage. A hot, sweat-inspiring series of images flashed through her weary brain. Dan making love to her . . . showering together . . . more lovemaking.

Her achy body, along with her sluggish pulse, reacted instantly.

The way she felt tonight, they wouldn't even have to take their clothes off. A good neck rub would work just fine for sending her over the moon – no pun intended.

That was the problem. Whenever she and Dan spent too much time alone – and she was weak, considering this insanity with Spears – they ended up breaking the rules of their working relationship. She was happy with where she'd landed careerwise. Dan had made her a good offer – one she hadn't been able to refuse. But that made him her boss. For propriety's sake rules were essential. Their personal relationship could not interfere with work. And until they worked out where exactly that relationship was going, flaunting it publicly was a huge no-no. The last thing either of them needed was for anyone in the department to latch on to the idea that she'd gotten the job because of their personal relationship or that she got any sort of preferential treatment *ever*.

Case in point: his incessant need to protect her. She was a big girl. A deputy chief, for heaven's sake. She could protect herself just like all his other deputy chiefs. Still, she was no fool. Eric Spears represented a serious threat. Just last week, she'd gotten a state-of-the-art security system installed along with nifty little motion sensors on the stairs leading up to her door. Add to that the top-of-the-line deadbolt and the Glock she kept under her pillow, and no one was getting near, much less into, her apartment without her knowing it and their regretting it.

God, how could her life be such a hot mess? Her lover was her boss. Her biggest nightmare was some malignant narcissistic freak who got off on torturing and murdering women, and now she'd gotten another admirer pretty much just like Spears, only this one targeted helpless children.

And that didn't even count the stone-cold reality that she was days late on her period – which was the reason she was having coffee instead of wine – or the scary-as-hell fact that her sister was suffering from some weird health issue the doctors couldn't yet diagnose.

With all that going on, how in the world could she be standing here fantasizing about neck rubs from her boss/lover? Not to mention if she was pregnant – she cringed – that would mean Dan was a father.

'Oh God.' She rubbed at her skull with her fingers to relax the tense muscles there.

Everything was out of control.

The decadent smell of a gourmet dark blend called Caramel Drizzle helped put those unpleasant thoughts out of her head. The warm mug felt good in her hands. There wasn't time right now to worry about personal problems. She had a very old, damned cold case to solve.

'If we're lucky it'll stay cold,' she grumbled.

Feet shuffling across the wood floor, she refused to consider the other option. If something had roused this killer's evil urges, he could be planning to strike again.

'One month.' The thought made her stomach roil. Thirty or so days from now there would be a harvest moon. Finding him before that was imperative.

An alarm chime, set to go off when someone started up the stairs toward her apartment door, jarred Jess from the troubling thought and sent a spike of fear right through her chest. Heart pumping, she almost dropped her mug of coffee getting to the small monitor that showed the landing outside her door. No matter that a cop was watching her apartment above a kindly old man's garage and that she had the fancy new high-tech security system, the reality was Spears had walked right up to the car of one of her former Bureau colleagues and slit his throat.

She had a new motto where safety was concerned: always be smart and never underestimate pure evil.

Harper.

A couple of deep steadying breaths were required before she got her fingers working well enough to release the locks. The instant her door was open he visually sized her up as if he'd feared the worst, just because she couldn't get the door open the first time he knocked. God, they were all on edge.

Pull it together. *Smile.* That she was barefoot and sported lounge pants and a baggy tee was no reason to feel embarrassed with Harper. 'Sergeant. What brings you out at this hour?'

'May I come inside, ma'am?'

Anticipation had her pulse picking up speed again. 'Is everything all right?' She backed up to allow him inside.

He waited until the door was closed and locked behind him. 'I did what you asked.'

The air in her lungs felt abruptly too thick to exhale. 'You sent the message?'

He nodded. 'The response came maybe twenty minutes ago.'

Jess hated to ask this next question but it was essential. 'Did you tell anyone else?'

He shook his head, regret on his face and in his posture. Jess understood she was asking a lot. Keeping this from Lori was difficult for him. For Jess, too. Detective Lori Wells had become a very close friend.

'What'd you tell her?' Lori was no fool. She would understand something was up with him coming over here at this hour.

'She went to see that new chick flick everyone's talking about with her mom and sister. They missed the seven o'clock showing, since we were at the office late, so she won't be home for a while. Today's her mom's birthday. They decided on a girls' night out.'

Jess nodded. 'I see.' She imagined Harper did as well. Her mom's birthday or no, Lori obviously needed girl time with the two women closest to her, probably to discuss her relationship with the man closest to her.

That wasn't necessarily a bad thing, but the two were

43

moving a little fast, in Jess's opinion. Like she had any room to talk. Just last week she and Dan had confessed their love for each other. They'd both known it was there, but somehow it was different saying it out loud, face-to-face.

As life-altering as that moment had been, there was no place for the distraction just now. Spears had responded to the message she'd had Harper send.

Three more seconds elapsed before Jess had the nerve to hold out her hand for the phone. The hesitation made her all the more furious at herself, but she was flat out worried. No point kidding herself. She was damned worried about what Spears would do next . . . and about this other monster who'd latched onto her recent infamy.

More than anything else she was terrified for three young women who might very well have no idea that one of them was about to become the main character in a terrifying and lethal game.

Holding her breath, Jess tapped the necessary functions and read the two text messages.

Why waste your time with more games, Eric? Let's do this.

Since Jess had been stuck with Dan and Black until she'd come home two hours ago, she'd asked Harper to send the text to the only contact number she had for Spears. Her detective hadn't liked it one bit, but he'd known she would find a way to do it herself if he refused her request.

Truth was, Harper had his own reasons for wanting the Player. Spears's protégé, Matthew Reed, had almost killed Lori. Harper had a big stake in this game, too.

Braced for another disturbing layer to this nightmare, she read the response from Spears:

Your impatience intrigues me, but this game is for you, Jess. Hold on, it's going to be a thrilling ride!

'Son of a bitch.' Jess struggled not to lose it in front of Harper. If she'd ever wanted to kill another human being in cold blood she had no recall of the time. She wanted to kill Spears. She wanted to watch him die, a slow merciless death by her hand.

'What now?' Harper's voice was strained with a fury he visibly struggled to conquer.

Anything she did carried some amount of risk. But she had to do something. 'I can taunt him with this new interest from the Man in the Moon in hopes he'll get jealous and make a move to take me out of this other perp's reach.'

That fury flattening his lips now, Harper shook his head. 'This is wrong, ma'am. You're taking too big a risk.'

'What should I do then, Sergeant? Tell me.' She almost sloshed coffee before she remembered the mug in her hand. The anxiety crushing her rib cage prohibited an adequate breath. 'How do I get his attention? Divert his path? Because if I don't figure out a way to intercept his plan, one of those women' – she pointed to the duplicate case board she'd created on her apartment wall – 'is going to pay for my lack of ingenuity.'

Harper took the coffee from her and carried it to the sink. Jess tore off her glasses and rubbed her eyes. She fought for the calm that had totally evaded her since the arrival of that damned package containing the photos.

As if he understood she needed a moment to pull it together, Harper steered her to the sofa and ushered her down. He sat beside her and waited a minute or two before he spoke. 'So what do we do?'

Jess stared at the prepaid phone in her hand and struggled to find the right words. Slowly she tapped the impotent letters into the text box. 'How about this?'

I'm a little busy with a new case. You aren't the only admirer of my work.

Harper read the warning. 'What if instead of coming after you, he just speeds up the game he's already set in motion?'

Pointing out the rest wasn't necessary. Jess glanced back at the photos on her wall. Three beautiful young women who had done nothing to deserve this. God knew this sort of push-the-killer strategy she was contemplating had backfired on her before.

'Thank you, Sergeant.' She deleted the words. 'You're right. You can't second-guess a psychopath. You'll lose every time.' She typed in a new message and then hit

Send. 'Okay.' She handed the phone back to Harper. 'You can dispose of that. I won't need it anymore.'

Harper read the message she'd sent. Simple and to the point:

I can't wait to watch you die, Eric. See you soon.

'Ma'am, I really am concerned about how this is going to end. What if we can't protect you? Or anyone else in his path?'

Jess mustered up a smile for him. 'I'm going to end this, Sergeant. The only variable is whether or not I can get the job done before he kills again.' If she accomplished nothing else before she took her last breath, she would get this done. She understood part of Harper's fear was for Lori. Being Jess's friend could be hazardous.

According to Agent Gant, her former boss at the Bureau and the man in charge of the Spears investigation, there was evidence the Player had slipped back into the country. He could be anywhere . . . right outside watching the cop who was watching her, for that matter.

Dear God, what if she was pregnant? That was another life she needed to protect.

Don't borrow trouble, Jess.

Harper gestured to the stacks of files on the floor. 'How you coming with this one?'

Jess took her place on the floor once more and picked up the file she'd reviewed last. 'The idea that this perp was able to get his hands on each child without obvious breaking and entering, without confrontation, and without anyone seeing him makes me believe he's a familiar.'

Harper joined her on the floor. Jess resisted the urge to grin at how totally uncomfortable he looked sitting there in that suit with one leg curled under him and the other bent for an arm prop. 'None of the families are connected – at least not in any way that was discovered in previous investigations. Different neighborhoods, schools, churches. Nothing in common at all was found.'

'The investigative work was relatively thorough.' She couldn't deny Black and his predecessor had done a pretty damned good job. 'But there will be something, Sergeant. We just haven't found it yet.'

'Like the girls, Andrea and the others, who were abducted by the Murphys?'

That was the case that had brought Jess back to Alabama – back to Dan. 'Yes, exactly like that. This unknown perp saw these children somewhere. Watched them. Maybe even interacted with them. Typically, a hunter has a preferred territory – a comfort zone. The Man in the Moon will have had a place he felt confident doing his hunting. That's the connection. All we have to do is find it.'

'Before September nineteenth,' he suggested.

'Preferably.' If his past record was any indication, once he'd taken the child there was little hope of stopping him or saving the child. Then again, they had only one set of remains. There was no way to be certain what had become of the other children. So far the remains, presumed to be Dorie Myers, had told them nothing as to the manner of death. However the little girl died, she hadn't suffered any broken bones. Still, there was a whole array of other ways to die that included tremendous suffering.

Not to mention the fear the child must have felt.

Jess shuddered inside.

She felt bad for Dan that he'd had to face those parents only to tell them basically nothing. And then to do the same in the press conference. But it was the truth. They had nothing, and until those remains were officially identified there was nothing to tell other than that some freak had decided to play with the department's newest deputy chief.

Sucked to be popular.

'Why reach out to you, Chief?' Harper thumbed through a file. 'After all these years of silence, why now? Why you?'

She considered his questions. They'd talked about this in the briefing, but Harper wanted her gut instinct. Problem was, she didn't have much of one yet.

Jess hunched her shoulders, let them drop. 'I wish I could answer those questions, but I don't have enough information to create an accurate assessment. Burnett could be right in that the perp is ill and wants to be caught.

Sometimes they want someone to stop them but this guy appears to have stopped himself. The one thing I can say with real accuracy at this point is that there's been some sort of change, more than once, in his life. First, there was a major change that prompted him to stop killing, assuming he has. Something else has occurred more recently to prompt his coming out like this.'

'Maybe he was in prison? Or maybe he lived somewhere else for a while.'

'Prison is a possibility,' Jess agreed. 'But if he lived somewhere else and continued his same pattern of abductions, we'd likely know about it. There'd be something in one database or another.'

'Yeah, I did a search on similar cases,' Harper said, sounding as dejected as Jess felt. 'I didn't find anything relevant.'

'Changing an MO isn't entirely unheard of.' But Jess knew the stats. 'It's highly unlikely unless there's a compelling reason. An injury or abrupt change in circum-stances can put a killer off his game. Sometimes the change is calculated, more often it's not.'

'So he didn't go anywhere, he just went dormant for some reason,' Harper proposed.

'Yes, I believe he's here.' Jess thought of all the evils she had studied in the past. It never got easier, and she never ceased to be amazed by their relentlessness and their resourcefulness. 'He's always been here. Something just awakened that old urge, that's all. He may have reached out because he doesn't want to kill again. But there would have to be a very compelling reason he finds himself in this quandary.'

'A .38 slug to the brain would take care of the problem.'

Jess laughed, though the sound was a little weak and a lot dry. 'It takes a certain level of courage to put a muzzle to your head and to pull the trigger to save someone else, Sergeant. The one thing I can guarantee you this very sick individual does not have is that kind of courage. Some of the most evil are the most self-absorbed and the biggest cowards when it comes to personal sacrifice. Their own self-value is far too overinflated to consider harming themselves.'

'Even if he doesn't want to keep killing, he wouldn't end it that way?'

'Probably not.'

Harper pushed to his feet. 'I'll never get that.'

Jess wished she could just spring up like that. She was feeling every day of her forty-two years tonight. Thankfully she didn't have to shame herself since Harper offered his hand. 'Don't bother trying to get it, Sergeant. You're one of the good guys. Self-sacrifice is in your DNA.'

'I should get back before Lori comes home and wonders where I am.'

Jess stopped him at the door. 'Thanks, Chet.' She rarely used his first name, just didn't feel right. At the moment, it felt exactly right. 'It means a lot to me that you were willing to indulge my desperation.'

He nodded. 'Yes, ma'am.'

The outside alarm sounded again. 'Maybe Lori's already looking for you.'

Harper made a face. 'Hope not. She won't like that we're keeping secrets from her.'

Something else for Jess to feel guilty about. The less Lori knew the better. Jess didn't want her dragged back into this any deeper than she already was by just being a part of Jess's life.

The monitor showed Dan approaching. Irritation niggled Jess. 'My surveillance detail must have told him you were here. Dropping off a file I forgot,' Jess added with a hitch of her head toward the piles on the floor.

One quick rap on the door later, she went through the paces, unlocking first one then the next lock. As she opened the door, it occurred to her that there could be a new development. Spears may have struck . . . or Lily could be in the hospital again. Renewed fear had Jess's heart ramming against her sternum.

She was definitely putting the wear and tear on the old ticker. Just one more thing to worry about. Her sister's sudden health issues had been a major wake-up call about mortality for both of them.

'Has there been a breakthrough in your investigation?' Dan asked, looking first at Jess then Harper.

Jess made a frustrated sound and rolled her eyes. 'Harper dropped by the file I left in his car, since he has to drive me everywhere I go.' She heaved a breath. 'Thank you again, Sergeant.'

'Any time, ma'am. I'll see you in the morning.' He gave another nod to Dan. 'Chief.'

Still visibly unconvinced, Dan stepped aside. 'G'night, Sergeant.'

Jess headed back to her work. Dan's relentless hovering was making her crazy. She'd thought she could deal with it, because she knew his compulsion came from the heart, but the last couple of days had been too much. But what really bugged her was the idea that he was immediately notified when a member of her own team stopped by.

'Did you have dinner?'

'Didn't your spy tell you I ordered pizza?' Not that she'd been able to get more than a few bites down. The rest had gone into the fridge. She had no appetite.

'What're you talking about, Jess?'

'Obviously the cop watching me called to tell you I had company.' She snatched open a folder and stared at the photo of the innocent young girl inside. God, how could she be worrying about Dan and his overprotectiveness when there were nineteen more little girls out there whose families wanted desperately to bring them home again?

Dan peeled off his suit jacket and joined her on the

floor. She realized then that he'd apparently just left the office. 'You haven't been home yet?'

'No. I've been at the morgue.'

'Why didn't you tell me?' If there was news he should have called. Damn it. Those frustrating feelings of desperation and helplessness warred with her determination to stay focused and strong. How was she supposed to do this if he kept treating her like she was a porcelain doll instead of a cop?

'That's what I'm here to do, Jess. Somehow I thought it was important to tell the parents first.'

'Oh my God.' The few bites of pizza did a somersault in her belly, and she felt like a total ass for feeling sorry for herself. 'Then it is Dorie Myers?'

He nodded. 'It was pretty simple. We already have dental records on file for all the missing children in that case. Over the years when we had unidentified remains we checked for these kids.' He stared at the piles of folders. 'Sylvia stayed late to do the confirmation.'

Sylvia Baron was a new and unexpected friend . . . sort of. She was also the associate coroner. And Dan's ex-sister-in-law. More small-town coincidences.

'I'm sorry. I know that was difficult.' No one wanted to have to tell a parent their child was dead.

He shrugged those broad shoulders of his. 'It's been thirteen years. This outcome was what they were expecting. They just want to bring her home.'

Somehow Jess had to make sure this Man in the Moon never got the chance to take another child ever again. 'Did you figure out how word got out to the parents who showed up at your office?' The last they spoke about it he was still furious with Gina Coleman.

'The receptionist at Channel Six. She went to school with the mother of one of the missing kids. She made the call.' He heaved a weary breath. 'I had to apologize to Gina.'

A hint of jealousy pricked Jess. Gina and Dan's sort of relationship had never been a big deal, he insisted, just recreational sex between two consenting adults. Still . . . she was another of his exes. The man seemed to have one on every corner. *God, Jess, get over it.*

Men who looked like Dan Burnett and had the kind of financial and public power he wielded were always highly sought after. Not to mention he was kind and a gentleman and sweet . . . and charming as hell.

Unlike frumpy ex-special agents who were persnickety and grouchy and thought they knew everything.

'She wants to be more closely involved in this case,' Dan said. 'Maybe do a special on the Man in the Moon mystery.'

Jess's hackles rose hard and fast. 'Who?' He'd better not say what she thought he was going to say.

'Gina.' He shrugged, trying to play it off. 'She could be a useful resource, Jess.'

Jess opened her mouth to lower the boom but quickly snapped it shut. Allowing any trickle of jealousy to get between her and a possible *resource* was just dumb. She was tired. She needed to sleep. Otherwise she would never be slipping down such a petty path. And she wouldn't be half as mad about him showing up when Harper was here if she hadn't felt guilty. He would blow a fuse if he found out she'd sent those texts to Spears.

'Gina seems to be okay after what happened with her sister,' Jess ventured, feeling contrite. Last week's big case revolving around a tight-knit little group of Birmingham elitists who called themselves the Five had left the city's upper crust a little ragged around the edges. The best part was that an old case involving bullying and murder had been solved.

What was happening to this world? Where were all the normal people?

Never mind. Considering she was a little south of normal herself, she wasn't about to start throwing any stones.

'She's dealing with it.'

'Gina might need a strong shoulder to lean on.' God! There it was! The green monster making a midnight appearance. She resisted the urge to chew off her tongue.

'Well, she didn't ask for mine – if that's what you're suggesting.'

Jess busied herself with the file on Sierra Campbell, the little girl abducted two years before Dorie Myers, to prevent saying something totally ridiculous about how his shoulders were only for her. 'I wasn't suggesting anything, just feeling bad for a friend.' She glanced up at him and smiled innocently.

'So the two of you are friends now.'

That his tone suggested he doubted it prompted her to tug at his tie. 'That's right. You have a problem with me befriending one of your old girlfriends?'

He moved his head side to side, a grin sliding across those tempting lips.

Time to pull the plug on this simmering moment before it reached a boil and she dragged him straight to her bed. 'You look tired, Dan. You should go home and get some sleep.'

'That's the pot calling the kettle black.' He reached out, nudged her chin up with his forefinger. 'You should get some sleep yourself.'

For a whole five seconds he stared at her lips and she ached for him to kiss her. But they had rules . . . this was a work night and there was a cop outside keeping watch.

'You're right.' She leaned away from him, closed the file she'd been reviewing and somehow got to her feet without assistance and fairly gracefully. 'I'll see you out.' She went to the door and waited for him to follow, every part of her screaming for him to stay.

Just watching him move toward her stole her breath. It didn't matter how tired he looked or how many exes he had, she just wanted to lean into him and have him hold her. To forget about serial monsters and innocent little children who'd had their lives stolen . . .

But that would have to wait until another day.

'I wish you'd change your mind and come home with me.'

The worry in his eyes almost finished undoing her resolve. 'The whole department, the Bureau, the media – they're all watching us right now, Dan. We have to be professional about this. My apartment is secure. There's a cop outside and I've got my Glock. I'll be okay.' Deep down, where she wouldn't let him see just now, she wasn't nearly so certain, but this was the right thing to do. For him. For her.

'If you change your mind I can be here in fifteen minutes.'

'I'm counting on it.'

'Night, Jess.'

She managed a smile. 'Night.'

He stood there staring at her for another long moment. Part of her hoped he would just do it – sweep her into his arms and stalk back to that big old bed waiting across the room. To hell with rules and the cop keeping watch outside.

Then he brushed a swift kiss across her cheek, opened the door, and walked out.

She closed and secured the door before collapsing against it.

She was so tired but that brief kiss would help her sleep better tonight.

Her cell vibrated on the wood floor.

She jumped. Had Harper gotten home to find Lori waiting for an explanation?

Jess hurried to snatch up her phone.

Not Harper.

The room shifted around her.

Your sergeant is quite hot, Jess. I bet he'd be a handful. Maybe I'll find out.

Terror exploded in her veins but the white-hot fury that immediately descended won out. Her hands shook with the urge to send Spears a message for him to go to hell or something equally clever . . . but that was what he wanted. He wanted her to react.

She threw her phone on the sofa. 'I'm not playing anymore, Spears.'

All she needed was one more shot at getting close to him, and then he wouldn't be playing anymore, either.

Chapter Four

Wednesday, August 18, 7.31 A.M.

Jess sat on the toilet and stared at the spotless panty liner.
'Start, damn it.'

Since her last pill packet had gotten screwed up she couldn't pinpoint with any certainty what day this was in the oh-my-God zone, but at least day three. Maybe four. Each day that passed pushed her closer to a certainty she was in no way prepared to acknowledge this morning.

'Fine.' She went to the sink to wash her hands. 'It won't be the end of the world,' she told the woman in the mirror with the raccoon eyes and the new wrinkles that weren't there yesterday. 'Lil managed to get two kids through high school. How hard could one be?'

Agony or desperation or something of that order groaned out of her. If only it was that easy. But it wasn't. Not at all. Lil had her husband. Jess . . . oh God. She groaned. She had Dan, no question. He loved her and she loved him but . . . they weren't ready for this. They were just now taking baby steps in their relationship. They were miles away from this milestone.

How did she tell him? Would he really be as prepared as he'd looked on Sunday at his niece's christening? Looking all starry-eyed while holding someone else's baby was entirely different from staring in the face the fact that a baby with your name stamped in its DNA was on the way.

'Just stop.' She braced her hands on the sink. There was no need to say anything yet. They both needed to be focused on work right now. Besides, she didn't even know for sure. Finding out one way or the other would be easy enough. All she needed was an at-home test.

Jess stared at her reflection and tried to breathe past the surge of anxiety that jammed into her throat. If she didn't take a test she didn't have to face what came next . . . just yet. It would actually be easier to get through the rest of the week, particularly with two cases hanging over her head – three, if she counted Captain Allen still being MIA – without having to deal with anything else.

However it turned out, she could do it. What woman didn't want to be sitting at her child's high school graduation when she was sixty? Jess shuddered. 'Don't think about it.'

Period or not, she had to get to work. She ran the brush through her hair. Harper would be here before she was ready, and explaining to him that she might have managed to be on time if she hadn't been so busy bemoaning the absence of her monthly visitor was not an acceptable excuse.

'Ha.' If she mentioned anything related to menses he'd probably rush back home and send Lori to pick her up. Bring up tampons or anything remotely related to the subject, and the strongest tough guys were out the door. Men were wimps when it came to discussing the female reproductive system.

And yet from puberty until the day they died it remained their top priority.

Jess sighed. If she were completely honest with herself, men – the good ones and the bad ones – were the bane of her existence. There was Dan and her ex Wesley and Spears and this Man in the Moon. And the missing Captain Allen along with his pal drug kingpin, Leonardo Lopez. She was Miss Popular when it came to man troubles, it seemed.

Then again, if she didn't stop thinking like that she might just end up single and alone the rest of her life. Her favorite high school teacher, Frances Wallace, had warned her about thinking she didn't need anyone else. Sometimes it was best to let someone else be the strong one.

'Enough with the psychoanalysis this morning.' She

tossed the brush onto the sink as she reached for her freshly laundered dress. The brush hit the floor and skidded across the vintage black-and-white tile, taking the toothpaste and mascara with it.

'Damn it!' She forgot the dry cleaner's plastic over her dress and reached for the junk scattered on the floor.

'That's what happens when you hit the snooze button twice, Jessie Lee.' Frustration wiring her nerves, she jammed the toothpaste and the brush behind the faucet to prevent it from going off the edge of the pedestal sink yet again. 'And then linger too long in the bathroom as if sheer force of will would garner a little cooperation from your womb.'

She scrambled past the toilet in search of the runaway mascara. 'Get over it,' she muttered. She'd been through a lot these last few weeks. Changing careers . . . moving back home. Stress screwed up periods all the time. She was overreacting in a big way.

'Gotcha.' She nabbed the mascara and braced to push up from the floor. Something dark and round near the baseboard between the toilet and the claw-foot tub captured her attention. Had she dropped something else?

She touched the object but it wasn't a thing . . . it was a tiny hole in the floor. Leaning closer, she tried to get a better look. She needed her glasses.

Pushing back from her knees to her feet, she stood and padded to the table where her bag waited. She dug through the mass of notes and junk to unearth the eyewear that appeared to be more and more necessary to daily life.

She jammed them on her face and hurried back to the bathroom. On her hands and knees, she peered at the spot. Definitely a hole. Perfectly round. No matter how close she stuck her face to the floor, she couldn't see if the hole went all the way through to the garage below or not. Maybe the plumber had made the hole with one of those special drill bits. It wasn't that far from the water supply line which also came up through the floor.

'Nothing a little caulk won't fix.'

Something else to ask her landlord about . . . or maybe she'd just pick up some caulk and take care of it herself. Dear old Mr Louis had already hired an electrician to accommodate her hair dryer. No need to bother him with this. She crumpled and rolled a square of toilet paper into a little ball and chunked it in the hole.

'That works for now.' She dusted off her hands and went back to the business of removing her dress from the dry cleaner's plastic.

She slipped into the blue double-breasted button-down and belted the waist with her favorite wide leather belt, which matched her black Mary Jane pumps. As she cinched the leather, the idea that her waist could be expanding even now made her flinch. She swallowed back a new gob of emotions trying to clog her throat.

The warning that she had company and the inevitable rap on her door saved her from going down that depressing road all over again. She pulled her hair free of her collar, straightened her lapels, and grabbed her shoes. She dragged on one and then the other as she made her way to the door.

She'd unsecured the dead bolt when that little voice she ignored more often than not warned her to check the monitor.

Annoyed with herself and the situation, Jess strode over to the monitor sitting atop the fridge. With her apartment being just one big room, table and counter space were a premium. Harper was supposed to be picking her up, and there was a cop outside watching her place. Both of which were irrelevant. She knew this. Spears was too clever for her to pretend he might not devise a way to get to her.

The face staring back at her on the monitor took her by surprise. Not Harper.

'What in the world?'

Ignoring the straps of her shoes she'd yet to fasten, she stamped back to the door, unlocked and opened it. 'Mr Louis, is everything all right?'

With her luck he was here to kick her out. The hole in her bathroom floor flitted through her mind, but she dismissed it. What sane human wanted a tenant in their backyard who came with her own personal police stakeout? She wasn't about to complain about something as trivial as a little bitty hole.

He stared at her from beyond those thick-lensed glasses of his. 'Everything's fine. I just came over to say good morning.' His lips lifted into a small, bashful smile.

Who was she kidding? George Louis was far too nice to even ponder the concept of kicking her out. The man was always doing something to help her out. The lovely antique glider on the landing outside her door . . . the sensor on the porch light that ensured it came on at dark.

He was truly a very nice man. And she was so, so late this morning.

As if the universe wanted to kick her stress level a little higher, Mr Louis presented her with a brown bag – the ones some folks still used for their lunches. 'I was in the mood for home cooking this morning. Home-ground sausage and biscuits – my sister's special recipe.'

Before she could say a word, he added, 'There's enough for you and the young fellow who picks you up. I've already given the gentleman outside a sack full with coffee. I think I have a fan for life now.'

Jess somehow kept her smile in place. How could she not? 'You are too kind, Mr Louis.'

'George,' he reminded. 'You're supposed to call me George.'

'George, thank you so much.' The alarm warning of yet another arrival chimed. 'That's probably my ride now.'

He nodded. 'Enjoy your day.'

'Thank you again, George,' she called after him.

While he and Harper exchanged greetings as they passed on the stairs, Jess fastened her shoe straps.

'Good morning, ma'am.'

'Good morning, Sergeant.' As Harper closed in on the door, Jess shoved the brown bag at him. She had no appetite. 'Let me get my bag and keys and I'm ready to go.' She and Harper had to talk about that text she received last night.

'What's this?'

'My landlord made you breakfast.' She grabbed her keys and slung her bag onto her shoulder as she hurried to the door. 'He called you a young fellow.'

Harper grunted. 'Smells good.'

After locking up, Jess headed for the stairs. 'I'm sure it is.' The barbecue she'd had with him last week had been the best she'd ever eaten.

In the driveway she hailed a good morning to the officer sitting in his car with a biscuit in one hand and a cup of coffee in the other.

What was she going to do with George Louis? She couldn't decide if he was getting too attached, was extra nosy, or plain old lonely.

You have spent too much time with the depraved, Jess. Some people are just nice.

Jess thanked the officer before settling into the

passenger seat of Harper's SUV. Her stomach felt weird. Not quite nauseated . . . just unsettled. Didn't mean a thing, she assured that little whiny voice that wasn't prepared for motherhood. Could be that pizza she had last night.

They were scarcely a block away when Harper groaned in pleasure. 'The old man makes a killer biscuit.' He chewed some more. 'The sausage is . . . *wow*. Did you eat one of these?'

She shook her head. 'I'm not hungry.'

'That's a shame. This is . . .'

He made another pleasurable sound that explained his feelings, Jess decided, far better than the words that might have completed his statement. Next he'd be expecting Lori to whip up biscuits from scratch. Oh yes, and to grind their sausage. That was what Publix was for, to Jess's way of thinking.

She dug out her phone and checked her calendar for the day. Dan and his PR guy, Trent Ward, who was back from parental leave – was everybody having babies? – were taking care of any media issues so Jess and her team could focus on the case. She assumed that was more about keeping her out of the limelight than anything. Suited her just fine.

Despite being disappointed he wasn't assigned the Man in the Moon case, Deputy Chief Black had agreed to be available for consultation if Jess needed him; otherwise, he remained focused on coordinating the BPD's resources with the Bureau in support of the Spears investigation and overseeing the Allen case.

The rustling bag drew her attention back to Harper, who was struggling to dig out another biscuit.

'Here, let me do that.' *Before you run us off the road,* she kept to herself. She opened the bag and reached inside. There were three more biscuits in there. How much did the man think they could eat? She unwrapped the foil from one of the biscuits and handed it to Harper.

'Thanks.' He scarcely got the word out before he tore off a bite.

She had to admit the scent coming from that bag was undeniably mouthwatering. Her stomach abruptly rumbled loud enough to have Harper glance her way. She winced. 'I guess I'm hungry after all.'

He made a sound of agreement. Conceding, Jess unwrapped one for herself. She'd barely chewed off a bite when, surprised, she let out a little moan of her own.

By the time they reached the office, Jess had consumed two of the flaky biscuits and juicy sausage sandwiches.

'Told you,' Harper pointed out.

She could feel the belt she'd cinched tightly to prove her abdomen was as flat as ever cutting into her waist.

No way could she be pregnant.

No way.

Before they got to the office she warned Harper about the message from Spears.

He stalled, looked directly at her. 'I get my hands on that son of a bitch, he'll know just how much of a handful I can be.'

The sausage roiled in her belly.

She had drawn yet another of those around her into this sick game.

Birmingham Police Department, Special Problems Unit

'Good morning, Chief,' Officer Chad Cook called from his desk.

'Good morning, Cook.' Before she could get out a greeting to Lori the detective was on her feet and following Jess to her desk.

'I had a couple of scenarios about the Man in the Moon case I thought you might be interested in hearing.'

Jess smiled. 'Good morning to you, too.'

'Sorry.' Lori tapped the folder in her hand. 'I got a little excited about this. Good morning, Chief.'

'Pull up a chair.' Thank God for work. She needed to work. She needed to be with her team. Whatever else was upside down or sideways in her life, it would straighten out in time. Solving this case was long overdue.

Harper strolled over to join them. A good kind of tension instantly started to hum between him and Lori. The smile she attempted to hide was priceless. 'Chief Black dropped off a list of retired and former cops who worked on the Man in the Moon case. If you're going to be in the office for a while,' Harper offered cautiously, looking from Jess to Lori and back, 'Cook and I could start the interviews.'

'Get on it,' Jess said without hesitation. 'If I need to leave the office Detective Wells will accompany me.'

When he hesitated, Lori sent him an evil eye.

He held up both hands, conceding the idea he hadn't dared to suggest out loud. 'Okeydokey. We're gone.'

Jess exchanged a look with Lori. There would be more.

Just as she suspected, both men paused at the door. 'If you need either of us,' Cook offered, as he held his hand to his face in the call-me gesture, 'you know what to do.'

'We'll be fine,' Lori assured him.

With the testosterone out of the room, Lori huddled closer to Jess. 'Before we get to the case, I told Chet I went to the movies with my mom and my sister last night, but what we actually did was talk to his mom. His birthday is Sunday.'

So that was what the girls' night out was about. Maybe there wasn't any trouble in paradise. The vibes Jess had picked up between them hadn't suggested problems.

'Are you planning him a surprise party?' Jess wasn't so sure how their work schedules would go this weekend, but she didn't want to miss whatever Lori had in mind.

'With the Spears case and this one I didn't consider anything that complicated.' She gave a hopeful shrug. 'I thought maybe lunch Sunday afternoon at his favorite restaurant. His mother traditionally prepares dinner for him, so I don't want to step on her toes.'

Jess opted not to ask about his son and ex-wife. Life was complicated these days. Seemed everyone had one kind of baggage or another.

'Count me in.' Even if they were working they had to eat.

'Do you think it would be okay to ask Chief Burnett?' Lori ventured.

'I'll ask him.' She and Dan spent most weekends together, when they weren't on duty. Why kid herself about the upcoming one, on duty or not?

She'd tossed and turned last night wishing she were in Dan's big old bed at that fancy house of his in Mountain Brook. No matter how hard she tried convincing herself that they could continue with this charade indefinitely, the truth was they needed to make some decisions. Soon.

'Thank you. I thought this could be a kind of work-friends get-together.'

Which meant she wasn't inviting the ex or the kid. 'Sounds great.'

'So.' Lori held the folder in both hands and tapped it against Jess's desk, leveling the thick contents. 'I could hardly sleep last night trying to figure out a connection between the children. There has to be one.'

'Absolutely.' Jess had tossed and turned herself. Missing Dan and this case were the primary reasons. And the text from Spears. She pushed that subject aside and still a shiver stole over her.

'According to the official reports from over the years,' Lori continued, 'the usual connections have been ruled out. It's not the schools, churches, doctors, or any sort of extracurricular community program.' She shook her head. 'It's almost as if these girls weren't even from the same planet despite the fact that they were all residents of the Birmingham area, Jefferson and Shelby counties.' She inclined her head, her gaze narrowing. 'Yet their lives didn't seem to cross paths at all before their disappearances.'

'The parents insist there's no contractor or handyman connection,' Jess noted. That was generally the next tier of suspects considered. Like Lori, it was driving her nuts not to be able to lay her finger on at least one connection. 'No beauty shops, boutiques, or grocery stores in common. Nothing other than the Galleria mall that some say they rarely visited and others went to with more regularity.'

'The Galleria employees were interviewed during the investigations of the final four victims,' Lori reminded her. 'Backgrounds checked. Other than the routine traffic troubles and a few who'd had misdemeanor possession charges and one three-year-old DUI, the investigators got nothing there.'

That was the hardest part in a case like this where there was no evidence and no witnesses. 'The potential for contact is unlimited, really,' Jess confessed. 'Even when you think you've covered all the bases there's usually one more you didn't think of.'

'True.' She tapped that file on Jess's desk again. 'So true.'

Jess felt a little trickle of anticipation. Lori had found something. Something important. 'It almost always narrows down to something small,' Jess went on. 'Something no one was even looking for.'

'Exactly.' Lori grinned outright then. She opened the folder and placed a crime scene photo from thirty years ago in front of Jess. 'The one thing every one of these families had in common was public utilities.' She pointed to the meter base right next to the missing child's bedroom window.

Her heart thundering, Jess moved through photo after photo and it was the same in each one. The angles were different but in every single photo of every damned window belonging to a missing child there was a power company meter base.

'I want the name of every meter reader whose territory

covered these homes during the past thirty-five years.'

'Already made the call.' Lori gave a little acknowledging nod. 'We should have the list by noon.'

Jess surveyed the case board across the room and the sweet faces there. This was another monster she intended to get.

He wasn't taking another little girl on her watch.

Chapter Five

Pelham, 1.05 P.M.

'I spent thirty years with Alabama Power.' Lawrence Patrick leaned back in his rocker. 'Went to work there right out of the army. I'd just turned twenty-two.'

Jess had learned that in interviews like this one far more could be gleaned by allowing the person of interest to talk about her- or himself for a while first. In this case, the tactic allowed Mr Patrick to relax and feel as if he were in charge of the information exchange and that he was providing input to the investigation versus being questioned as a potential suspect.

'Thirty years.' Jess made a note on her pad. Next to her Lori did the same, using the notepad on her smartphone. The old-fashioned way suited Jess just fine. 'That's an admirable accomplishment, Mr Patrick. You retired last year?'

'I did.' He cocked his head and studied Jess. 'Do you really believe any of my meter readers could have been involved with the disappearance of those little girls?'

Now they got to the heart of the matter. Jess had been waiting for him to get there before she launched the first direct question. She'd started with the top-ranking name on the list Alabama Power provided. A field supervisor. 'We have to retrace the steps of anyone who visited the homes of the children on a regular basis. Someone who might have known all the families involved.'

'Well.' He shrugged. 'I'll tell you the same thing I told the other cop who made that same statement thirteen years ago.'

Jess stalled the frown that wanted to furrow her brow. 'You were interviewed by someone from the Birmingham Police Department before?'

He nodded. 'Sure was. When that last little girl went missing, the Myers child, a Detective Corly or Corlon. He asked me about the meter readers for the routes that covered the Myerses' home as well as the others that devil stole children from. Me and that detective went over each address, one by one, all the way back to the first abduction thirty-three years ago. The first two kids went missing before I started with Alabama Power,' Patrick pointed out, 'but by the time the Myers child disappeared I was a supervisor, so I had access to the personnel files, knew the guys who'd worked those routes personally. Not one of those men would dream of hurting a child. I'd bet my life on it.'

Unfortunately it wasn't his life at stake.

If the BPD interviewed this man, why wasn't there a report? Jess had specifically looked for that connection after Lori suggested the possibility. She could ask Black about the discrepancy. Meanwhile, she wanted to talk to that detective. 'Could the detective who interviewed you have been named Corlew?'

'This is a photo of Detective Corlew.' Lori showed Mr Patrick the image on her cell. 'Is he the man who interviewed you?'

'Yes, ma'am, that's him. He was a little younger, of course.' Patrick pointed to the screen. 'I remember now, there was some kinda hubbub in the news about him a few years later. Got fired, I believe.'

'Why don't we go over the statement you gave Detective Corlew?' Jess suggested. 'Perhaps you've remembered something you didn't think to mention at the time.'

Patrick shook his head. 'I don't mind going over what I told him but nothing about what I said then has changed. For the twenty or so years in question there were a total of six full-time meter readers and two fellows who filled in from time to time to take care of those particular routes during vacations and illness. Four of 'em have passed on since then.'

'What about the other four?' She'd come this far, and she wasn't going to leave a stone unturned just because Mr Patrick felt confident there was nothing to find along that path. 'They're still alive? Working?'

'Fergus Cagle took my place as supervisor. The other three, Mike Kennamer, Jerry Bullock, and Waylon Gifford, are still reading those meters. All upstanding men with children and grandchildren of their own.' He shook his head. 'You won't find the devil you're looking for among 'em, Chief Harris.'

That was the problem with the devil: most folks didn't recognize him until it was too late. Sometimes not even then.

Half an hour later Jess thanked Mr Patrick and followed Lori to her snazzy red Mustang. 'Before we move on to the interviews with Cagle and the others, I'd like to find out why Corlew's interviews with these guys weren't in the case files.'

'We could ask Chief Black,' Lori suggested, as she opened the driver's-side door.

Jess sent her a skeptical look. 'I was thinking something a little less volatile. He's still stinging from last week's revelations about the Five.'

'I was hoping you would say that.'

When they'd settled into the oven Alabama's August sun had transformed the car's interior into, Lori snapped her seat belt into place. 'Corlew's having lunch at Jim 'N Nick's. He invited us to join him.'

Yet another reason Jess felt so fortunate to have Lori on her team. Knowing Jess would want to talk to Corlew – even before she'd said as much – Lori had already confirmed his location. Technology was an amazing thing. While Jess had continued to question Mr Patrick, Lori had obviously been communicating via text messages with Buddy Corlew. One of these days Lori needed to give Jess a few lessons.

Since Harper and Cook were whittling down the list of cops who'd worked this case in the past, Jess wondered if they had already interviewed Corlew. 'Any word from Harper?'

Lori revved the Mustang's engine. 'They haven't gotten to Corlew's name on the list, if that's what you're asking.'

'That's the answer I was hoping for. I'll let Harper know we're taking that one.' Jess tapped in the message and hit Send. For someone who hated text messaging, she'd become quite adept at it. Still, she had a long way to go to catch up with her detectives.

She relaxed into the seat and considered Patrick's statement as well as his demeanor during the interview. He felt confident none of his people were involved with the abductions. He'd gone as far as to ask Jess if she'd considered the telephone companies and the cable providers, since most of the families involved had one or both.

The answer was yes. But the phone company didn't make regular visits to the homes, and none of the victims' families had listed work by the telephone company in the two or three weeks prior to the disappearances. Same went for the cable companies.

'Looks like every light's going to get us,' Lori grumbled. She'd had to stop for the last two traffic signals.

'If one gets you, they all will.'

'Annoys the crap out of me.'

Lori brought up Harper's birthday again, but the sporty car waiting in the lane next to them had snagged Jess's attention. The windows were darkly tinted – illegally so, she would wager – making it impossible to see the driver. But that wasn't what garnered her attention. That creepy-crawly sensation she experienced whenever someone was watching her had goose bumps spilling across her skin.

Paranoia. If she allowed herself to be distracted by what-ifs she might miss important details in this investigation. She needed to be completely focused. Determined to make that happen, she turned her attention back to the traffic signal. Was it never going to change to green?

An engine revved. At first Jess thought it was Lori. The sound was very similar to her high-octane Mustang's roar . . . but it wasn't Lori. Another rumbling had Jess turning toward the car waiting next to them. Camaro. Black. She couldn't see the driver through the heavily tinted windows, but the feeling that he could see her and wanted her attention was undeniable.

Was he baiting them?

'Just wait until the light changes, smart-ass,' Lori warned. 'We'll see who has the fastest top end.' She shook her head at Jess. 'When you drive a sports car everyone else driving one automatically assumes you want to see who can piss the farthest. Especially guys.'

Jess tried to relax. That was as good an explanation as any. 'Maybe he's flirting with the driver.'

'Maybe.' The light changed and Lori eased forward. 'Since you're in the car I won't make an ass of myself.'

'Don't hold back on my account.' To Jess's supreme irritation, rather than taking off, the other car kept pace with theirs.

She glared at the tinted window running right along-side hers. The idea that the driver could be armed – like last week when she'd had a weapon pointed at her from a car trailing her – had her barely resisting the urge to squirm.

Deciding she'd had enough of the other driver's tactics, whatever the motive, Jess opened her mouth to tell Lori to floor it when the other car abruptly lunged forward, leaving them behind.

'It's a rental,' Lori grumbled. 'What an idiot.'

Jess breathed a little easier.

For the rest of the drive back to Birmingham she

comforted herself with the notion that Lori was probably right when she mentioned the competitiveness of sports car drivers.

Then again, denial was a common escape . . . even for those experienced enough to know better. Spears had used rentals before. And there was Captain Ted Allen. His family hadn't heard from him. His body hadn't been found, though his vehicle had been. Maybe he was driving that rental. Maybe he still wanted revenge for Jess busting into his case, which seemed totally irrational unless his connection to Lopez was a financial one. That avenue, as well as several others, was under investigation.

Don't let your imagination run away with you, Jess. Ted Allen was one of two places, in her opinion: soaking up rays on a sunny beach somewhere south of the border, or pushing up daisies right under their noses.

Dread sent a shudder rocking through her.

'You cold?' Lori reached for the AC control.

'No.' Jess shook her head. 'I'm fine. Just fine.'

Jim 'N Nick's was on Eleventh Avenue in Five Points, near Lori's old apartment. The atmosphere was casual, and the aromas coming from the kitchen were incredible. Jess's mouth began to water as soon as they walked through the door. She'd had no idea she was so starved until she walked into the place. Usually she had to be reminded it was time to eat.

No one was going to have to remind her at the moment. Food just tasted better lately – except for that pizza last night.

Corlew waved them over to his booth. 'I ordered burgers and sweet tea. You won't get better anywhere in town.'

'Thanks,' Lori said, as she waited for Jess to slide into the booth first.

Corlew assessed her for a second or two too long. 'How's it going, Jess?'

Jess would have to be deaf not to notice the way his voice softened when he spoke to her. Good Lord, *they* had been a long time ago. And even then there really hadn't been a *them*. She had already been with Dan. But there had been something between her and Corlew. A spark . . . a glimmer of something that might have been had circumstances been different.

A close call for any female. Buddy Corlew had been a womanizing shit. A damned handsome one, but a shit nonetheless. He had, however, been a friend on occasion. She was hoping this would be one of those occasions.

Mostly, she surmised, today's thoughtfulness was about making up for trying to make the BPD, Dan in particular, look bad last week. By all accounts, he'd spent a lot of time trying to make the department look bad. Not so unusual for ex-cops, especially ones who'd been fired. But he should get over that, Jess thought. Corlew was a PI these days. Carrying around a grudge wasn't going to win him any respect, much less friends.

'Going just great, Corlew. How's the PI business?' As a private investigator he did basically the same work she did, just without all the rules and the ultimate arrests. Like her, he'd never been very good with rules anyway. The main difference between them was that she would never use anyone else to get ahead. Corlew would use anyone, anytime, for anything that might benefit him.

'I heard you almost lost your ponytail,' Lori chimed in when the silence dragged on. 'You made today's early morning news.'

He laughed, the sound rumbling from deep in his chest, something Jess shouldn't have noticed. 'That was a close one,' he agreed.

Maybe it was an inside joke, but Jess had no idea what the two were talking about. Apparently she needed to watch the early morning news while she rushed about getting ready in the mornings. Never going to happen.

As if he'd gathered her confusion from her expression, he explained, 'I promised a client I'd bring her no-good cheating husband back to Birmingham for prosecution. He'd cleaned out her bank account and run off with the housekeeper.' Corlew shook his head. 'I told her she could chop off my hair if I failed. That bastard was halfway across Texas headed for Mexico when I caught up with him. Got him back here about midnight last night.'

The ponytail was vintage Corlew. He'd had it all through high school. Jess imagined the only time he'd been without it was during his stint in the Marines and his tenure with the department.

Their burgers arrived, and Jess lost herself in the food that strangely tasted better than anything she'd ever eaten in her entire life. She couldn't remember when she'd enjoyed a simple burger more. If she'd been at home alone she would've licked her fingers when she finished. If she kept eating like this she was going to outgrow the new wardrobe she'd been forced to buy when her motel room and all her stuff was vandalized a couple of weeks ago.

'What can I do for you ladies today?' Corlew asked when he'd knocked back the last of his sweet tea.

The way Jess heard it, booze was his refreshment of choice. His inability to abstain when on duty had helped kill his career. Maybe he was one of those who resisted until after five o'clock.

'You interviewed a Mr Patrick from Alabama Power as well as several of his meter readers thirteen years ago after the last abduction associated with the Man in the Moon case.' Jess dug out her spiral notepad and surveyed the scribbling she'd done there. Corlew wouldn't be surprised at the question. Even if he'd missed Dan's press conference last night he no doubt had contacts on both sides of the law.

'I did. Patrick was the field supervisor over the meter readers who worked the routes of the victims' homes in that case, including the little Myers girl's house.'

That he fiddled with his glass and checked his cell as he spoke set off warning bells. 'Why isn't there a report in any of the case files you worked?' Reports got lost or misplaced occasionally, but on a case this high profile and well documented with Black in charge – Black was a stickler for the rules – an error this big didn't seem likely.

Corlew frowned, shrugged one shoulder. 'I did several reports.' He leaned to the side as if looking for the waitress. 'I interviewed every damned one of those meter readers. Not that it mattered. Harold Black was right about that – it was a dead end – but we wanted to make sure we covered all the bases.'

And yet, the reports of those interviews weren't in the files. That her old friend appeared so fidgety seemed all the stranger. 'You didn't feel any of the men you interviewed were potential suspects?' Jess was really hoping to find a lead. Soon. Whatever Corlew knew, he didn't appear ready to give it to her just yet. That was, she decided, his new MO. Then again, knowledge was power. Corlew had made plenty of bad decisions in his life but no one could accuse him of being dumb.

'A couple were a little peculiar,' he said finally. 'Religious zealots. But this is Alabama – you see some of that from time to time.' Corlew pointed to his glass for a refill as the waitress made a pass around the tables in their section. 'But you have to ask yourself: How would they get to the kids? What would make a child open her window to a meter reader she probably hadn't seen more than once or twice in recent memory? These guys do their meter reading during the week. School-age kids aren't likely to be around except in the summer.'

'What if the windows were unlocked?' Jess challenged. 'None of the homes, not even the Myers home, had a security system. The abductions were in early fall, the perfect time of year for windows to be raised to conserve energy while enjoying the cooler nights.' Not to mention a meter reader would know which homes left windows unsecured and raised and which didn't. As well as which children were friendly opposed to the ones who were particularly shy and who had pets.

'That's true.' Corlew smiled for the waitress who refilled his glass, but it wasn't his A-game killer grin.

He was hiding something. Jess could feel it.

When the waitress had moved on, Corlew picked up where he'd left off. 'But I didn't get that kind of vibe from any of those guys. Their supervisor was adamant that his crew was above reproach, and I think he was right.'

'Not one of the men you interviewed stands out?' Jess asked again. 'No one made an impression?'

He shook his head. 'You're wasting your time if you think you'll find the Man in the Moon among that group.

Not brilliant enough to pull it off, no offense to meter readers. Think about it, Jess. The guy who did this had to be able to lure each kid out of her room without anyone else hearing or seeing anything. Most of the homes these kids were taken from were rural but not all. This guy was slick. Slick as hell.'

'Maybe so.' Jess couldn't argue the point, since she hadn't interviewed the persons of interest in question, but she intended to do just that.

'Must creep you out to have some sick bastard like that sending you gifts.'

There was that. 'I guess I just have that kind of charisma.' Though her name and the specifics on discovery hadn't been mentioned in the press conference she wasn't surprised that he knew most of the details.

'Oh, you've got plenty of that, Jessie Lee,' Corlew accused. 'The mayor had better watch out or next thing you know you'll have his job. People like you. They like your guts and those cute brown eyes.'

Jess managed a smile, but it was time to go. He clearly didn't want to talk further about his work with the BPD just now. Like the case last week, he'd give her what he wanted her to have when the timing was right for him. She couldn't depend on Buddy Corlew. They weren't friends anymore. Maybe they never had been.

'Is there anything else you'd like to share from your days at BPD that might help with this investigation?' Jess searched his face for any indications he was holding something back, not that she held out much hope for spotting a slip. The man was an expert in the art of lying. That he seemed nervous at her questioning was way out of character.

He turned his hands up. 'Nothing but the usual. The BPD had more than three decades to clear up this investigation and they didn't. That says it all, doesn't it?'

Enough. She wasn't listening to one of his rants. 'Thanks for lunch, Corlew. You give me a call if you think of anything that might actually be useful to my investigation.'

She and Lori were out of the booth before he could bluster an argument about their hurry. Jess kept going, waving as they hit the nearest exit.

'I think the guy has a crush on you,' Lori teased as they crossed the parking lot.

'What he has,' Jess argued, 'is a massive crush on himself.' Some things never changed. 'Let's get that new supervisor over at Alabama Power, Fergus Cagle, to line up interviews with the three remaining meter readers.'

'Corlew may have missed something,' Lori suggested.

'Or maybe he just wasn't looking for the right something.' It always paid to have a firsthand look. Unless Corlew's issues with the department had something to do with this case, she didn't have time to care what he was hiding.

If he kept anything relevant from her, he would rue the day he tried playing games with her again. She had one too many psychos inviting her to play as it was.

Her cell clanged. She fished it out of her bag and frowned at the name on the screen. Her former boss at the Bureau. 'Harris.'

'Jess, can you be at the Birmingham office in fifteen minutes?'

Supervisory Special Agent Ralph Gant wouldn't ask unless something was up that he didn't want to discuss by phone. She glanced at Lori and considered her lead foot. 'Sure, I can be there.'

'Good. We'll conference.'

1000 Eighteenth Street, Birmingham, 3.45 P.M.

Jess was surprised and slightly unnerved that she and Lori were ushered so quickly through security at the Bureau offices and straight to the conference room. Agent Todd Manning showed them to their seats and settled at the head of the table.

'Chief Burnett is en route,' he informed her. 'We'll wait for his arrival before we begin.'

This definitely was not standard protocol. Where was everyone else? And why the heck was Manning being so nice to her? He never had been before. 'Coffee would be nice while we wait,' Jess said, beaming a smile at him.

He hesitated but then scooted back his chair. 'Sure.' He stood. 'Coffee for you, Detective Wells?'

'No thank you, Todd. I'm good.'

He cleared his throat and walked out of the room.

'What's going on?' she asked Jess, keeping her voice down. 'There's no one here except Todd. Is that weird or what?'

Jess glanced at the door. 'That just means no one else needs to know. And, yes, that's weird considering it has to be about Spears.'

'Exactly,' Lori agreed. 'Why wouldn't everyone working the investigation need to know? Like Chief Black?'

'I guess we'll find out when Gant tells us. Get a message to Harper so he's aware of what's going on.'

'Did that while you were schmoozing with Todd.'

The woman was good. She had a knack for anticipating the right steps.

Todd returned, coffee in hand, and with Burnett right behind him.

The burger she'd enjoyed so much a few minutes ago wasn't sitting so well now.

Burnett took the seat next to Jess then passed her the coffee from Manning. He didn't look at her. Whatever news she was about to get, he had already been briefed. And it wasn't good. The *thump, thump* in her chest bumped into a faster rhythm, and her palms started to sweat despite the chill that had abruptly dropped her body temp.

'We're ready on this end, sir.'

Jess jumped at the sound of Manning's voice as he informed Gant they were standing by.

The wall-mounted monitor awakened, displaying Gant in his office at Quantico. 'It's good to see you, Jess.'

'Gant,' she acknowledged. Any hard feelings they'd had were over and done with. Life was too short to hold a grudge. Yet she couldn't manage a corresponding pleasantry just now.

Burnett exchanged greetings with Jess's former boss and then Gant got to the point.

'We believe Spears may be involved with a rather wide network of others with similar interests.'

A tight laugh slipped past the lump in Jess's throat. 'Are we talking about a cult following or just the usual obsessed fans? I believe the recently deceased Matthew Reed already proved the latter.' If Gant and the rest of what had once been her team at Quantico had listened, they would have known this weeks ago.

'We're not talking about an isolated follower here or there,' Gant clarified. 'We're talking about a whole network of worshippers.'

The tension in Burnett's posture grew more palpable, matching her own. Jess could feel his leg bouncing with apprehension under the table. There was a lot more . . .

'Okay.' Jess suffered another chill but managed to formulate the proper questions. 'Will this development help us narrow down his whereabouts? Have you discovered a reliable source? Someone who's a part of this We Love Eric Spears club?'

'We've discovered a source of information, but we don't know how reliable it will prove.' Gant shook his head. 'This development will make finding him far more difficult, maybe even impossible.'

Big surprise. Spears specialized in anonymity.

'Get to the point, Gant,' Burnett growled.

Jess stared at the man next to her. Why the hell didn't Dan just tell her what this was about? He could have called her before Gant did. Or brought her up to speed as soon as he got here. That he had done none of the above worried her more than anything Gant had said thus far.

'We picked up some chatter about you, Jess,' Gant explained. 'A few images of you, but most were from a considerable distance, and we couldn't determine the dates and locations without Chief Burnett's assistance.'

A sort of numbness settled in her bones. 'Are you saying that Spears and his friends have been sharing pictures of me?' All the times she'd felt like someone was watching her suddenly tumbled one after the other through her head.

'We think,' Burnett said, turning toward her, 'the driver who pointed the gun at you last week on that exit ramp was someone doing Spears a favor. Maybe gaining brownie points for the effort. Spears may be watching you with the help of *others*.'

'Spears has stirred an interest in you among these *others*.' Gant heaved a heavy breath, the sound echoing in the silence of the room. 'They're applauding his taste and offering their services in whatever capacity he requires.'

Jess stared at him, her heart starting to pound even harder. 'Spears might not be here at all. That's what you're saying,' she said, just to make sure they were on the same page. The numbness was playing havoc with her ability to assimilate the information. 'But he has friends here, is that it?'

'Yes,' Burnett admitted, a truckload of worry crammed in that one word. 'Friends who might also be killers.'

Chapter Six

Southpointe Circle, Hoover, 6.01 P.M.

'I don't have to go in.' Lori hoped to come off as a martyr when she really was a total coward.

She did not want to go in that house – the home of Chet's ex-wife, Sherry. Her domain. *Her* territory, where she had the home field advantage.

The last time Sherry dropped by their apartment to pick up little Chester she'd acted more indifferent than usual toward Lori. Chet's ex had been all smiles and congratulatory when she first heard the news about Lori and him moving in together. Those first couple of meetings after that had been all sugary sweet. Not anymore.

The ex-wife and mother to Chet's only child had decided she wanted or needed to hold her ground for reasons Lori couldn't fathom.

Wasn't it always that way? Sherry had wanted the

divorce. The sooner the better. The ink was barely dry on the paper when she turned up engaged to another man – a big, powerful executive, according to Sherry, named William. Chet, however, tried not to hold it against her. For his son's sake, he insisted, they needed to remain friends.

'I want you to come in,' Chet assured her softly. 'We're together now. Partners in more ways than one.' He smiled. 'In every way. Don't let her make you feel unwelcome. I gave her that power for a long time, but I'm over it now. Come on.'

He climbed out and rounded the hood to Lori's door.

She sighed and did what she had to do. The one thing she wasn't going to do was allow her insecurities with Sherry to hurt Chet. Or Chester. The kid was starting to grow on her.

'Just so you know,' Lori said quietly as they strolled up the walk, 'I got the distinct impression on Saturday when we picked up Chester to go to the zoo and then again on Sunday that your ex doesn't like me very much.'

Chet took her hand in his and squeezed. 'Sounds like she has a problem.' He hesitated at the door. 'But we don't.' He grinned as he pressed the doorbell.

Lori relaxed then. He was right. Sherry's problems weren't their problems. If she didn't like Lori that was too bad.

The door opened and Sherry, looking stunningly fit and tanned in a white dress, made a face. 'Didn't you get my message?'

'What message?' Chet's posture stiffened as if he feared the worst. 'Is Chester okay?'

'William and I had to cancel our dinner plans. Chester has a fever. He's resting in his room. I left a message at your office with Chad Cook. Didn't he tell you?'

Chet shook his head. 'Did you take him to the doctor?'

'He has a fever.' She waved it off. 'It's probably a virus. He'll be fine tomorrow, but tonight he needs to stay home.'

Sherry avoided eye contact with Lori. The slightly higher pitch in her tone she couldn't hide. If Lori were a betting woman she'd wager the part of her savings that wasn't earmarked for her sister's college fund the woman was lying. Making a scene by suggesting as much wouldn't do any good. The fact that Sherry had left the message at the office rather than just calling or texting Chet spoke volumes. She set up this moment to make Chet feel helpless. To show Lori, in person, who was boss.

'Since Chester isn't feeling well,' Lori offered, forcing Sherry to acknowledge her presence, 'why don't you go on in and give him a kiss good night?' She gave Chet her best smile. 'I'll wait here. He may not feel up to seeing us both.'

Chet looked from Lori to Sherry and back. 'I'm sure you can come inside. You don't need to wait out here.'

'He's asleep,' Sherry announced. 'Didn't I say that?' She pressed her fingertips to her temples in exasperation. 'I don't know whether I'm coming or going. The thing is, Chester needs to rest now.' To Lori she pointed out, 'When small children are sick, company of any sort can be a problem. He can call you tomorrow,' she informed Chet before stepping back to close the door. 'Sorry about the mix-up.'

'It's all right,' Chet relinquished. 'If he wakes up, tell him I love him.'

'Of course. Good night.'

The door closed.

Side by side Lori and Chet returned to the car. She kept quiet, waiting to see what his take was on the situation. Sharing custody of a child was tough enough. She didn't want to add to the angst. The disappointment he felt now was obvious as hell.

What a bitch.

Chet didn't say anything at all until they were driving away. 'I don't know why Sherry lied to us that way. She hasn't always been the easiest person to deal with, but she's never done that before.'

'That's the impression I got, too.' Lori was glad he saw through the ploy. 'Maybe she doesn't want Chester around me.' The idea kicked Lori in the gut but she couldn't pretend that wasn't a strong possibility.

'I hope that's not the case.' Chet glanced at her as he navigated the intersection that would take them away from his son's neighborhood. 'If it is, she's in for a rude awakening.'

His words should have made Lori feel better about his ex's blatant dislike for her, but somehow they didn't. The last thing she wanted was to become an obstacle standing between him and his son.

For the second time in the last half hour he reached for her hand. 'You're beautiful and smart, Lori. It's natural for her to be a little jealous, especially of the idea that Chester might fall in love with you, too. Sherry isn't a bad person. She'll come around when she's had time to think about the futility and pettiness of her behavior. I remember how I felt when she and William moved in together. I was certain he would try to take my place as Chester's dad, but the fact is, he hasn't done that at all. Sherry may be going through a similar reaction.'

One thing Lori knew with complete certainty: the woman had never deserved this man. Not for a minute, much less for the years she'd made him miserable.

'Thanks. I needed to hear that.'

He raised her hand to his lips and kissed her there. 'I'll never tire of telling you how beautiful and special you are.'

They needed a subject change, or she was going to climb

over that console and show him a little of her gratitude. 'This new development with Spears has Jess pretty rattled.'

'It's a bad situation. I don't know how the hell the FBI will ever find and stop this guy. As much as I want to see that happen, our priority has to be keeping her safe – even when she doesn't want us to. Chief Burnett is damned worried.'

Lori would never forget the look on the chief's face in that conference call with Special Agent Gant when he gave Jess the bottom line about Spears and his friends. 'Spears's followers could be anywhere.' The whole concept was totally insane. How could they hope to protect her or anyone else from that kind of threat? 'Watching her and waiting to do that bastard's bidding.'

They couldn't fully protect her. No one could. Not even the chief of police.

'How was she holding up when you took her home?' Harper asked.

'She's in denial.' No matter how incredibly smart and experienced Jess was, this was personal, and personal had a way of rendering the smartest, most experienced person a little off balance. 'She'll never admit it in a million years, but this has shaken her big-time. I think deep inside she's scared.'

'You think everything's okay between her and the chief? She seems a little flustered, more so than usual, when he's around.'

Lori had noticed that, too. 'She hasn't mentioned anything.' Not that she necessarily would. 'Anyone who knows her can see she's really edgy lately.'

'She has a lot on her plate,' Chet agreed. He glanced at Lori, his eyes somber. 'I have a bad feeling this is going to get a whole lot worse before it gets better.'

Chapter Seven

9911 Conroy Road, 9.28 P.M.

Jess had a list a mile long that she intended to get started on first thing tomorrow morning. Harper and Cook would continue moving forward with interviewing the cops involved in the Man in the Moon investigation over the past three decades. She and Lori would interview the surviving meter readers and start with the victims' families.

The Myers family would be her preferred starting place, but she'd have to see about that. As badly as she wanted to find some answers in this case, she understood that family in particular needed time to grieve one last time for the child stolen from them, no matter how long ago it happened. There were final steps – burial arrangements and maybe a memorial service – they needed to take for closure.

Thirteen years was a long time, but when it came to losing a child it was nothing. She might not have any children of her own, but understanding the concept that losing a child went against nature wasn't rocket science. Some parents never recovered from that kind of anguish. The Murphys, the case that had brought her back to Alabama, were textbook examples of how the anguish could deepen and become a whole other tragedy.

Having a child changed a person. Reset priorities and perspectives. Facing the loss of that child didn't reverse the process . . . it ate at the person from the inside out like a cancer.

Jess rubbed at her bleary eyes. This was not a good time to be focused on a case about murdered children.

What was she saying? Was there ever a good time?

Certainly not.

Above all else, this case deserved the very best the department had to offer. Jess worked hard at meeting that standard and even raising the bar. She wasn't about to start falling down on the job now just because some psycho had his friends watching her.

'Screw you, Spears.' She had far more important matters to see after. He and his friends could just go to hell.

He wasn't sending her into hiding. Burnett had suggested a vacation but she'd ignored him. She had cops watching her 24/7. A surveillance detail that followed her around, no matter that she was always with Lori or

Harper. And now another cop remained here, keeping an eye on her place, whenever she was not home to ensure no one got past her new security system and left her any more presents.

Mr Louis probably stayed glued to his windows day and night to make sure he didn't miss anything. Poor man.

'What a disaster.' She readied her files for jamming into her bag. One less thing she'd have to do in the morning.

Another good reason to stay home instead of with Dan or anyone else: her presence wouldn't put the people she cared about in danger. It was bad enough that Spears was playing with the lives of three innocent women simply because they met his preferred criteria. Jess had no intention of leading any of his *friends* to her sister's house or to Lori's or Dan's.

No one was safe from him. Not even Dan. Her hands stilled in their work as she thought of the scars on his abdomen from his one up-close encounter with Spears. Spears had stabbed him. Dan and Lori both almost died that day just because Spears wanted to make Jess suffer.

She couldn't let that happen again. For all her complaining about propriety and what everyone at the department would think, deep down her biggest worry was that Dan would get between her and Spears and lose his life trying to protect her. Her heart twisted with the thought.

Her hand went to her belly, as the reality that the ability to make a decision like that might no longer be solely hers. Depending on how this turned out, Dan would have a say in the matter . . .

The muffled sound of her cell reached out to her. Jess snapped from the worrisome thoughts, reminded herself to breathe and padded over to her sofa. She checked the screen. *Lil.*

A bubble of apprehension formed in her chest. It was late for her sister. She went to bed with the chickens. 'Hey, sis, what's up?'

'Jess, I didn't want to bother you with this until morning but Blake insisted I call. There's a box on my front porch. He says it's addressed to you. Should we be worried?'

Her apprehension expanded into outright fear. 'Don't touch it, Lil. Stay in the house and keep the doors locked. I'll be right there.'

Jess ended the call before her sister could say goodbye. She tapped Harper's name in her contact list and gathered up a pair of jeans and a tee while she waited through two rings. 'I need you and Lori at my sister's house as quickly as possible. We'll need evidence techs and maybe a bomb tech to be safe.' Just because the last package hadn't contained any explosives didn't mean things hadn't changed. 'Someone left another package for me.'

'Should we pick you up en route, ma'am?'

'No, Sergeant, head that way now. You're closer to Lily than me. I'll call Burnett and hitch a ride with him.'

'Yes, ma'am.'

Jess changed out of her PJs while she made the call to Burnett, then she got Lily back on the line to ensure she and Blake didn't get nosy and decide to check out the package before she could get there.

As she listened to Lily ramble about how worried she was, Jess closed her eyes and tried to calm her insides.

This wasn't the toughest or most complicated case she had faced. Spears wasn't even the most heinous killer she had encountered.

But . . . for thirty-plus years the Man in the Moon had evaded identification, much less capture. Spears so far proved equally evasive but at least they knew who he was.

The Man in the Moon's elusiveness made anticipating his next move a hell of a lot tougher.

You couldn't stop what you couldn't see.

Lakefront Trail, Bessemer, 11.49 P.M.

The bomb squad commander cleared the package. No explosives or other destructive substances.

Just like before.

Jess felt grateful for that part. She suspected that the families on this block, including Lily and her husband, who had been ushered from their homes at or past bedtime were simply ticked off. BPD uniforms had questioned the folks and were already shepherding most back to their respective addresses. Lily and Blake would have to wait a little while longer.

In the middle of the front porch the evidence techs settled the box onto a trace sheet so all the contents could be inspected. Portable lights had been set up to ensure they could see what they were doing. Jess, decked out in shoe covers and gloves, crouched down to have a look first. Deputy Chief Black had arrived and was waiting outside the perimeter with Burnett.

The news hounds who monitored the police band were already on the street, and camera crews were waiting for an opportunity to get a clip or a sound bite on the story. Jess hadn't seen Gina Coleman in the growing mob, but she would show eventually.

'Ma'am, would you like me to start?' Harper asked.

Jess shook off the surrounding distractions and refocused on the package. 'Go ahead, Sergeant.' That way, he and the evidence techs wouldn't have to see her hands shake. She hoped her stomach settled soon. That peanut butter and banana sandwich she'd scarfed down after she got home was reappearing in a most unpleasant manner.

The box, a plain old brown cardboard one, about twenty by twenty inches square, found any day of the week at Walmart for a couple of bucks and sealed with shipping tape, had been opened by the bomb tech. As before, plastic, burlap and newspapers swathed the items inside.

Human remains. *Bones.*

Again.

As the small bones were removed from their wrappings, an ache tugged at Jess. Another family who had waited so very long would finally be able to stop wondering. But dear God, what kind of answer was this?

Unless this victim's remains showed otherwise, there was no clue as to cause of death. No way to know what this child may have suffered before dying.

Then again, maybe the parents didn't really want to know.

Was it better not to hear the horrific details?

Was it enough to simply have some sort of closure?

Jess had reviewed photos of all the victims over and over, knew them by heart. Was this the cute little blonde-haired girl with the curly locks and the big gap-toothed smile, or the dainty child with the long brown pigtails that hung all the way to her waist?

If she were pregnant . . . the lump in her throat expanded . . . would she have a little girl? How could she possibly hope to protect her from evil like this? Before she could stop herself she glanced to where Dan waited. Would their little girl have dark hair and blue eyes like her father?

'You all right, Chief?'

'Of course.' She tried again to clear that damned lump from her throat. 'It's just hot under these lights.'

'Here we go.' Harper gently removed the small plastic sleeve she'd been looking for from between layers of the burlap. 'Looks like we have a pattern, Chief. He wants us to know who he is.'

Harper placed the protected newspaper clipping in her open hands. The plastic sleeve was a common four-by-six photo protector – the multi-pocket kind that came in sheets. He'd cut the photo pockets apart to use them individually. The newspaper article was folded in such a way to display the missing child's photo. The little blonde girl with her big gap-toothed smile.

Emma James.

A blast of outrage propelled Jess to her feet.

Harper stood as well. He passed the preserved article with the photo to an evidence tech. Jess had to walk away.

'Do what you have to do,' she heard Harper instruct, 'but let's get the remains ready to move as quickly as possible. We don't want this to drag out and have the families of victims showing up here.'

Those were directions she should have given. Instead, she'd had to take a minute to catch her breath. Her head was spinning; her stomach was twirling and teetering like a drunken ballerina. Somehow she had to find her footing here. Then she'd make sure her sister was okay and head to the morgue herself. Sylvia Baron had the necessary dental records; she was overseeing the identification personally rather than passing the job off to the lab. Jess needed to be there, too. She couldn't do the job these families deserved if she let this killer or any aspect of this case continue to rattle her so.

For a moment, she scanned the growing crowd beyond the yellow tape that marked her sister's yard and home a crime scene. Was the bastard here? Observing? Salivating as he watched her deal with the nightmare he'd created? Fury swept through her. For a second she considered barging into that crowd and demanding IDs.

Harper caught up with her. 'I'll put in a call to Dr Baron.'

Jess had to clear her mind yet again. *Deep breath.* 'Tell her I'll be there as soon as I can.'

'Yes, ma'am.'

When Harper had rejoined the techs, Jess stretched her neck and took a couple more good, deep breaths. 'Okay.' She braced for the fuss her sister would no doubt launch. 'Let's get this part over with,' she grumbled.

In the house Lily and Blake were questioning Lori. Jess wasn't surprised. Knowing Lori, she had managed to get her questions in first in spite of these two.

'You're not giving my detective a hard time, are you?' Jess asked, hoping to lift the mood just a little. Her sister had enough to deal with trying to find some answers to the medical issues plaguing her. She didn't need to worry about Jess and some crazed killer on top of the mountain already in front of her.

'Is it another of those little girls?' Lil demanded. 'Your detective won't tell us.'

'We won't be able to confirm that until we officially identify the . . . remains.'

Lily's hands went over her mouth. She shook her head and a new wave of tears bloomed on her lashes. Blake draped his arm around her shoulders and tried to comfort her. Jess fought the need to cry herself. She wasn't doing those little girls one bit of good getting all emotional like this.

'I'll be outside,' Lori offered.

'Thanks.' Jess waited until Lori had gone out through the kitchen door. The front porch was a crime scene there would be no using that door until sometime tomorrow.

'Why is he sending these to you?' Lil's lips trembled.

Jess steeled herself against her own emotions and hugged her sister hard. 'I don't know. But I'm going to do all I can to find him and stop him.'.

'It's not fair,' Lil murmured. 'You already have one freak taunting you.'

112

A pathetic excuse for a laugh rumbled out of Jess. 'I guess I have a target painted on my forehead that only the freaks can see.'

Lil drew back and searched Jess's eyes, tears still slipping from her own. 'I don't like this, Jess. What if he gets lucky and somehow gets close enough to hurt you?'

Jess hugged her sister again. 'That won't be lucky, sweetie.' She drew back to look Lil in the eyes once more. 'That'll be the last thing he ever does.'

Lil required a few more minutes of persuasion before she relented and allowed Jess to leave so she could do her job.

They agreed on one point – the situation provided a tangible reason to be thankful both Lil's kids were away at college. Jess was most grateful her sister didn't seem to hold that against her. So far, her homecoming had disrupted the lives of everyone close to her.

'Way to go, Jess.'

Outside, Burnett waited for her. He looked as weary and troubled as she felt. Who wouldn't be? They only had about eighteen more to go. Her entire being ached at the thought. The need to collapse in Dan's arms was so strong she had to look away from him to hold herself back.

Having the killer continue to make deliveries to her wasn't half as worrisome as the idea that he could start to eye replacements.

'Where's Black?' she asked. He'd been talking to Dan when Jess went inside to reassure her sister.

'He'll meet us at the coroner's office.'

'We should get over there. There's nothing else I can do here.' Except fall apart for the viewing pleasure of all those watching, maybe including the evil being who did this.

Dan nodded, but there was more on his mind. He looked so worried. She ached to just close out all those prying eyes and go to him.

Do your job, Jess. 'We can talk on the way,' she suggested. If he was going to blow up and lay down the law again about how she should be in hiding, she didn't want that to happen here with all those reporters buzzing around on the street. Fact was, she was barely hanging onto her composure here.

He nodded again.

As they moved toward his SUV, the reporters clamored for statements and Dan gave them all they were going to get for now: 'No comment.'

Chapter Eight

Jefferson County Coroner's Office,
Thursday, August 19, 2.29 A.M.

Dan stared at the tiny bones arranged on the coroner's table and his chest ached. What kind of evil preyed upon little children like this? Humans made mistakes. But this was no error – no spontaneous event that was later regretted. No. This bastard repeated his heinous deed over and over. Year after year.

'How long will it take you to make the official identification?' Jess asked. 'I'm not trying to rush you, Dr Baron, but as soon as this news hits the street, those parents are going to want to know which one of them this child belongs to.'

If the bastard who'd done this stuck to his previous MO, the remains would prove to be Emma James. Jesus Christ. Dan had to look away a moment.

'I uploaded the dental records of the other victims to our database after the first set of remains found their way to you,' Sylvia Baron explained. 'I wanted to be prepared . . . just in case.' She nodded to the computer screen on the credenza and then rested her attention on Jess – waiting, Dan suspected, for a thank-you.

Jess didn't disappoint her. 'I appreciate your hard work. I'm certain the families will, as well, even if saying so isn't on their minds just now.'

When she didn't get on with it, Dan prompted, 'You want a drum roll, too?'

Sylvia shot him a glare. 'Emma James. The little girl in the photo.'

'She went missing the year before Dorie.'

'That's right,' Dan said in answer to Jess's observation. She looked so tired. He hated that some sick fuck was doing this to her. 'He's taunting us with a trip down memory lane.'

'The delivery was made personally this time,' Jess said quietly, as if she were thinking aloud. Her voice was thin, anguished. No one wanted to investigate cases like this, but these children deserved the best on their side.

'He may have paid someone to make the delivery for him,' Dan countered. Walking up to Lily's door when she was home was taking a risk. Then again, at that time of night most were distracted by television or preparing for bed.

Jess shook her head. 'He wouldn't share any part of this with anyone else. I'm certain he made the delivery himself. His every step is careful, methodical.'

Dan laughed, a painful sound even to his own ears. 'And he wants to share his accomplishments with you.' How the hell was he supposed to protect her until they found this bastard?

'We will find him, Dan,' Jess said as if she'd read his mind. 'He doesn't know it yet, but he's helping us along.'

Dan held up his hands. Couldn't say what was on his mind in front of Sylvia. The associate medical examiner knew too much about him and his relationship with Jess already. She didn't need to know he was out of his mind with worry. Hell, he hadn't slept at all last night. From the looks of her, Jess hadn't, either.

'I have to tell you, Harris,' Sylvia said, as she folded her arms over her chest and pointed an accusing look at Jess, 'you certainly know how to keep life interesting. In all my years in this office, I have never had so many back-to-back – how shall I put this – completely bizarre cases. You should have your own reality series.'

Jess forged a quick smile. 'I've made it my mission in life to make sure you're never bored again, Doctor.'

'What're your preliminary conclusions on the remains?' Dan decided this might be a good time to draw the conversation back to the case. He was relatively certain

Jess was not in the mood for pithy remarks. He definitely wasn't.

Sylvia took his pointed question in stride. 'No visible fractures or damage.' As she spoke she studied what she had to work with on the table. 'I'll do what I can, but there's really nothing left to give us any firm answers. There are other tests that take time which might give us something, but I wouldn't count on it.'

'I guess we'll know what happened when I catch him,' Jess announced. She turned to Dan. 'I thought Chief Black was meeting us here.'

'He's here,' Sylvia answered before Dan could. 'He got a call just before you arrived. He's using my office.'

'I'll give him an update and find out what's happened now.' Dan headed for the exit before Jess could decide to tag along. He needed a few minutes alone with Black. What he really needed was some distance to get his emotions in check.

The long white corridor was deserted. Dan hated the smell and the total absence of color. If he had the time he'd step outside for some air. It was driving him crazy to have Jess trapped in the crosshairs of two damned killers. She refused to listen to reason. She wanted to work. He had tried every way under the sun to dissuade her but that wasn't happening.

Harold Black exited Sylvia's office just as Dan reached the door.

'It's Emma James. Sylvia just confirmed.'

Harold exhaled a weary breath. 'I suspected that would be the case. What is this monster doing?'

'Whatever it is, I don't think he's anywhere near finished.'

'He has at least eighteen more victims,' Harold agreed. 'Enough to make a delivery about every other night until the harvest moon.'

'I'm just praying he doesn't do any shopping.' How the hell were they supposed to find him in the next month when dozens of cops hadn't been able to in the last thirty years? Dan wanted to kick something.

'I hope we'll be so lucky.' Harold scrubbed his hand across his face. 'On top of that, we have a development in the Allen investigation. I got a call from Detective Roark. With this' – Harold gestured toward the room Dan had just left – 'and the Spears case, I put Roark as lead on Allen's disappearance.'

They could use a break in that case as well. The idea that one of his cops may have been in bed with the very criminal element he was tasked to investigate was tough to swallow. Yet that was one of the avenues that had to be investigated. Jess's clash with Allen and Lopez complicated matters. Certain circumstantial evidence indicated Allen had a grudge against Jess and had attempted to act on it. Whatever he'd been up to, finding him was the first step in getting some answers.

'A jogger found Allen's cell phone this afternoon. Called the contact listed as "wife."'

Dan perked up. This could turn into a solid lead. 'Anything on the phone salvageable?'

'We don't know about that yet, but Roark has delivered it to Vernon at the lab.'

If there was anything to be found on the device, Ricky Vernon would find it. 'This could be the break we need.'

Harold nodded. 'It could be. You're right.'

The other man's inability to maintain eye contact warned there was more. 'But . . .' Dan prompted.

'The troubling part is where they found the damned thing, Dan.'

Dan's spine went rigid. 'Where the hell did they find it?'

Harold frowned. 'Was today trash pickup day in your neighborhood?'

What was he getting at? Dan was too damned tired for beating around the bush. 'As a matter of fact, it was – what about it?' And then he knew. As if the thought had slammed into his brain like a bullet . . . he understood what his friend was getting at.

'Your trash can was overturned, some of the contents scattered over the end of your driveway and into the street.' He managed a dim smile. 'You know how sanitation workers are, they aren't picking up what falls out. So, this jogger spotted the phone. There was blood, Dan. The lab has already confirmed it's a match to Allen's blood type. We'll know more in a day or two.'

In other words they'd had this phone for hours. Harold had known it was found in front of Dan's house but he hadn't bothered to tell him until now. The urge to laugh came hard and fast. Instead, he held up a hand to stop whatever Harold had to say next. 'Just let me know when Vernon gives you something.'

Harold nodded. 'Will do.' He scrubbed at his jaw. 'If you don't object, I'd prefer to notify the James family personally. I worked this case when that little girl went missing. I know these people.'

'Of course. You should take care of that.'

'I hate to wake anyone at this ungodly hour,' Harold confessed with a sigh, 'but I don't want them hearing this any other way.'

Every one of those families would be watching and waiting for more developments. They had the right to know as soon as humanly possible. The anguish on the faces of those who had showed up at his office would haunt Dan for the rest of his life.

Harold hesitated. 'There's one other thing, Dan.'

For the love of God. He hoped it wasn't more questions about how Allen's cell phone ended up in or near Dan's trash. His bullshit meter was maxed out. 'What else?'

'Some of the parents have retained Buddy Corlew's services.' Harold shook his head. 'I don't have to remind you that we got our first glimpse that he wasn't cut out to serve the citizens of Birmingham back when he was involved in the Man in the Moon investigation. We made a serious mistake by underestimating how far down he would go.'

Dan remembered all too well. Corlew had been a respected detective when Emma James went missing. Nine years later Dan was tasked with the unsavory job of firing him. It was a sad day when a cop was kicked off the force. But he wasn't wasting any sympathy on Corlew. If he kept pushing the idea that the department was the problem, Dan was going to personally see that he got the message to back off.

Maybe he should have done that a long time ago. Truth was, he'd pretty much ignored the guy until he started trying to draw Jess into his schemes.

'His involvement concerns me,' Harold said, pulling Dan from his troubling thoughts.

'You're worried about what exactly?' Dan needed him to be specific. Though he hated for any of the victims' families to throw their money away on the likes of Buddy Corlew, it was a free country.

'I'm concerned that in his continued attempts to make the department look bad, he'll hurt these parents, and they've already suffered the unthinkable. He's carrying a grudge, Dan. He will use anyone or anything to bring us down.'

Dan held up both hands. 'All right. I'll talk to him.'

'I'd feel better if you did.'

'Consider it done.'

When Harold was on his way, Dan went in search of Jess. He hadn't gotten far when she found him.

'Sylvia's going to stay with Emma. Since she has two sets of remains now, she's hoping to find some common characteristics. The tiniest speck that might provide insight into how or where these children died.'

'Maybe we'll get lucky and she'll find something.' He hesitated but decided there was no reason to talk about the update he'd gotten from Black. No use adding that to her plate tonight. 'Why don't I take you home with me? We'll get a few hours' sleep and then we'll swing by your place before going to the office.'

'My place will be just fine,' she informed him with a look that warned she wasn't fooled by his avoidance of the subject. 'Did Black have news I should know about?'

Hiding anything from Jess was futile. He should know better by now. 'They found Allen's cell phone.'

Her eyes gave away the dread before she said a word. 'Where?'

'That's the interesting part.' He guided her toward the exit. 'In my trash.'

Shock widened her eyes. 'What?'

'That's what the man said.'

In the parking area she hesitated before climbing into

his SUV. 'Now maybe everyone in the department will stop looking at me as if I killed him.' She smiled up at Dan. 'They can look at you that way instead.'

'Get in,' he ordered, not amused.

'Just saying.'

By the time he'd navigated onto the street, she'd relaxed into the passenger seat and closed her eyes. She was tired. He didn't see how she was holding it together. After all those years living away, he'd talked her into coming here to help with a case. Once that case was done, he'd persuaded her to stay.

For this. One nightmare after the other.

He fought the anger, mostly at himself, and then the new burst of fear dumped another layer of emotion on him. He wanted to put a bullet right between Spears's eyes. But first he wanted to find this so called Man in the Moon and tear his heart out with his bare hands.

He gritted his teeth. *Dial it back a notch.* Between now and daylight he needed to find control again. Maintaining his cool had never been a problem. Until now. He glanced at his passenger. But then he'd never had to worry about keeping Jess safe before. It was one of the hardest tasks he'd ever faced.

That old-phone ringtone jangled from the big bag she carried. Jess snapped her head up and dug for her phone.

It was only a couple of hours before daybreak, and they didn't need any more trouble tonight.

'No, Sergeant. It's okay. I'm not home yet.'

Harper. The evidence techs had found something. Dan's pulse rate accelerated.

'All right.' She listened for a bit. 'Thank you. See you at eight.'

She put her phone away and sat quietly for a moment before passing along the news. 'The perp left us another clue as to why he's come forward after all these years.'

Dan frowned. *The newspapers.* Oh hell.

'Like the ones with Dorie Myers's remains, the newspapers all contained headlines about the disappearance of Emma James. No fingerprints yet. But he used a pencil to circle letters and words on some of the pages. Harper put the letters together and came up with a message.'

Her voice was so thin that Dan almost stopped the vehicle so he could look her in the eyes. When she didn't go on, he pushed, 'Just tell me.'

'This is all for you, Jess.'

Neither said a word the rest of the way to her place. Dan knew if he said anything he'd say too much. When he turned into the drive on Conroy Road, the surveillance cruiser was in place. He wished that made him feel even one iota better. The Birmingham Police Department was staffed with the best, from the patrol cops to the deputy chiefs. But Spears had bested all who had attempted to catch him, from the FBI to local law enforcement. He had endless resources and backup plans for every imaginable scenario. And now he had *friends* watching Jess.

'You don't need to walk me to the door,' she complained as he came around to her side of the vehicle. 'It's almost daylight.'

'You don't want the officer over there to think I'm not a gentleman, do you?' He moved ahead of her and led the way across the yard.

'Fine,' she grumbled, tagging along behind him.

At the top of the stairs leading to her apartment she handed him the keys. Once inside, he entered the code for the alarm. He was glad she'd gotten the security system installed. He wasn't convinced that would be enough but it helped.

Without a word she dug her weapon from her bag then dropped the bag on the floor. When she'd tucked the Glock under her pillow she started peeling off clothes. She kicked off her sneakers and wiggled out of the jeans. If he hadn't been so mesmerized by her every move she might not have turned around to find his jaw gaping.

'There's a spare key in the freezer. Lock up on your way out, Dan. I'm done.' She climbed into the bed wearing nothing but that old gray tee and flashy pink panties.

Had to be the exhaustion speaking. She'd just given him a key to her place. He wasn't sure whether to be pleased or worried. 'You need anything?'

'No.' Her voice was muffled by the mound of pillows she'd burrowed into.

'G'night,' he offered.

This time all he got was a grunt.

He reached for the quilt to cover her up but hesitated. He should be ashamed of himself but he couldn't help admiring those long, toned legs and the curve of her bottom. The desire to crawl in bed beside her was nearly overwhelming, but she was armed and he wasn't taking any chances.

Careful not to disturb her, he covered her and left a kiss against her hair. After he'd reset the alarm and locked up, he turned out the lights and stretched out on the sofa.

She might just shoot him in the morning anyway, but at least he would get a few hours' sleep without worrying if she was safe.

Chapter Nine

9.20 A.M.

Jess considered each photo Spears had sent her. Each woman looked to be early to mid-twenties. All had long dark hair and would comfortably fit into the category of gorgeous.

Spears wouldn't be interested if they weren't beautiful, intelligent, and gifted in some way. He always chose women who intrigued him. Since Jess didn't know their names or anything else about these women, it was impossible for her to hazard a guess as to which one would end up a part of his deadly game.

She had inspected these photos again and again in hopes of noticing something that made one of the women stand out, but there was nothing.

'You ready?'

Startled by the sound of Lori's voice, Jess jerked to

attention. 'I'm sorry. What did you say?' It wasn't until she looked around that she realized they were no longer moving. Lori had parked the Mustang.

'This is the Myerses' residence. Are you ready to go in?'

'Yes. Sorry. I was lost in thought.' Jess shoved her cell phone into her bag. Where was her mind?

With Spears, apparently.

'Are you okay, Jess?'

She hesitated, her hand on the door handle. Lori rarely called her by her first name when they were on duty. 'I'm fine.'

'If there's anything you need to talk about . . .' she offered, worry darkening her green eyes.

Jess wondered if her friend would regret having asked if Jess just flat out told her all that was on her mind. From the never-ending nightmare with Spears to this new horror with the Man in the Moon. Or what if she just up and announced that a new day had come and there was still no sign of her period? Would Lori look at Jess differently then? After all, she was unquestionably old enough to know better than to allow this to happen.

Forty-two, divorced . . . how stupid could she get? The Pill had been a mainstay in her life almost as long as she'd had a driver's license. How had she allowed this to happen?

Daniel Burnett had no idea how lucky he was to have

DEBRA WEBB

escaped this morning with his hide still intact. It wasn't so much that he'd slept on her couch that made her mad as hell, it was the idea that she hadn't gotten even a minute of privacy to bemoan the fact that her period remained MIA.

'Thanks.' Jess marshaled a smile she hoped covered a multitude of worries. 'I'm just a little distracted.'

Lori reached across the console and patted her arm. 'You're a hell of a lot stronger than me. I can tell you that. I don't see how you're keeping it together to proceed with this investigation. I'd be running for the hills, screaming at the top of my lungs.'

'If I stopped working,' Jess assured her, 'I'd really lose my mind. Then I'd be running for the hills.' She surveyed the rambling farmhouse that sat on thirty acres well outside Birmingham proper. 'Stopping isn't an option. Not for me and not for those little girls. Come on –' she opened her door '– let's get this done.'

Mrs Myers had agreed to an interview. She and her husband lived alone in the big old house. Their only other child, a son, was away at college, like Lily's kids. God, how fast they grew up. And Jess had missed so much.

She had a lot of making up to do with her small family.

Keep your mind on the task at hand, Jess. After this interview, she and Lori would tackle the meter readers and see if Corlew had missed anything.

130

'Mrs Myers taught school until Dorie went missing,' Lori said. 'After all these years of hoping she might be found, do you think she'll be helpful under the circumstances?'

'The survivors often withdraw.' Jess took the steps up onto the big shady porch. 'Sometimes it's easier to just stay someplace safe in your mind so you don't have to touch the pain. For others it helps to touch the hurt often. To review every last detail time and time again until it's bearable. We all have our own way of grieving.'

'That was my way.'

Jess wasn't sure who jumped the highest, her or Lori, at the sound of the woman's voice. She sat on the porch swing deep in the shadow cast by a large, flowing Lady Banks rose which had long ago overtaken the far end of the porch.

'Mrs Myers?' Jess waited for a response before introducing herself or moving toward where the woman waited.

'I'm Rita Myers. My husband's at the barn, but he'll be along.'

Since Rita seemed content to remain on the swing, Jess walked slowly in that direction. 'I'm Deputy Chief Jess Harris and this is Detective Lori Wells.'

'I thought we'd sit out here.' Rita looked around as if seeing her porch for the first time. 'It's still cool enough to enjoy the morning.' She gestured to the table nestled between two wicker chairs. A tall sweating pitcher and two glasses waited on a tray. 'I made lemonade.'

'Thank you.' Jess took the chair closest to the swing. Lori settled in the other. 'Your home is so peaceful.'

'Thank you.'

Jess poured a glass of lemonade. 'This summer has sure been a hot one. According to the weatherman there's no relief in sight.'

'Keeps folks looking for ways to cool off.' Rita gave a push with her bare toe, setting the swing in motion. 'I've made a lot of lemonade this summer.'

Jess sipped the cool drink. 'Hmm. It's delicious.'

'My grandmother always said lemonade wasn't lemonade if you didn't leave the pulp in the lemon juice.'

Jess smiled. 'I think your grandmother was right.'

Lori poured herself a glass as well. 'I love your roses, Mrs Myers.'

The ghost of a smile touched the woman's lips. 'I planted that Lady Banks the year my son was born. The next year I planted a pink Angel Face climber on the east end of the house to celebrate my daughter's birth. You'll have to take a look before you leave. It's more beautiful this year than ever.'

'My mother loves roses.' Cradling her glass in both hands, Lori relaxed in her chair. 'She planted roses when my sister and I were born as well. That's a nice tradition.'

Jess had no idea if her mother had planted anything for her and Lily. Both their parents had died when Jess was only ten. Unfortunately she and Lil didn't know much at all about either side of their family. There was the aunt on their mother's side, for what that was worth.

Jess decided to start her questions with a good memory. 'When did you and your husband buy this farm?'

'He bought it as a wedding present for me. My parents were city dwellers, and I had all these fond memories of my grandmother and her little country home.' That tiny smile was back. 'He wanted me to have my heart's desire.'

'He sounds like a keeper,' Jess suggested. 'Those are few and far between.'

'After twenty-five years I guess it would be kind of silly to decide he wasn't.' Rita picked at the hem of her blouse. 'Dale got our son through his teenage years alone. After what happened I couldn't be there for him. I owe my husband a huge debt for picking up my slack.'

'You wanted to find your daughter.' Jess had read the reports about how often Rita Myers had attempted to nudge the investigators along on the Man in the Moon case. She didn't want to believe the children were dead. About five years ago she had stopped making queries. Maybe that was when she'd finally found that place she could bear.

And now the pain was back.

'It was my job,' she insisted, as if they should have known this. 'I'm her mother. I couldn't just sit back and wait for the police to find her. I had to do something.'

'Rita,' Jess said, choosing her words carefully, 'when your daughter went missing, you stated to the police that you had often felt like someone was watching you and Dorie. Can you tell me about that?'

'For about six months before she ... disappeared, every time we'd go into town to shop for groceries I'd feel like someone was following us around the store.' She shrugged, her fingers busy with that hem. 'I tried to catch whoever it was, but I never could. Dale thought I was losing it. Dorie didn't seem to notice, so I tried to ignore the feelings.' She shrugged. 'But it was there every time. My grandmother used to say that some people felt things others didn't. A sort of knowing. After Dorie went missing, I decided I must've been sensing what was coming.'

'You could never pinpoint any one person who always seemed to be there when you got those feelings?' Jess knew exactly the feeling she meant. For weeks now she had felt as if someone was watching her. Unfortunately her feelings had nothing to do with a sixth sense. Spears had pals of his keeping an eye on her.

Rita shook her head. 'Never did. And after that night, Dale cried and cried because he hadn't believed me. He felt like he'd failed our daughter. Failed me.'

'Did Dorie ever mention anyone talking to her at school

or at any time when she may have been out of your sight? A stranger or someone she didn't know well?'

Another defeated shake of her head. 'There was nothing. For years after she was gone, I would play every moment of those last few weeks over and over in my mind. My friends stopped coming by or calling because that's all I wanted to talk about.'

'But you had to do what you had to do.' Jess understood. It was a coping mechanism she'd needed to survive an inconceivable tragedy.

Rita nodded. 'Some don't understand. I hope they never have to.'

'It's routine procedure to consider anyone, whether friends of yours or Dorie's or even family members, as suspects. Was there anyone who you felt could have been involved in her disappearance? Someone maybe the police overlooked or cleared too hastily?'

'That part was extremely difficult.' She stared at her glass of lemonade for a long moment. 'Even Dale was questioned so many times that he was sick of the whole process. I tried to explain that we didn't know anyone who would do anything like that, but the detectives kept telling us they had a job to do. It just seemed like a waste of time to me.'

Most people felt that way, and yet more often than not they knew the person who had taken their child. 'May we see Dorie's bedroom?'

135

'Sure.' Rita pushed up from the swing. 'I thought you might want to look around in there so I opened up the window to air it out.'

The house wasn't fancy by any means. Just large rooms with much-loved wood floors and walls covered with family photos and collections of cherished finds. The sofa and chairs wore slipcovers, and someone had taken a coat of paint to the old farm table. The place could have graced the pages of a chic decorating magazine.

At the back of the house, there were two bedrooms separated by a bathroom. Rita led them to the one on the left.

It wasn't necessary to have visited the home before to know they had stepped back in time thirteen years. The daffodil yellow walls of the bedroom were adorned with Barbie posters and princess pictures cut from magazines. The covers on the bed were drawn back; the pillow was rumpled as if someone had slept there last night. But Jess instinctively knew no one had slept in this room since the night Dorie went missing.

The once bright sunny rug next to the bed was a little dingy. A pair of little girls' sneakers lay on the floor next to it.

'You don't mind if we look around?'

Rita looked surprised by Jess's question but then she nodded. 'Look all you want.' She glanced at the door. 'I should go see what's keeping my husband.'

'We'll be right here,' Jess promised.

As soon as the mother was out of the room, Jess tugged on a pair of gloves and whispered, 'Look inside and under everything.'

'You got it.' Lori pulled a pair from her slacks pocket and snapped them on.

Working quickly, they examined every doll, stuffed toy, drawer, the closet – top to bottom, even inside the pockets of clothing. Jess wiggled her head and shoulders under the twin-size bed and had a look. She checked between the mattress and the box springs and beneath the fitted sheet.

'What about this?'

Jess joined Lori at the rear window. The room had two windows, one to the left as you entered the room and one on the south side, at the back of the house that overlooked the big yard and the woods beyond.

Striped floor-length curtain panels hung on each side of the large window. But it wasn't the cheery curtains that had garnered Lori's attention. It was the deep scratches in the window stool.

'I don't remember seeing anything about this in the reports from this scene.' Jess had read them all. There was no tampering whatsoever listed. She peeled off her gloves and stuffed them in her bag.

'It was Samson.'

Jess turned to the man who'd spoken from the doorway.

Dale Myers lingered there, his wife at his side.

'Samson?' Jess asked as she moved toward the couple.

'Our Labrador retriever,' he explained. 'We got him as a pup the Christmas . . . before. He was supposed to be for both the kids but he loved Dorie the most.' He motioned to the window. 'Dorie knew the dog wasn't supposed to come in the bedrooms. He was supposed to sleep outside at night and be a guard dog. But she'd sneak him in after we all went to bed. She'd keep urging him until he'd jump in through the window. He left a few marks.'

The reports had mentioned a dog, which Jess found odd. Dogs usually barked. A guard dog who didn't bark was like having a car that didn't start. 'Samson didn't bark that night?'

'That's the part I'll never figure out,' Dale admitted. 'He's a good dog. To this day he barks when a stranger comes around. But he didn't bark that night. The only reason he didn't rush to meet your car and bark like crazy when you drove up was because I had him in the barn with me. He growled and whined to let me know you were here.'

That answered what would have been her next question. 'Was he in Dorie's room that night?'

'We're pretty sure he wasn't.' Rita looked to her husband as if wanting to confirm her answer.

'We don't think he was,' Dale explained. 'He was

missing the next morning. That's why we thought at first that Dorie had gone looking for him in the woods and gotten lost.'

'He was missing that morning,' Jess repeated. Why hadn't that information been in the official reports? 'When did he come home? Or did you have to search for him?'

Dale and Rita looked at each other again. 'He was gone for about two days,' Dale finally said. 'We told the police but they didn't seem to think it was all that important.' The lingering fury burned in his tone.

'One of our neighbors spotted him down by the creek,' Rita picked up where he left off. There was no anger in her voice, just defeat. 'Every once in a while since she . . . left us . . . he'd be gone all day and we'd find him there. He and Dorie liked to play in that creek. We figured he was missing her, too. Since she wasn't here anymore, he kept looking for her at their other favorite place.'

'They dragged the creek,' Dale said, his voice thick with emotion. 'Didn't find anything, of course. We don't really know how he ended up down there that night. Maybe it didn't have anything to do with . . . *anything*.'

As if he'd sensed they were talking about him, Samson poked his head in the room. He eyed Jess and Lori suspiciously.

'Hey, Samson.' Jess decided Samson had been a pretty big fellow even at only eight months old back when Dorie went missing. His sleek black hair was peppered with gray now. Somehow seeing him made Dorie all the more real. She had lived in this room and loved that big old dog.

It took all the willpower Jess possessed to hold back the tears. What in the world was happening to her?

'He sleeps in here every night, even now.' Rita scratched him behind the ears. 'I think he spent all these years hoping she'd come back the same way we did.'

Dale's arms went around his wife and he held her close as she regathered her composure. He brushed his lips across her temple and whispered soothing words to her. Watching him comfort her was the most tender yet the most painful thing Jess had ever witnessed. She blinked back the renewed sting of tears. Lately she was having a heck of a time controlling her emotions.

Rita managed a watery smile. 'Sorry.'

'No need to apologize,' Jess assured her. She took a deep breath to loosen the knot in her chest. 'Was there anyone who came around the house that Samson wouldn't bark at? Besides family, I mean?'

The detectives' reports confirmed how thoroughly the family, neighbors, and friends had been investigated. Deputy Chief Black and his team had gone above and beyond to rule out each person who might have had access to the child.

'I'm telling you he barks at most everyone. He did then

and he does now,' Dale maintained. 'If you weren't a part of the family or a friend who came over pretty regularly he was gonna bark at you.'

'What about the meter readers and telephone repairmen, folks like that?' No matter what Corlew said, Jess intended to follow that lead. Something may have been missed. A fresh look never hurt. As much as she didn't want to believe he would purposely botch an investigation involving a missing child, she couldn't risk that she was wrong.

Dale looked to his wife again. 'Most of them are scared of him, wouldn't you say?'

She nodded. 'They don't get out of their vehicles until they see that one of us is home.'

Taking into consideration the couple's absolute certainty, there was only one explanation for why Samson didn't bark that night.

Either Dorie was taken by someone she knew – someone Samson knew – or she and the dog had been lured away from the house so no one would hear a sound.

Jess leaned forward in her seat. 'That's it. Turn right after the speed limit sign.'

Dale Myers had given clear directions to the creek where they had found Samson after Dorie's abduction. Still, they would have missed the turn if not for the speed limit sign he'd mentioned in his directions.

The car bumped off the highway onto the narrow gravel road.

Jess cursed under her breath. 'Why don't we park here and walk down to the creek? He said it's not far. I don't want to damage your car.'

Lori surveyed the woods that had already engulfed them only a few yards from the paved road. 'I don't know if we should get out of the car. There's a whole lot of opportunities for someone to hide in these woods.'

Good God, Burnett had drilled Lori and Harper about protecting her until they could scarcely do their jobs. With a big sigh for emphasis, Jess powered her window down. 'Do you hear that?'

Lori frowned. 'Hear what?'

'Exactly. I think we'll be able to hear anyone coming once they turn onto this gravel road.'

Lori removed the weapon holstered at her waist. 'Well, alrighty then.'

Jess palmed her Glock and shouldered her bag then climbed out of the car. She moved carefully down the gravel road. It was a bit slow going at first, since the road dipped steeply downward before leveling off and cutting toward the creek. Dale Myers had said they went fishing here. Lots of folks who lived along this road did. It was walking distance from the Myers farm, not more than a mile and a half or two.

'I think I'll start keeping a pair of sneakers in the trunk,' Lori grumbled.

'Keep two,' Jess suggested. High heels, no matter how stylish or what designer label they sported, just didn't go with gravel roads.

The bubbling and trickling of the water revived her determination. Jess moved more quickly toward the sound. As she got closer, the road widened into an area good for parking two or three vehicles. Nearer the water the thick shade canopy blocked most of the sun and weeds grew along the paths leading to the water's edge.

'If you like to swim, this would be the place to be on a hot summer day.' Lori surveyed the creek from a safe distance. 'Wide and deep enough for a paddle canoe or a flat-bottomed boat.'

Lori was terrified of water. Jess hadn't talked to her about it, but obviously she had no desire to get too close to the water's edge. Jess turned around and studied the road that led to this spot. The main road wasn't visible from here. The Mustang, either. Once a vehicle pulled down into this flat area, no one passing on the road would know it was here.

The story Myers had told about their dog and how he'd been found here two days after Dorie went missing kept niggling at Jess That dog had come here and then waited for a reason.

'This is where he parked,' Jess decided.

Lori's gaze collided with hers as if the same epiphany had just struck her. 'He walked through the woods and approached the Myers home from the rear. He walked straight up to Dorie's window.'

'But Samson didn't bark,' Jess countered.

'He used one of those training whistles or whatever,' Lori suggested. 'Called the pup to him and gave him a treat. He'd probably done it before just to be sure Samson would go for it. Then they went to the house together.'

'He used the dog to lure Dorie out through the window and he brought her here.' Jess's heart pounded so hard she could no longer hear the trickling water or the whisper of the breeze shifting the leaves of the trees.

'Only he hadn't counted on Samson following them this far or refusing to go back to the house.'

'Poor thing probably tried to follow the bastard's vehicle but ended up back here when he couldn't keep up.' Jess played the scenario over and over in her head. 'Or the perp could have left him the treats or a pile of dog food then drove away while Samson was occupied with an unexpected windfall.'

'Samson hung out right here, assuming they'd come back.'

Emotion swelled in Jess's throat. 'Only they didn't and he just kept waiting.'

A twig snapped and Jess whirled around, swung her weapon upward, adopting a firing stance. She scanned the tree line and then the gravel road where it rose toward the paved highway.

'Get down, Jess!'

Lori's voice echoed around her at the same instant the man came into her line of sight . . . dark hair . . . dark glasses . . . tall . . .

Jess lunged into the tree line.

Lori rushed up the gravel road. 'Police! Hands away from your body!' she ordered.

'Damn it, Lori,' Jess muttered, scrambling from the underbrush.

An engine roared to life and tires squealed as Jess made it to where Lori stood, feet wide apart, weapon aimed on the retreating vehicle.

'Did you get his license plate number?' Jess was breathing hard. Her feet were killing her and the bastard who'd just scared ten years off her life was long gone.

Lori shook her head as she lowered her weapon. 'He had mud or something smeared across it. I couldn't get even one digit. Four doors. Dark in color.'

The road was deserted now as far as Jess could see in either direction. 'Definitely not a local looking to cast a fishing line. Not in a business suit.' Jess hadn't gotten any real details on the face, not behind those dark sunglasses. But that cocky body language of his had her instincts zipping into high gear. 'Did you get the make?'

Lori turned to her and Jess knew the answer before she

said a word. 'An Infiniti.' Her shoulders sagged in frustration or defeat. 'I should've taken a shot at his tires. Maybe I could've stopped him.'

'No.' Jess shoved her Glock back into her bag. 'You had no compelling reason to take a shot. You didn't see a weapon and you couldn't be sure it was the same guy.'

But Jess was sure. A man matching his general description, dark hair and dark glasses, driving a blue or black Infiniti had aimed a weapon at her just a few days ago. But he hadn't been wielding a weapon today. Probably didn't want to get his ass shot sneaking up on two cops like that. It seemed incredible to Jess that the guy would dare to get so close. But then again, he was one of Spears's followers. He might do anything to impress his pal. Spears's former protégé, Matthew Reed, had gone so far as having cosmetic surgery to look like his mentor. There were folks in this world who were truly, deeply damaged.

'Damn that bastard.'

Jess dragged her mind back to the present. 'Did he do something to your car?' Lori's dad had left her that car. Jess joined her on the driver's side of the Mustang.

'He left you a gift.'

Dread coiled deep inside Jess as she stared at the bouquet of flowers wrapped in tissue paper that lay on the hood. Before Jess could do so herself, Lori donned gloves and picked up the accompanying envelope addressed to Jess, opened it and withdrew the card.

Love and Kisses, Your Secret Admirer

'Shit,' Lori muttered. She scanned the highway again. 'We have to call this in.'

'And be stuck here waiting for an evidence tech.' No way. What was the point? She shook her head. 'Let's bag the envelope and card and put the flowers in the trunk. We'll figure this out later. I need to interview those meter readers today. Supervisor Cagle was good enough to get them all rounded up for a meeting. I don't want to miss it.'

'You're the boss.'

Dan would throw a fit, but he'd just have to deal with it.

Jess had an investigation to conduct. Some scumbag sending her flowers wasn't going to stall her search for the monster who'd taken all those little girls.

Chapter Ten

Hoover Medical Plaza, 11.01 A.M.

Chet flipped through another magazine. Kim, the receptionist, had promised he wouldn't have to wait long. He hoped she didn't let him down. He needed this appointment. But he and Cook were wasting valuable time, and as nice as Chief Harris was, she wouldn't be too happy about that.

Cook, his partner on this task, jammed his cell back into his pocket. 'We need to grab lunch after this, man. I'm starving.'

'You're always starving.' Chet closed the magazine he'd thumbed through and set it aside. He stared at the back of the receptionist's head beyond the sliding glass that separated the lobby from the sign-in desk, hoping she would turn around and notice that he was still waiting.

He didn't have time for this . . . but he had to know.

Worry wrapped around his chest and squeezed like a vise.

'What's the deal with the uptight coroner lady? Sylvia Baron?'

If Cook hadn't said her name as if he were relishing a thick, juicy steak, Chet might have thought nothing of the seemingly innocuous question. But Chet could see where this was coming from and, worse, where it was going.

He looked to see that the other four people in the waiting room were buried in magazines or their cell phones. 'What the hell, Cook?' he whispered. 'Dr Baron is so far out of your league you can't even smell her perfume.' He made a face and shook his head.

Cook leaned closer. 'No, no, you got me all wrong. I'm just curious, that's all.'

Chet lifted his eyebrows. 'Don't bullshit me, *Officer* Cook,' he said under his breath. 'The woman is the daughter of a senator. She was born with a silver spoon up her ass. That's what makes her so *uptight*.'

Cook grinned. 'I was thinking it was the absence of a good lay. I'd be happy to take care of that particular problem for her. She is *hot*.'

'She is about eighteen, twenty years older than you, bro,' Chet reminded him.

'I got no problem with that,' Cook assured him. 'I love older women.' He looked around as if he feared he'd just been overheard. 'Not the chief, of course. I mean she's hot and all but she belongs to Burnett.'

Chet shook his head again. 'You should never repeat any of that out loud ever again. Trust me, if you want to live, you should keep all that to yourself.'

He hoped he'd never said anything that stupid when he was Cook's age. Depression set in on the heels of that thought. God, he was old. Thirty-one this coming weekend.

Damn.

'You just wait,' Cook said with all the cockiness of a twenty-three-year-old who didn't understand how life worked just yet. 'If I get the chance, I'll have the doc loosened up in no time.'

Chet laughed. 'That's assuming you can get close enough for her to even notice you're breathing.'

'I'll get close enough,' Cook guaranteed. 'She'll be noticing a lot more than my respiration.'

Fortunately, the nurse popped her head out and called Chet's name. 'I'll be back.' He hesitated before following the nurse. 'We are not here. Don't forget that.'

'Yeah, yeah.'

'And how are you today, Mr Harper?' the nurse asked, as she led the way to an exam room.

'Great. Thank you.'

He hoped.

After being weighed, having his vitals taken and

waiting ten more minutes, Dr Bolton finally showed up.

'It's not time for your physical,' she said, surprised to see him.

Chet was lucky. He never got sick. 'Next month.' Now for the touchy part. 'I have a question about that surgery I had after Chester was born.'

'The vasectomy?'

Chet's gut felt queasy. 'Yes, ma'am. I was wondering what the protocol is for getting it reversed.'

She studied him a moment. 'I see.'

He felt like a total sleazeball. What was it about having a doctor say *I see* that made a person feel like they'd done something wrong? Maybe because most of the time, they had? What the hell had he been thinking? Worse, how the hell was he going to explain this to Lori? She insisted she wasn't interested in having kids for now. Didn't even want to discuss the possibility. But there was a big difference between choosing not to and having the option taken off the table.

He should have looked into this before. He'd heard of guys getting the procedure reversed. He'd figured that was what he'd do if the need ever came up. When he'd started doing his research a few weeks ago, the possible complications were a big nasty surprise.

'I met someone and the relationship is progressing and I . . . need to know.'

'You haven't told her?'

151

Why was it those four words, far worse than *I see*, sounded like a death sentence? The thought of telling Lori made him want to throw up. Mainly he just didn't want to make a mistake by not being adequately prepared for the next step. The other night they'd even talked about the kind of house they might buy together one day. He hoped he hadn't waited too long already.

'Well, as you will recall, both the urologist who did the surgery and I counseled you about that. It was a big decision, not one that should have been taken lightly.'

'It's what my wife wanted.' Why couldn't he just have an answer? 'I was trying to save my marriage.'

Dr Bolton didn't say anything to that. She didn't have to. The marriage had fallen apart anyway.

'Okay,' she finally said. 'There is a procedure, as I'm sure you know if you've done your research, for reversals. It takes several hours of surgery to reconnect the plumbing, so to speak, and then some time in recovery before you can go home. Usually, if there are no complications, you can be in and out in a day. There's considerable pain and some downtime from work. A day or two. Sexual activity can be resumed in about three weeks.' She gave a little shrug. 'If you're asking me can it be done, the answer is yes.'

'What's the success rate?' According to his research, since it had been only three years there was a higher success rate.

'Considering the short time since your original surgery, there's a good chance. Fifty per cent or better in most cases. There's a test to see if your body has started producing sperm antibodies. If it has, then the likelihood of success is very poor.' She placed his chart on the exam table they wouldn't need today. 'There are risks involved with any surgery. We would need to get you in to see a good surgeon and have him discuss those issues with you, work up the necessary labs before moving forward. The surgeon who did your vasectomy is retired, but there are several others I would recommend.'

'How soon can we do that?' He was anxious to learn all he could so he and Lori could talk about this. He didn't want to tell her until he knew what they were up against. The idea of her finding out before he told her scared the hell out of him.

What really terrified him was the possibility of her being hurt because he kept this from her. To keep a secret from the woman he wanted to spend the rest of his life with was just wrong.

'I'll have Kim take care of it.' Dr Bolton hesitated before moving on. 'Chet, you're a good man, and if this woman is the kind of woman who deserves you, you need to be completely honest with her. There is no other bigger killer of relationships than deceit.'

'Thank you, Dr Bolton. I'm going to make this right.'

Back at the desk and feeling like a cad, he waited for

the appointment to be made and paid his copay. Cook wasn't in the lobby. That made him nervous as hell. By the time he was out the door, Chet was sweating bullets. He found Cook in the parking lot near the car talking on his cell.

Instantly, Chet's heart rate doubled. He'd had to silence his phone. He slid it from his pocket to ensure Lori hadn't called.

She hadn't. He managed a breath. Damn, he didn't like this sneaking around. He didn't see how guys cheated.

When Chet walked up, Cook ended the call. 'I called in lunch over at Pete's Subs. He's holding a table for us.'

Chet shook his head as he climbed into the driver's seat. How nice it must be to have just one worry – when he would eat next.

'Guess who eats at Pete's Subs every Thursday?' Cook dropped into the passenger seat.

'You're kidding.' This guy had it bad. Maybe food wasn't his only worry.

'At twelve thirty on the dot with her boss.'

Chet started the engine. 'Did you ever consider that maybe she's already getting what she needs from her boss? Leeds is rich. Being the county medical examiner gives him some amount of power in the community. Ladies like Baron go for old guys like that.'

Cook harrumphed. 'No way. He's gay. I checked.'

'I don't even want to know how you check to determine another man's sexual preference.'

'I have friends who are gay and bisexual,' Cook informed him. 'Now who's uptight?'

'Just making you aware of how a statement like that can be misconstrued,' Chet pointed out.

'Did you get your shot?'

Chet had told Cook he needed a tetanus booster. 'Good for another ten years.'

He just hoped the plumbing was still good for more than shooting blanks.

Chapter Eleven

Garage Café, Tenth Terrace South, 12.52 P.M.

Dan hadn't been to the Garage in ages. Most of his lunches involved work, and the Garage didn't fit the bill when it came to the necessary atmosphere for dealing with Birmingham's political hierarchy. A little bohemian and a lot funky, the place was perfect for guys like Corlew.

His nemesis had taken the little table way in the back, in the corner, of course.

Some things never changed.

'Well, well, Danny boy, how's the Magic City's top cop?' Corlew mouthed off as Dan pulled out a chair.

'I might bother with an answer if I thought you actually cared.' Dan waved off the waitress who started their way. 'But I caught most of your interview with Gerard Stevens the other day. Since bashing the department and me appeared to be the crux of the broadcast I'm relatively certain you couldn't care less.'

'You should order.' Corlew motioned for the now-confused woman to come on over. 'The food here is like fine wine – it's gotten better with age.'

'You would know.' Dan silently chastised himself for stooping to this guy's level.

'Bleu cheese burger, medium rare, and a Bud draft.' Corlew gave her a wink. 'My friend here will have the most expensive bottle of water you have in the house. And he's picking up the tab.'

'You got it, Buddy.' The young lady gave him a big smile and a nice view of her hips swaying as she sashayed off.

When she was gone, Corlew's smile disappeared. 'What's the deal, Daniel? You have something you need to say to me?' He shrugged. 'I don't know, like I'm sorry for being a dick or something?'

'Keep dreaming, Buddy.' Irritation worked its way into his voice, and Dan hated that Corlew could so easily rile him. It was like being back in high school again and facing off after a pivotal football game. 'We need to talk about the Man in the Moon case.'

Corlew laughed. 'I gotcha. You heard I've been re-tained by some of the parents who would actually like someone to find out what happened to their children.' He held his arms out in a search-me gesture. 'I got nothing to hide. I did my job when those last two kids went missing.' He dropped his hands back to the table. 'Can the BPD say the same about all its detectives? I don't think so, or this case would've been solved years ago.'

Oh yeah. The guy still had a hard-on for making the department look bad. 'It's been a long time, Corlew. Four years.' Dan leaned across the table, his frustration getting the better of him now. 'You fucked up and I did what I had to do. Drinking on the job, dragging in late, failing to file reports, shall I go on?'

Corlew said nothing, just stared straight at him as if Dan hadn't said a word.

'If you genuinely want to help those parents, then you help them. But don't use those people for your own selfish agenda.'

Fury flared in Corlew's eyes. Oh yes, he'd hit a nerve with that one.

'You're a politician, Dan. Politicians see what they want to see. Say what they think folks want to hear.' He did the leaning across the table this time. 'Problem is, you're not a liar and a cheat like most politicians. You're one of those people who wants to believe the best in everyone – except me, naturally – so you see what you want to see. That's gonna be your downfall, Daniel. Mark my words.'

Like he gave one shit what this jerk thought. 'Just don't

make this about you,' Dan warned. 'If you'll excuse me, I have a department to see after.'

Corlew grabbed his arm when Dan would have pushed back his chair. 'I'm through waiting for you to do the right thing, Danny boy. This freak's decision to start digging up bones is a sign, my friend. I'm paying attention. Are you?'

Dan stared at him for a long moment before pulling his arm free. 'This city and the citizens who live here always have my full attention.'

'And what about Jess? With all your attention on work, can you take care of her too?'

Dan reached across the table and grabbed Corlew by the shirtfront. He jerked him close. Stared straight into his eyes to make sure the man got the full intent behind his words. 'If you do anything,' he snarled, the urge to do more than warn this asshole a living, breathing urgency inside him, 'to hurt her or upset her in any way, I will hunt you down and beat the hell out of you like I should've done a long time ago.'

Corlew didn't flinch. 'Jess and I go back a long way. She knows she can count on me when the chips are down. We're cut from the same cloth, me and Jess. You'll see. She won't turn on me.'

Dan smirked. 'Jess knows what you are. You're trying to play her just like you did back in high school. It won't work. Save yourself the trouble. Stay away from her. Do we understand each other?'

'Hell, Danny boy.' Corlew laughed. 'I didn't know you still had it in you.'

Dan shoved him away. 'You remember what I said and we won't have a problem.' He stood and dropped a twenty on the table. 'Enjoy your lunch.'

Struggling to regain his composure, Dan strode out of the restaurant and headed for his SUV. What he really wanted to do was to go back in there and beat the hell out of the guy on principle. If he had something on the department then he should give it up. This dancing all around it, throwing about innuendos and then dropping the ball until the next time he wanted to stir the stink was bullshit.

Be that as it may, it was Dan's duty to make sure that all his people were clean. For the past four years he had ignored Corlew's insinuations about Harold Black and his division. It was time to put those allegations to rest once and for all.

Might as well start with his latest off-the-cuff remarks about how the last two cases in the Man in the Moon investigation were handled. Dan put in a call to Harper for a private meeting in his office ASAP.

Harper was a good man. He could do what needed to be done without prejudice. Jess could do the same, but she had enough going on right now. Dan didn't want to weigh her down with any additional complications.

When Dan reached the city parking garage, Harper and Cook were just pulling in.

Couldn't ask for better timing. He climbed out, shut the door, and secured his vehicle. Harper waited in the aisle between parking lanes.

'I sent Cook to the office to complete reports.'

'Good.' Dan surveyed the garage. 'I need you to look into a situation that's been festering for a while.' As much as he needed this done, he wasn't looking forward to it. Maybe that was why he'd put it off all this time. It was easier to despise Corlew than to think there was some truth to his allegations.

Maybe the history between them was the reason it had been so easy to believe the worst about Corlew four years ago.

Don't even go there, Dan.

'Buddy Corlew insinuated that we fell down on those last two cases, James and Myers, in the Man in the Moon investigation. He's been retained in his capacity as a private investigator by one or more of the victims' families. I don't know which ones yet. At any rate, if the department is culpable in some way, I need to know it, and I need to make it right if that's possible. Chief Black swears it was all done by the book, but he was so close to the investigation his judgment may be skewed. I don't want any question about this. I want to be absolutely certain.'

They'd been down this road with Corlew before. The trail was getting worn and rutted.

Harper considered his words for a moment. 'Cook and I've been interviewing the cops who worked the case, from the beginning.'

'Have you picked up on some thread that's nudged your instincts?'

Harper shook his head. 'Not at all, sir. What I've gathered is that we did everything possible to do the impossible – find a ghost.'

That eased Dan's tension a fraction. 'Look closely at those last two cases. If there were any mistakes, I want to know.'

'Yes, sir.'

Dan's cell vibrated with an incoming text. He slid it from his pocket as they continued toward the BPD offices.

A man should always send his beloved flowers.

He stalled. 'What the hell?'

An image came next. A bouquet of flowers with a card. He zoomed in on the card. It was addressed to Jess. His gut clenched. He zoomed back out. The flowers were lying on what appeared to be the hood of a car . . . a red car.

He turned to Harper. 'Where's Chief Harris?' His pulse rate went off the charts.

'She and Detective Wells are conducting interviews in the field. Parents of the victims.'

'In Wells's red Mustang?'

Harper nodded.

Fear pumped through Dan's veins. 'We need to find them. *Now*.'

Chapter Twelve

Sixth Avenue North, 1.05 P.M.

Jess was just about ready to show her shield and wave her Glock if Fergus Cagle didn't show up in the next sixty seconds.

The man had kept them waiting in his office for more than an hour. If not for the secretary sitting right outside the door, she and Lori could have reviewed every drawer and file the man had in his office.

'Chief Burnett is still demanding that you come back to the office.' Lori looked from her cell to Jess. 'Harper says he is beyond furious.'

Well hell. He'd been clamoring for them to return to the office for the past fifteen minutes. 'Step into the lobby and let him know that I'm in the middle of an interview and I can't get back there until I've finished.' Not only was she meeting with Cagle, but there was Bullock, Gifford, and Kennamer to boot. She had waited this long, and she wasn't leaving without these interviews.

'Will do.'

Jess refused to even take her phone from her bag. She'd set it to silent after Dan's first phone call. She had a job to do. Lori was with her. He needed to back off.

'Chief Harris.'

Jess looked up just in time to see Fergus Cagle striding into the room. She didn't have to wait for the formal introduction. He was tall and thin with gray hair. Nice eyes and a friendly smile. She recognized him from the case file photos. He hadn't changed one bit.

'I apologize for keeping you waiting. That confounded budget meeting just didn't want to end.' He shook his head. 'With all the cutbacks, we're having a time keeping our employees properly compensated. From the looks of things we'll be laying off more workers at the beginning of the year. That's why I'm jumping through hoops trying to be in too many places at one time.'

'You're here now.' Jess propped a smile in place. 'Why don't we get started?' She frowned. 'The other three gentlemen are here?'

'Yes, ma'am. I was under the impression you wanted to speak to them separate from me, so they're waiting in the employee lounge.'

Lori reentered the office. The look she gave Jess warned

that Burnett hadn't been pleased with her answer. What was new?

'Mr Cagle, this is Detective Wells. If there's an office free, she could interview one of the other gentlemen. We'll make quick work of this formality so you can get back to the business of keeping our city's power flowing.'

And they could get to the office before Dan sent SWAT to collect her.

'Why sure.' Cagle stepped to the door and instructed his secretary to show Detective Wells to an office and then have Kennamer meet her there.

When he returned to his desk, he placed his hands palms down on the cluttered surface and released a big sigh. 'Now I'm all yours, ma'am.'

'According to the statements you gave fourteen and then thirteen years ago,' Jess began, 'you didn't recall seeing Emma James or Dorie Myers in the weeks prior to their disappearances.'

He gave a succinct nod. 'That's right. I was a reader back then but I didn't work either of those routes normally. Once in a while I subbed for Bullock or Kennamer. The route that included the Myers house belonged to Jerry . . . Bullock. I might have taken Mike's – Kennamer's – route that included the James property once. We try to keep a reader on a particular route. He learns the idiosyncrasies of the homes along that route. Gets to know

166

the routines of the families. We can spot problems easier that way.'

'What sort of problems?' Jess readied her pad and pen for taking notes.

'We can tell if a home is using more resources than usual; that can sometimes indicate a problem that the homeowner doesn't know about. Sometimes there are deaths and we might not hear about it here in the office. The last thing we want to do is turn off someone's power when they've lost a loved one and just forgot to pay the bill. We like to believe that we're building relationships, Chief Harris. This is more than just about business.'

'I imagine a good knowledge of the route protects the reader as well.' As he considered the question she watched his face, his hands. He appeared very much at ease, very open.

'That's true also,' he agreed. 'We want our employees to be safe on the job. Some of the folks, especially those in the rural areas, have dogs that run loose. We've had more than our fair share of dog bites. The readers make it a point to get to know which houses have dogs. If possible they try to befriend the family pets. That makes their jobs easier and generally keeps everyone happy.'

'Do readers carry treats for the dogs in hopes of winning them over?' Jess stopped breathing in anticipation of his answer. Whoever had taken Dorie Myers had known how to handle her dog. That was a given.

'We don't recommend or encourage feeding the pets. That kind of thing can end up in a lawsuit. It's pretty much up to the reader to deal with each individual and unique situation. As long as he gets permission from the owner to give treats, I don't see the harm.'

That was a yes in Jess's opinion. She hoped her next question wouldn't offend him. 'In all your years working in the field and then in your capacity as a supervisor, have you ever known any of your employees to get involved with a customer? Attached, maybe, in an inappropriate or overzealous manner?'

Cagle leaned back in his chair and appeared to thoroughly weigh the question. 'There was one time about twelve years ago that Roger Fowler got a little caught up in an affair with a female customer. Wouldn't have been an issue except that the woman was married and she accused him of taking some jewelry from her home. In all my time in this department I have never known any of the men here to cross that line. Except that once. We keep an eye on each other, Chief Harris. None of us wants to lose the community's trust by allowing a screwup. That's just plain old good sense and job security. Roger retired after that. It was best.'

Jess made a note of Roger Fowler's name. 'Were any legal charges filed against Mr Fowler?'

Cagle shook his head. 'She and her husband chose not to file charges.'

'Do you have an address and phone number for Mr Fowler?'

'We have the address and phone number he had when he worked here. My secretary will find that for you,' he offered. 'Anything we can do to help.'

Jess appreciated the cooperation. 'Do you have any pets, Mr Cagle?' She knew he did, because there were pictures of him and a couple of dogs on the credenza behind his desk.

'I sure do.' He turned his chair so he could see the photos that had caught her attention. 'I have two Golden Retrievers and an old cat. They keep me company. After my wife passed on, I needed a companion. The next thing I knew I had three of 'em. I guess the good Lord knew I was lonesome.'

Jess scribbled a few notes mostly for show. 'What about children? Do you have children at home?'

'No, ma'am. My daughter's all grown up. But I do have two beautiful grandchildren who visit regularly. A boy who's thirteen and a nine-year-old granddaughter. I am truly blessed.'

'I'm sure you can sympathize with the parents of all these missing children. Little girls around the same age as your granddaughter. That's why I'm here, Mr Cagle. We're going back through all the steps to ensure we haven't missed anything. We have to find and stop the person responsible for these tragedies.'

He nodded. 'I do understand. Like most folks, I thought we'd seen the last of this nightmare thirteen years ago. That's one prayer I'm hoping will still be answered.'

'It does make you wonder, why now? After all these years?' Jess watched his face, his eyes for the slightest hint of any emotion beyond what appeared to be genuine regret.

He sighed, his expression somber, then he surveyed his desk and glanced at the clock before meeting her gaze once more. 'I hope you'll know the answer to that question soon. I know we're supposed to love all God's creatures, but this is one creature that needs to be stopped for his own good as well as the community's. Seems like the whole community's counting on you to do that, Chief Harris.'

Jess thanked him for his time and moved on to interview the final man on her list, Jerry Bullock. Cagle was accommodating enough to allow her to use his office. Lori had already finished her interview with Kennamer and was talking to Gifford.

'Mr Bullock, besides Mr Cagle, you've worked the longest for Alabama Power.'

The man nodded. 'That's right.'

Bullock was fifty-eight, a little on the heavy side. He had a friendly demeanor but he seemed distracted or nervous.

'Can you tell me what you remember from the days

170

and weeks around the Man in the Moon abductions? The last two in particular. I believe Dorie Myers was on your route.'

He lifted his shoulders in a shrug. 'We all talked about what a shame it was. I didn't know any of the victims personally. Like you said, the Myers home was on my route at that time. I knew the parents, but I only saw the kids once in a while. They were usually in school when I came by the house.' He looked at her, his expression pained. 'I felt for the Myerses. Still do. They're good folks. The whole community was pretty torn up when that little girl disappeared.'

'Did you or any of your coworkers or friends have any theories on who might be taking all those children?'

He pursed his lips and appeared to consider her question at length. 'Back then I think everybody considered everybody else a suspect. Hell, we didn't know what was going on. I just kept hoping the police would find some evidence but they never did.'

'Was there any reason at that time or now for you to be concerned for your job or your safety, Mr Bullock?'

Startled by her question, he sat up straight. 'No, ma'am. No way.' He shook his head adamantly. 'Why would you ask that?'

Jess made a few notes on her pad just to make him wonder. 'Standard procedure, Mr Bullock. Now.' She gave him a big smile. 'Do you remember Roger Fowler?'

Bullock gave a halfhearted shrug. 'I knew of him, but we didn't pal around or anything.' He looked away, scratched the back of his head. 'I heard he got into trouble and had to retire early.'

Obviously that was a subject he didn't want to talk about. 'Do you have anything else you want to say or any questions for me?'

He hesitated a bit but then asked, 'You think you can catch him, ma'am? I mean, if this starts up again . . .' He shook his head. 'If half the CSI stuff you see on TV is accurate, surely you can find him. He don't need to get away with this anymore.' He cleared his throat. 'You will catch him this time, won't you?'

'We're doing everything possible to find him,' Jess assured him. 'You have my word on that.'

When he'd left, Jess gathered her things and stopped by the secretary's desk for Fowler's last known address.

The stories of the surviving meter readers hadn't changed in thirteen years, it seemed. Considering how often they'd had the opportunity to discuss the past and rehash those memories, it was a miracle each one told his version exactly as he had over a decade before. The one new thread was Roger Fowler. Of course his illicit workplace affair hadn't happened until the year after Dorie Myers was abducted, so there was no reason he would have been mentioned.

The fact that the man had no qualms about sleeping

with another man's wife didn't make him a killer, but it certainly prompted a closer look at whatever else he might have been up to during his tenure at Alabama Power.

Jess left Alabama Power feeling as if she'd just exited a well-choreographed stage production where not a single character forgot his lines.

'We have ten minutes to get to the Jameses' home.' Jess chewed her lip. 'Should I call and let them know we'll be a few minutes late?' The Jameses lived all the way out in Pelham, and not even Lori's Mustang could go that fast.

'I think you'll have to take care of that roadblock first.'

Jess followed her gaze to the Mustang, where Burnett waited. A BPD cruiser had Lori's car blocked in its parking slot.

Outrage rushed up Jess's spine. 'Give me a couple of minutes. See what you can find out about the meter reader who was fired, Roger Fowler.'

'Yes, ma'am.'

Jess stalked up to where Dan waited. For about three seconds and despite her fury, she couldn't help being drawn to his strength. It was distracting enough that he was tall and handsome and that damned blue suit, the one she liked better than all the others, made those eyes of his glitter. On top of being plain old handsome, he had those broad shoulders and those strong arms that could make her feel safe . . .

But right now she was as mad as hell and she was not playing with him about this. 'You have two minutes and then I'm on my way to interview the James family.'

He held out his phone, screen first. She glared at it, then surrendered and dug out her reading glasses. How was she supposed to stand her ground when she had to stop and get her damned glasses? She snatched the phone from his hand and had a look. Spears, the bastard, had sent him a text and the image of the flowers her self-proclaimed secret admirer had left on Lori's car. Confirmed once and for all that the guy in the Infiniti was working for the obsessed serial killer.

She shoved the phone back at Dan. 'The flowers are in the trunk. The card and envelope have been bagged for turning in to Evidence. What of it? We barely got a glimpse of the person who made the delivery.'

Evidently he was just as mad as she was. She could have used a jackhammer and not made a dent in that stony jaw of his. As she spoke, his posture had gone just as rigid. But it was the fire in those blue eyes that told her he was way, way ticked off. This might end up taking a few minutes longer than she'd anticipated.

'But you can't be sure he wasn't armed,' he said tightly, every word vibrating with fury.

'It's possible.' She shrugged. 'If he was, he ran like a coward, since Wells and I were definitely armed and ready.'

He dropped his phone into his jacket pocket and seemed to have trouble summoning whatever he intended to say next. Never a good sign. 'How many times did I call you after I received that text?'

She supposed her ignoring his calls added insult to injury. Daniel Burnett hated to be ignored. 'I was in the middle of interviews.' She gestured to the building behind her. 'In case you haven't noticed, I'm working a case that involves twenty missing children. I wasn't exactly sitting around waiting for you to call.'

'In the future,' he said, 'when I call, *answer*.' That lethal tone was one she hadn't heard before. 'I don't care where you are or what you're doing, answer the damned phone.'

'There are times—'

He moved his head firmly from side to side, shutting her up. 'There is no time that excuses your refusal to answer. If you are conscious, you answer. Are we clear?'

'Yes, sir.'

'Why did you and Detective Wells leave this morning without your surveillance detail?'

Oh hell. 'I forgot.' That was the truth. She completely forgot she needed to let them know when she left the office. 'It won't happen again.'

He pointed to the waiting cruiser. 'They will be following you the rest of the day. A two-man team will be watching you every minute of every day and night until this is over.'

'Fine.' Geez. He didn't have to be such a hardass about it.

He turned to walk away and she called after him, 'Dan, wait.'

When he'd turned around she suggested, 'Since you're here, why don't you take this stuff to Evidence and save me a trip.'

Before he could respond she passed him the bag containing the card and the envelope. Lori opened the trunk to retrieve the flowers.

He glared at Jess as he took the flowers then he just walked away. No *goodbye*, no *see you later*, nothing.

'He is *pissed*,' Lori said, as she rounded to her side of the car. 'I don't think I've ever seen him that angry.'

'Seriously.' Jess dropped into the passenger seat and exhaled a chest full of frustration. 'I'll call Mrs James en route. And, for God's sake, whatever you do, don't lose that tail.'

'By the way,' Lori said, as she backed out of the parking slot, 'Roger Fowler's dead. He had a heart attack last year. His ex-wife said she hopes he's rotting in hell.'

'Guess he's not our guy.'

Unless there were two.

* * *

Pelham, 3.30 P.M.

Erin James sat on the sofa next to her husband, Roy, and kept quiet as Jess asked the questions she hoped would prompt some new memory . . . some seemingly insignificant fact that had been left out of their statements fourteen years ago.

Again, the answers were exactly the same as the ones given all those years before. Jess tamped down her mounting frustration. She would find the missing piece. All she had to do was keep going over the puzzle.

'Did Emma like dogs?' she asked. According to the case file, the family hadn't owned any pets at the time of their daughter's disappearance. Since previous investigations found no connection between the victims – little girls – Jess was reviewing any possible link. Dorie Myers had a dog she adored, and that dog had gone missing that same night. Maybe it was a long shot, but it wasn't outside the realm of possibility.

'She was afraid of dogs,' Roy answered.

His wife rarely even blinked. Jess suspected she had required medication after the news they'd gotten last night. No matter that fourteen years had passed, if the tiniest light of hope had still lived deep inside these parents, it was extinguished now.

'So no pets?' Jess repeated for clarification.

The husband shook his head. 'No pets.'

Erin's gaze abruptly shifted to meet Jess's. 'There was a cat.'

'A cat?'

The husband stared at his wife as if she'd lost her mind. 'We didn't have a cat, sweetheart. Emma was allergic to cats.'

Erin's head went up and down, the move a little uncoordinated. 'I know.' She drew in a big breath. 'But she liked them anyway. Every time we visited anyone who had a cat, Emma would ask me why couldn't she have one. "I don't mind sneezing," she'd say.' Erin's lips trembled into a smile as she swiped at her eyes. 'But we didn't want to aggravate her allergies, so we never let her have one.'

'You said there was a cat,' Jess reminded her softly.

'A stray, I guess,' Erin said, her voice barely above a whisper. 'It showed up a couple days before . . .'

'You didn't tell me about a cat,' Roy said accusingly, as if she'd broken a marriage vow.

Jess understood his reaction. It was a common one among those left behind after a devastating tragedy. Those tender memories were so precious, the idea that he'd been left out of one was too painful to bear.

'I knew you wouldn't like it,' Erin admitted. 'I let her play with it in her room. We fed her some milk. She was really hungry.'

Roy stood and stepped away from the sofa. 'I can't believe you kept this from me.'

Erin ignored him. She just kept on talking to Jess as if the dam had broken and she couldn't stop the outpouring of words. 'She was white with black spots. Long hair, like a Persian. We knew she had a good home somewhere, because she was plenty fat and her coat was shiny.' Another smile tugged at her lips. 'Emma wanted to name her Spot if no one claimed her. I laughed and told her Spot was a dog's name.'

'What happened to the cat?' Jess wasn't sure how the stray cat fit into the child's abduction, but she wasn't going to pretend this couldn't be relevant. She just wasn't sure how yet. The slightest detail could make the difference.

'We were going to talk to Roy the next day. I told Emma that her daddy would come around. He loved her too much to deny her anything.'

Roy turned back to her then, his face damp with emotion.

'When she said her prayers that night she included the cat.'

'Why didn't I ever see this cat?' Roy asked gently. He resumed his seat next to his wife.

'The cat was gone the next morning, just like Emma.' Erin swiped at her eyes again. 'I consoled myself with the idea that the cat was with her wherever she was.'

'You didn't see the cat after that night?' Jess asked again. The cat had come from somewhere and chances were if it was lost it would hang around where it had gotten fed last. 'It didn't belong to any of your neighbors?'

'Never saw it again.'

Jess looked from Erin to her husband. 'I know you've both relived those days leading up to the night Emma disappeared over and over. I also know it's difficult to keep going back and revisiting those painful memories. But the smallest forgotten detail could make a difference. If you think of anything at all that you may have overlooked before, or if a question comes to mind, please call me.' She placed her business card on the coffee table.

'You still want to see her room?'

The hope in the mother's voice squeezed Jess's heart. 'I do, yes.'

The Jameses' home was a three-bedroom ranch in a quiet neighborhood that backed up to a wooded area. Like Dorie's room, Emma's had been left exactly as it was the night she disappeared. The bed was unmade, the My Little Pony comforter cast aside. Above the bed, pictures of colorful ponies and spotted cats drawn in crayon were thumbtacked to the wall, the edges yellowed and curling. Dolls and stuffed animals adorned the shelves along one wall, but it was a big, stuffed, very pink pony sitting atop the chest of drawers that drew Jess's attention.

'She got Prissy for her birthday that spring,' Erin explained, stroking the pony's thick mane. 'She said when she grew up she intended to keep a pony in her backyard.'

'She was quite the artist.' Jess surveyed the crayon drawings above the bed. A girl who knew what she wanted and didn't mind putting it on paper for anyone to see.

'She always got an A in Art.'

Jess turned to the father standing in the middle of the room, looking lost with his quiet comment echoing around them. 'Before we go, Mr James, if it's no trouble, do you mind if we have a look at your backyard?'

'No trouble.'

He led the way through the house and out the kitchen door. Jess trailed behind Lori, listening to Erin go on about what a smart little girl Emma was. Always did her homework. Cleaned her room and minded her manners. Her voice prompted images of that gap-toothed smile and those long blonde locks of Emma's. How had these people managed to go on after losing that precious child?

How could she possibly ever prepare herself for motherhood?

Jess pushed the thoughts aside and wandered around the yard. Emma and the others were depending on her.

She noted the location of the old swing set and the fact that there was no fence separating the backyard from the woods. She made a mental note that there were woods behind Dorie's house, too. Then she moved to the window that looked into Emma's bedroom. Even as short as Jess was, she could see the drawings on the wall above the child's bed.

The Man in the Moon would have seen them, too. The drawings told him about how much Emma loved ponies . . . and about the spotted cat.

Jess turned back to the parents watching her so intently and mustered a reassuring smile. 'We should get out of your way now. Thank you for helping with our investigation.'

'Do you think you can find him –' Ray James looked away, cleared his throat '– after all this time?'

This was the second time today she'd been asked that question. 'I can promise you one thing, Mr James,' she said. 'I will give it everything I've got and then some.'

Emma's parents followed her and Lori to the front of the house before going inside and closing the door.

Once in the Mustang she and Lori sat for a minute before driving away. The air-conditioning fought valiantly against the August heat. The police cruiser waited on the street for their next move.

'Do you think he'll keep making these deliveries to you?' Lori's voice filled the quiet that had shrouded them like a funeral cloak.

Jess wished she could answer that question with any measure of certainty. 'His every step depends on what his motive is for suddenly reappearing.' She thought of the rusty swing set in the backyard that had waited fourteen years for the little girl who once played on it to return. 'I think we'll know by tomorrow night if he plans to continue. He seems to be on a pretty aggressive schedule.'

'Why do you think he's doing this? Getting your attention surely isn't his primary objective.'

Jess laughed though the sound fell flat of humor. 'I know I'm cute and lovable, but I agree that getting my attention is likely not his primary objective.'

'Remorse maybe?' Lori braced her hands on the steering wheel. 'Maybe he is old and dying and hoping to find absolution.'

Dan had suggested something along those lines. Jess doubted his motive was that simple or anywhere near that pure. 'If his motive was absolution, then why make a game of it? Why not just deliver each child's remains to her parents' doorstep?' Jess dug out her sunglasses and slid them into place. 'My impression is that he's a sociopath with a larger agenda and we're way behind the curve.'

Lori sighed. 'Where to now?'

Jess glanced at the BPD cruiser waiting to follow them. 'A couple more hours at the office and then I'm going home.' She relaxed into the seat and tried to evict the images of a little girl and a stray cat wandering off into the darkness.

If the Man in the Moon would just give her something . . . anything that pointed her in the right direction.

He wanted her to find him, or so he claimed.

Something Fergus Cagle had said to her reverberated through her now. The meter readers learned the idiosyncrasies of the homes ... got to know the families' routines ...

Whoever took these children knew the homes and the families. He wasn't afraid to approach the house and take what he wanted. Clearly he had watched his prey for days or weeks until he felt utterly confident.

Who else besides a meter reader had the opportunity to get that close on a regular basis without rousing suspicion?

Pest control provider? The mailman?

Not the mailman. His deliveries rarely took him to the door of a home and certainly not to the children's bedroom windows. Mailboxes were way out in front near the street ... nowhere near the windows on the backs of the homes.

Jess closed her eyes. She needed to clear her head ... then she could start over with a fresh perspective.

A long hot bath was in order.

And a glass of wine...

Or maybe not, since she still hadn't gotten her period. She groaned. How had she gotten into this mess?

She did a mental eye roll. Oh, yes. She remembered. One tall, dark, and handsome police chief was the answer.

The very one who might just need to learn to answer to 'Daddy.'

Birmingham Police Department, 6.35 P.M.

Jess stared at her cell phone through two more rings. *Gant.* She steeled herself and answered just before it went to voice mail. 'Harris,' she said by way of a greeting.

'You didn't think you needed to call me when those flowers were delivered?'

'That's what Burnett's for,' she countered. 'I'm sure he called you as soon as he finished chewing me out for not calling him.' He was still mad at her. Anytime he avoided her it was because he was too angry to trust what he might say.

Well she was mad, too. Mad as hell that Spears was out there playing a game that included three innocent women whose names she didn't even know yet. Gant and the whole bunch needed to be worried about those three women, not her. Jess could take care of herself.

'Your stalker in the Infiniti is getting bolder, Jess,' Gant cautioned. 'There's no way to anticipate what he might do next.'

'Have you identified the women in those photos?' That's what the supervisory agent in charge of the Behavioral Analysis Unit needed to have his energies and powerful abilities of analysis focused on. He was wasting time talking to her.

'We're close on one of the women. We've followed up on hundreds of names from callers. This time we may have gotten lucky in Mobile. I hope to have a confirmation within the next twenty-four hours.'

Jess sat up a little straighter. 'Have you actually found the woman?' That would be very good news. She wanted to hope . . . she really did.

'Not exactly. She – if this is one of the women in the photos – is unaccounted for.'

Jess groaned. 'Damn it. Where the hell are these women? Their faces are all over the news. Someone somewhere has to know them.'

'Bear in mind, Jess,' Gant reminded her, 'we only got the photos out to the media and in the national databases less than seventy-two hours ago. These things take time. You know this. It doesn't work like it does on TV.'

Jess reared back and glared at her phone. 'You did not just say that to me.'

'You know what I mean, Jess.'

'Yeah, yeah, I know.' She did. People, young and old, went missing all the time without being missed immediately by friends and neighbors. She also knew that Spears would take advantage of those least likely to be missed. 'Am I still trending among his friends on the Net?'

Wasn't that every woman's dream? To be the subject of discussion among killers and their fans?

'That's difficult to assess. There's indications that some have moved on to private chat rooms. But they're still out there, Jess, and they're talking about you.'

Lovely. 'As soon as you find out about the woman in Mobile, you'll let me know?'

'Count on it.'

When the call ended Jess decided it was time to go home. As if she'd summoned him, Harper strolled back into the office. He'd had a command performance with the chief of police.

Jess grabbed her bag and readied to go. Harper went about doing the same. That he didn't say anything had Jess wondering what Dan had to say. This was the first time since their college days that he'd gotten this angry at her. She remembered now why she hated so much when they argued. It made her feel empty and . . . afraid.

'You ready, ma'am?' Harper asked.

She cleared her throat and banished the memories. 'Is he still angry at me?'

Harper considered her question a moment. 'Not angry, no, ma'am. He's worried.'

Well, that made two of them. 'Take me home, Sergeant. I'm done for today.'

Sometimes a woman, even a cop, had to admit when

she was at an impasse and only a hot bath and chocolate would help.

And maybe an apology.

Chapter Thirteen

9911 Conroy Road, 7.15 P.M.

Jess stared at the interior of her fridge hoping something ready to eat and delicious would appear. There was nothing edible except a hunk of cheese and leftover pizza that needed to go in the trash. Somehow she just didn't have the wherewithal to shut the door and admit she had no food in the house.

Hadn't she just gone shopping and filled her shelves the other day? Relenting, she closed the fridge door and moved on to the cupboards. Yeah, there was food but all of it required some prep time and she just wasn't up for it.

Any other time she wouldn't even think about food unless someone waved it in front of her. Maybe it was the fact she was getting nowhere on this case that had her wanting to break open a box of Hamburger Helper and eat the uncooked noodles.

She grabbed her cell and shuffled over to the sofa. The suit she'd worn today was in the dry cleaner's pile. After a quick shower she'd dragged on jeans and a tee. Eventually she was having that hot bath just to relax her muscles and then heading straight to bed.

But she needed to eat first. Her belly wouldn't stop rumbling. Maybe that middle-age spread she'd always heard about had taken root and needed fuel for the necessary expansion. Other than chocolate, she'd never been a stress eater.

The third possible explanation bobbed to the surface of her other worries.

'Not going there.' The concept was still only a theory. With this case and the whole Spears thing, who'd had time to pick up a test, anyway? No need to worry until she was at least a week late. That was reasonable, wasn't it?

Let it go for now.

'Who around here delivers?' She prompted a Google search. 'Definitely not pizza.' She bypassed all the pizza joints. 'Steak-Out?' She shrugged. 'Maybe.'

The security system warned that she had company. Maybe it was Dan. Guilt gave her a nudge. She hoped it was Dan. Most of his points were valid. It wasn't fair for her to ignore him. She owed him an apology. If there was ever a time in her life she needed to stop being so damned hardheaded and independent, this was it. She and Dan were . . . a couple. Didn't matter that this particular status wasn't official. Work conflicts and ethics had to be considered. He was her boss, and everyone in the department was going to be gauging whether or not she gained extra privileges because of their personal relationship.

A firm rap on the door reminded her to check the security monitor.

She frowned. Not Dan. Gina Coleman and Sylvia Baron. What were those two doing here *together*?

Too curious to care that she'd already washed the makeup off her face and discarded her bra, she opened the door to greet her visitors. Maybe the world was coming to an end.

'Ladies.' She refused to feel inadequate with the two standing at her doorstep looking as if they'd just stepped off the runway in their formfitting designer dresses and spiked heels. 'Did I forget to mark my calendar?'

As if her own body were on a mission to undermine her confidence, her gut rumbled loud enough for all to hear.

Sylvia held up a take-out bag. 'Sounds like we're just in time.'

Mortified, Jess shrugged. 'I was busy. I forgot to stop for takeout.' And too lazy to cook. The grandiose plans she'd had when she went grocery shopping of creating culinary masterpieces in her little kitchen had fallen flat this week.

Maybe she needed those cooking classes Gina used for finding her zen. Haha.

Gina waved a bottle of sparkling water and another bag, this one pink. 'I brought the drinks and dessert.'

Jess frowned, confused and then worried. Why sparkling water? These two couldn't know . . .

'Don't be rude, Harris,' Sylvia chastised. 'Invite us in. This is our first official girls' night.'

Jess backed up, opening the door wider in invitation. 'Sounds fun.' What it really sounded like was an evening of listening to complaints about work and men. She stifled a groan. She hated those kinds of 'bash the bastards you sleep with' sessions. A total waste of energy and she had none to spare.

That was another thing . . . she was just exhausted every night lately. Maybe it was time to get on a good multivitamin.

One thing she knew for certain. As soon as these ladies were out of here she intended to Google the symptoms of early pregnancy. *Oh God*. She wanted to scream, and she couldn't even scream in her own house. She had company. The last two people on earth she would want to suspect she was . . .

Wait. Other than the mental confusion and achiness, she had several of her sister's symptoms. What if they were suffering from the same unidentified illness? Her mind went immediately to her bag, where the notes about any health problems Jess and Lil's parents might have had waited. Their Aunt Wanda had prepared them *after* claiming she couldn't remember anything.

Jess rolled her eyes. The woman's notes were as worthless as everything else she'd ever done for Lil and Jess. Ellen, their mother, had never been sick a day in her life – according to Wanda. She'd had perfect pregnancies and deliveries. Lee, their father, on the other hand, had issues, Wanda had suddenly recalled. But she couldn't say what. She hadn't even named symptoms. How totally useless was that load of crap?

While Jess was caught up in her own worries, Sylvia had taken over her kitchen, arranging the take-out containers of Chinese entrees.

Giving herself a mental kick for standing here like she was in a coma, Jess went to the cabinet and grabbed three plates. She loved Chinese. Between the rice and the four – no five – entrees, this was going to be a feast. No cooking time required.

So maybe this unexpected visit wasn't such a bad thing. It certainly smelled good.

Thankfully Wesley, her ex, had given her a set of lovely stemmed glasses that Gina was currently filling with sparkling water.

Jess had a good reason – that she absolutely would not share – for avoiding alcohol. But why were Sylvia and

Gina opting out? She'd learn the reason soon enough, she supposed.

They settled around the table and not too much conversation was made while they savored the sweet and spicy meal. Jess could deal with the occasional girls' night if the food was this good. No one had time to complain if they were stuffing their faces.

Sylvia stopped eating and held up her glass. 'Let's have a toast to us, ladies.' She shot Gina a look. 'Even if it is only water.'

'After what happened with my sister,' Gina replied, 'I drank myself to sleep three nights in a row. I realized this morning that I've always used alcohol for a sleep aid and I decided I had to do something about it before I woke up at fifty and discovered I was an alcoholic. Life is too short to spend it under the influence of mind-numbing drugs.' She glared at Sylvia. 'You satisfied?'

Sylvia harrumphed as the three of them clinked glasses. 'Suit yourself, but next time I'm bringing wine.'

Jess sipped the sparkling water and toyed with the idea of keeping her mouth shut for the rest of the night. She wasn't sharing secrets with *anyone* until she was ready, and then it would be only with Dan. And maybe her sister.

After a few more bites of scrumptious chicken, Jess couldn't take it anymore. 'When did we decide we were going to start having these little get-togethers?' No amount of mind-numbing drugs would have erased a decision like that from her memory banks.

Sylvia pointed her chopsticks at Jess. 'I made the decision this afternoon. I called Gina, and we agreed on tonight at your place. Do you have a problem with that? I didn't have to include you, you know.'

Well, there was that. 'I didn't—'

'Yes, you did,' Gina challenged Sylvia. 'How can we figure out this case without her?' She gave Jess a look that warned this wasn't about friendship. 'Besides, she owes me.'

Jess opted not to mention that she had repaid the woman already for using her to accomplish a certain mission her second week in Birmingham. Good grief. Gina needed to learn to let go of a grudge.

'The chief mentioned you had offered to help out,' Jess admitted. 'I intended to call but I've been *crazy* busy.' She looked from one to the other. 'I think it's a great idea.' Fresh perspectives could add the unexpected slant to a case.

'Thank God.' Sylvia looked heavenward. 'If you'd turned her down I was going to be stuck playing Isles to her Rizzoli. You're not a cop.' She pointed her chopsticks again, first at Gina then at Jess. 'She is.'

Both women stared at her. Jess cleared her throat as she twirled her chopsticks in the lo mein. 'I didn't know you two . . .' Jess suffered the heat of their glares '. . . socialized.'

'We both went to Brighton,' Gina explained. 'You don't just graduate and never look back. There's the social commitments and the reunions. Besides, we've known each other forever. It's a small school.'

'Excuse me,' Sylvia argued. 'Forever is a long time. I am not that old.'

Gina waved her off and dove back into her veggies.

'What she's trying to say,' Sylvia elaborated, 'is that Brighton graduates support one another. She's going through a hard time and I'm trying to be there for her.' She lifted a skeptical eyebrow. 'We take care of our fellow alumni. It's ingrained from kindergarten. Dan knows the deal.'

But Jess did not. Unlike Dan and all his fancy friends, Jess hadn't attended Birmingham's most swanky private school. 'That's nice.' She pushed a smile into place. 'There's nothing like good friends.' She thought of Corlew and almost laughed out loud. He was the kind of friend she'd made in high school. Didn't matter, though, because she had Dan.

Would Dan want their child to go to Brighton?

Jess blinked to clear away the thought. 'Do either of you have a new perspective or some ideas regarding the case?'

'I've asked a forensic anthropologist from the university to do an evaluation of the remains,' Sylvia announced. 'I'm hopeful he might be able to provide a more in-depth analysis.'

Jess was still waiting for further analysis from the lab on the burlap and the newspapers. So far, what they had wasn't much. The burlap wrapped around Dorie's bones had been enveloped in plastic for protection. They'd gotten no trace evidence to indicate where the bundle had been kept before being delivered to Jess. So far, they had even less on Emma's remains.

'I, on the other hand,' Gina told them, 'have something more tangible right now.'

Jess washed down a bite of spicy chicken. 'Don't keep us in suspense.'

Gina jumped up and crossed to where she'd left her bag. She removed a manila file folder and hesitated. She pointed to Jess's homemade case board. 'I love this, by the way.'

'Thanks.' Most people thought it was morbid, but it helped Jess focus. It was generally at night, after the day was behind her and she'd relaxed, that her mind opened up, allowing the missing pieces hidden amid the info she'd digested all day to float to the surface.

Folder in hand, Gina rejoined them at the table. She pushed her plate aside and opened her folder. 'I read everything I could find on the cases, all the way back to the first one thirty-three years ago.'

As a reporter Gina would want to capitalize on a case this big. Understandable. Besides, her television reporter nemesis, Gerard Stevens, had landed the interview with

Corlew last week. Gina probably wanted to show him who really had the best reporter chops. Helping to find the truth for these parents was a far better story than bashing the BPD with an ex-cop bearing a grudge. If it helped Jess find the Man in the Moon that was all the better.

'Sixteen years ago,' Gina went on, 'one of the residents in the area where victim number seventeen disappeared, insisted the Man in the Moon was someone in the construction crew building a new subdivision in the neighborhood. But nothing panned out.'

Jess scooted her chair around the table to sit beside Gina.

'Give us the condensed version,' Sylvia grumbled. 'We don't want to be here all night.'

Gina sent her a shut-up look. 'In fifteen of the twenty cases there was major construction in the nearby vicinity. Most often new subdivisions.'

'You think our man is related to a construction crew.' That was possible, but none of the families had mentioned any construction activities nearby. Looking at Gina's list, that was probably because the activities weren't actually that close to the victims' homes. But, hey, it was something to consider. At this point, Jess wasn't ruling anything out without due consideration. 'Did any particular crews come up every time?'

'Just one.' Gina grinned. 'A four-man crew.'

'Do tell.' She had Jess's full attention now.

'Atkins Electric. A family-owned business started thirty-five years ago.' Gina tapped the home page from the company's website she'd printed out. 'The business started out with four brothers, three of whom have died over the years. But their sons stepped into their shoes. The one remaining founding brother, Benny Atkins, is still going strong. He was in the general area of where the victim lived in fifteen of the twenty cases.'

Jess wanted to be excited. She really did. 'But not in the actual neighborhood where the child lived?' That was the rub. Nearby but not up close.

'That's true,' Gina allowed. 'But they were around. At the convenience stores. Driving past the homes where the kids lived. The kids had been on summer break for months, running around to neighborhood pools, yard-hopping to play with friends. There was opportunity.'

Jess couldn't deny that assessment. 'I'll set up an interview for tomorrow.'

She'd have to work Atkins in around the crazy day she already had scheduled. Or maybe she'd just show up at their shop before they opened. Tomorrow was going to be a long one. Dan was holding another press conference at six thirty tomorrow evening. Trent Ward, the department's PR rep, had issued a limited statement at noon today about Emma James. But the community wanted to hear from their chief of police. This time Jess was supposed to be there. Last she'd heard, Dan didn't want her in the limelight. Apparently he'd changed his mind.

She wouldn't know. Why the heck didn't he call? That empty feeling just wouldn't let go.

'I know one of the mothers,' Sylvia said, drawing their attention to her. 'We were in premed together. When she got pregnant she dropped out. We ran into each other from time to time over the years. When I saw her after her little girl went missing, she was a mess. It was like the life had gone out of her. She was an empty shell of the woman I'd known before.'

'I can't imagine,' Gina murmured.

'Personally,' Jess admitted, 'I don't see how anyone who's aware of the evil in this world can bring a child into it.' Her stomach roiled, as if to remind her that she might not have any room to talk about this particular subject anymore.

'You look at all the good,' Sylvia countered, 'not the bad. You believe good will prevail.' She laughed. 'As foolish as that concept is, that's what we do in most situations. Then we get slammed because we trusted the wrong person.'

Jess could understand why Sylvia felt that way. Her husband of ten years had cheated, ultimately leaving her for a younger woman.

'Kicked in the teeth because we tried,' Gina chimed in.

Jess knew nothing about Gina's personal life, other

than that she and Dan had gotten together occasionally, but she didn't think that was what the woman meant. In any event, maybe Jess had more in common with these two than she realized. They were all jaded and tired and yet determined not to give up on their career goals and maybe on life in general. Possibly even on love.

Damn, she wished she could have a glass of wine . . . or two or three.

Gina stared at the water in her glass. 'I've had to do a lot of soul searching lately. I'm right where I wanted to be careerwise, but my personal life is in shambles. It's time to face reality and move on with who we really are and where we want to be.'

'Hear hear,' Sylvia agreed, as she started to lift her glass but then changed her mind. 'To hell with it. It's just not the same with water.'

'Don't be a bitch,' Gina tossed back. 'I've taken the first of many important steps to make my life better.'

'Good for you,' Jess offered. Seemed a neutral enough statement.

'When are you and Dan going to stop pretending you're not still in love with each other?' Sylvia nailed Jess next. 'Watching the two of you try to pretend you aren't in a relationship is becoming tedious.'

'Oh' – Jess pursed her lips – 'maybe around the same time you and your boss confess about whatever it is you have going on.'

Sylvia and Gina burst into laughter.

Jess hated when that happened. When everyone else seemed privy to some knowledge that only she was unaware of.

'Jess, sweetie, my boss is gay,' Sylvia pointed out. 'He only loves me for my incredible skills with the dead.'

'See,' Gina piped up, 'doesn't she sound just like Maura Isles?'

'Dr Leeds is gay?' Jess had no idea. 'Doesn't he have a wife and two or three kids?'

'He does,' Sylvia confirmed. 'But he also has a lover. A surgeon, no less. A gorgeous man who prefers his privacy and is perfectly happy to share a secret life with Martin.'

Why did Jess always miss that stuff about her colleagues? She rarely missed a thing when it came to the bad guys, thankfully. Maybe the good guys were just too boring for her to pay attention.

'Well, what do you know?' Jess held her palms up in surprise. 'I had no idea.'

'Besides,' Gina teased, 'Sylvia likes younger men these days.'

'The ones my age are all asses,' Sylvia proclaimed, 'like my ex.'

Jess knew Sylvia's ex and he was a nice man, but that didn't mean he'd been a good husband to her, so she gave Sylvia grace. You never really knew a person until you lived with them. Jess was a good person but she'd made a terrible wife.

Then again, maybe she'd just married the wrong man.

'Now you know all our secrets,' Gina announced, 'what are yours?'

The varying sauces from the entrees did a little churning in her belly as both women stared at Jess.

Across the room, deep in her bag, Jess's cell clanged.

Thank God.

'Excuse me, ladies.' She jumped out of her seat and hurried across the room.

Dan's name and face flashed on her screen. Her heart performed a little skip and several hops.

'Hey.' She glanced at the two women at her table who seemed caught up in their own intense conversation.

'I wanted to apologize for being such a jerk today,' he said. 'I was angry and I went a little overboard.'

He sounded tired. Tired and defeated. Made her ache to hold him. The idea that the two women across the room were right nudged her. She and Dan needed to stop pretending.

As if she hadn't just had that epiphany, she gave him what for. 'You sure did.' If she cut him too much slack, he'd just use it against her by going even more overboard the next time. 'But your apology is accepted.' Just do it, Jess. 'And I'm sorry for ignoring you. It was thoughtless and it won't happen again.' She made a face, hoped she could stick to that promise.

'You okay?'

'I'm good.' She hugged her arm around herself and wished she knew for certain what was going on with her body. Not true. She wasn't ready to know. She needed to focus on this case. 'You?'

'I'll be okay.'

There was a lot he didn't qualify that statement with, and Jess knew most of it. He wanted this over. He wanted Spears stopped. He wanted the monster who'd taken all those children to be caught and brought to justice. And he wanted Jess to be safe.

Then he'd be okay.

'We'll both be okay, Dan,' she murmured.

'See you in the morning. Night, Jess.'

'Night.'

The urge to call him right back and tell him she loved him was almost more than she could set aside. She left her phone on the coffee table and padded back to the table where Sylvia and Gina were cleaning up.

'I can take care of that,' Jess offered. They both shooed her away and kept doing what they were doing.

'I need to get going,' Sylvia announced when the last plate was rinsed and stacked neatly in the sink. 'I have to be up really early in the morning to meet the guy from the university.'

'He's about twenty-five,' Gina interjected. 'It takes a couple extra hours to prepare for that much staying power.'

'He's thirty,' Sylvia argued, 'and this is work.'

'That's perfect,' Gina argued back. 'No strings, just great sex.'

Jess grabbed a couple of the stemmed glasses and headed for the sink. She wasn't touching that one. She didn't need any more reminders of Gina and Dan's 'no strings' relationship. The silence in the room warned that everyone knew what Jess was thinking.

'Well,' Gina rushed to add, 'I'm out of here, ladies. See you at the press conference,' she said to Jess. 'Let me know what you find out about Atkins Electric.'

Jess promised to keep her posted as she walked her to the door.

Sylvia joined Jess there but didn't leave immediately. 'She's having a tough time getting past what happened with her sister.'

Seemed impossible that it had been just last week. It felt like a lifetime ago. 'It was a lot to swallow.' Jess frowned. 'She's lucky to have such a good friend.'

Sylvia shrugged. 'I can be good when I want to. Besides, I know what it's like to have something like this happen.'

Sylvia's sister Nina was schizophrenic. About eleven years ago Nina had been married to Dan. She'd gone over the edge, tried to kill him, for God's sake. Nina had been in an institution since. It was a sad story. One that clearly weighed heavily on Sylvia. Dan, too. He felt guilty to this day for failing to see what no one had told him about.

Jess smiled, trying to lighten the moment. 'And all this time I thought you were too stuck up to do something so nice.'

'Don't let tonight fool you, Harris. I am exceedingly stuck up and for good reason.'

With that Sylvia was gone with nothing more than a wave as she descended the stairs.

Jess closed the door, locked up, and set the alarm. That big old claw-foot tub was calling her name.

After turning the knobs to fill the tub, she dragged off her clothes and paused. She still looked the same. She smoothed a hand over her belly. But what if everything was different? How would she protect this child? The parents of all those missing little girls had done their best, and still evil had snatched their very hearts.

Jess was going to need Dan and Lil. Like Gina, she was also going to need to take a long, hard look at her life and consider changes.

'No more thinking.'

With her phone and her Glock on the floor next to the tub, Jess eased into the warm water and relaxed. She just wanted to close her eyes and forget the world for a few short minutes. Her muscles needed this reprieve.

Her cell clanged and vibrated on the floor.

'Damn it.' Couldn't a woman have her bath without being disturbed? She looked over the rim of the tub and glared at her phone.

Lily.

Jess snatched up the phone. 'Hey. You okay?'

'I'm okay,' her sister assured her. 'I was just feeling lonely. Blake's in bed already and I guess I got to thinking about the kids being gone . . . I just needed to hear your voice, Jess.'

Jess smiled and relaxed in the tub once more. 'Well, I'm right here, Lil. We can talk all night if you want.'

Lily told her all about what the kids were up to at college, and Jess decided she was the one who'd needed to hear her sister's voice. She really was glad to be home.

By the time the bath water had cooled, Lil was ready to go to bed. Jess said good night and set her phone back on the floor.

She reached to pull the drain plug and something tiny and white near the toilet caught her eye. She squinted and tried to make it out. It was the little ball of toilet paper she'd rolled up and stuffed in that hole.

She shuddered. If there was some sort of bug going in and out of that damned hole . . . she shuddered again. She'd just have to get some caulk or something more permanent to fill the damned thing.

Jess had no tolerance for bugs or spiders.

When she'd dried off and dragged on her robe, she

crouched down next to the toilet and had a look. She made another ball of toilet paper and stuffed the hole once more. 'Damned old houses.'

If she ever bought another house it would not be a *historic* one.

Too many creaks and cracks and critters.

She grabbed her phone and her Glock and went to bed.

She closed her eyes and wished for sleep . . . but that wasn't going to happen for a while. All those little faces on her case board were looking at her, waiting for her to find them. Add to that the three women whose photos Spears had sent her . . . were waiting for someone to find them.

How could Jess dare sleep when those women were targets because of her? When those children needed her to find them . . . to find justice for them?

She felt as if she were running in circles. There was nothing but vague leads on the Man in the Moon case, and Spears's followers were watching her, leaving her flowers and exchanging photos.

Jess admitted defeat and sat up. Whether it was the suggestion Gina had passed along about the construction crews in the vicinity of the victims or that one meter reader, Jerry Bullock, who had been so nervous during his interview, she couldn't shut her brain off yet and pretend she'd done all she could this day.

She threw the covers back and got up.

This was going to be a long night and she didn't want to do this alone.

She made the call. When he answered she said the words before she lost her nerve. 'Can you come over? I need a sounding board.'

For fifteen minutes Jess paced the floor. She studied those pictures and reviewed the reports she had read from all twenty abductions. Not the first clue or piece of evidence had been found, and the Man in the Moon had gotten off scot-free. What was he doing taking these kinds of risks now? Was he feeling remorseful, as she and Lori had discussed earlier? What life-changing event had occurred to trigger his need to reach out to Jess with these gifts?

Had her recent visibility on the news stirred an interest? Maybe he'd decided it was time and he wanted a high-profile cop to nail him.

'Doesn't make sense.' He'd said in his last message that this was all for her. 'Unless . . .'

The security system chimed, and she rushed to the door. She disarmed the system, unlocked the door, and yanked it open. It wasn't until she opened her mouth to speak that she realized what she'd done. Ice curled around her, made her body quake.

'Shit.'

'What?' Dan ushered her back so he could come inside and close the door. When he'd locked it and reset the alarm, he surveyed her, worry etched across his face. 'What happened?'

She blinked, felt like kicking herself for the stupid mistake. 'I knew you were coming so I . . . I forgot to check the monitor.'

No matter that a cop waited outside . . . no matter that she had known Dan was coming, she'd made a mistake.

And that was how easy it was to become a victim.

Dan put his arms around her and pulled her close. 'You're tired. That's all.'

She nodded against the warmth and strength of his chest. She knew this, but that didn't change the fact that she'd made a mistake. Somehow she couldn't get past that.

'Come on.' He guided her to the sofa. 'You said you needed a sounding board. What do you want to talk about?'

She stalled at the sofa. 'I changed my mind.' Her throat ached and she couldn't trust herself to speak anymore.

He looked disappointed. 'You want me to go back home?'

Was that what she wanted? She'd spent the last month and a half sending him home on work nights and beating herself up when she didn't. She searched his face, knew every angle and line. Her body hummed with need just standing this close to him.

She shook her head. 'I don't want you to go.'

His fingers dived into her hair and he pulled her close. 'I love you, Jess,' he whispered against her lips.

'Love you,' she murmured between fiery kisses.

He kissed her until she melted against him. All the fear and worries about what was coming next for them faded.

Dan was here and that was all that mattered.

Chapter Fourteen

11.55 P.M.

He stared at the moon and cursed himself.

His body ached with that relentless craving. A craving he had conquered for more than a dozen years. How could he be so helpless now . . . after all this time? Where was his strength?

He tightened the obedience belt to the final notch, screaming with the agony of the nails burrowing more deeply into his ribs. Still the urge would not be silenced.

She had done this to him. It was her fault. Jess Harris had become Birmingham's sweetheart and she had ruined his life.

And now, as he stared at the bones spread on the blanket beneath the moonlight, he could barely breathe.

There was no turning back. No undoing the evil.

Dropping to his knees, he folded the blanket carefully,

drawing the precious treasure into a protected bundle. He felt the blood oozing into his waistband, but he no longer cared.

Agony swelled again, bursting from his lips in low moans. He had been good for so long. His sweet Lucy and his Lord and Savior had given him the strength. The whore he'd married as a foolish young man had taken his baby girl from him. For years he had searched for a replacement to soothe his soul.

Satan had put that idea in his heart! He hadn't meant to do it.

He'd lost control. He was weak . . . so weak.

But none had ever taken the place of his sweet, sweet Lucy. He'd tried to teach them, but they resisted until he sent them to heaven.

Finally the whore had died, and Lucy had come back to him.

He had walked the path of goodness since that day.

Until now.

'Forgive me, Father,' he cried as he searched the heavens for a sign. 'I have broken our covenant. I am lost!'

But there would be no sign and no forgiveness this time. All was lost.

What if someone else had seen him take the girl?

Fear speared his heart. He jumped to his feet, the bundle held tightly to his chest, and rushed into the house. The dogs watched as he paced back and forth in hopes of working off some of the anxiety crushing him in its ruthless grip.

He'd always been so careful . . . every step meticulously calculated. Not tonight. Tonight had been filled with chaos and complications.

Complications he should have seen coming.

Think! He had to think. He'd had to move this treasure from beneath the burying tree sooner than he'd intended. The order had come and he'd had no choice.

Then he'd lost control and taken a new one.

'God, why have you forsaken me?' he wailed.

The police could be coming for him now! *Harris* could be coming for him!

He'd made a terrible, terrible mistake. This wasn't part of the plan.

He hadn't wanted to do this. But he'd seen her playing in the street . . . watching her . . . listening to her voice had roused the demon. He'd been weak and he'd lost control.

It wasn't his fault . . . not his fault at all.

He moaned, the sound low and deep in his throat.

She was responsible.

Penelope curled around his leg, trying to comfort him with her rubbing and purring. He nudged the cat away. He had to think.

The basement! He could hide this precious delivery in the basement just in case there was trouble tonight.

He hurried to the closet and his secret door. He didn't bother with the flashlight. The darkness was his ally.

He felt his way down the steep stairs that descended into the basement. It was safe down here so he pulled the string that lit the bare bulb dangling from the ceiling. Taking his time he scanned the shelves and the boxes for the perfect spot.

The Christmas box. Yes, that would serve his purpose. He gently placed the precious bundle atop another sturdy box, one that contained old photographs he no longer cared to look at. He should have thrown it away a long time ago. He swiped the dust from the Christmas box and opened the flaps. After moving aside the piles of colorful balls and strands of shiny tinsel, he placed the precious bundle inside, positioned tinsel over it and quickly closed the flaps.

'There.' His body twitched with relief. This little one was safe now.

He turned off the light and climbed the stairs. Quickly, he assured his secret door was hidden once more. Just in case. His heart continued to pound as sweat slid down his body, joining the blood soaking into his trousers.

He closed his eyes and fought the longing to touch the *new* treasure.

He slowed his breathing and focused his mind on Lucy.

Whimpering brushed his senses. His breath hardened to rock in his lungs, stiffening his spine.

She was awake.

'Shhh,' he urged. 'You mustn't cry.'

Her cries grew louder and he cried with her. 'Please,' he begged, 'don't cry.'

She sobbed harder.

He sank to the floor, the demon inside him howling with need. He banged his head against the wall . . . fought the urges . . . but it was too late.

It was done.

Chapter Fifteen

Atkins Electric, Homewood,
Friday, August 20, 7.45 A.M.

'The lights aren't on yet.' Lori powered her car window down and leaned her head out. 'Nope. No lights.'

'Let's drive down the back alley,' Jess suggested, 'see if anyone's parked back there. I'd like to get in the door before they open for business.' She had no desire to stand around waiting for the owner's attention.

This was a long shot. A really, really long shot, but Jess couldn't ignore the lead.

The storefront had a typical retail façade. Big plate-glass display windows with a double glass door in the middle. The parking out front was limited, since the store sat so close to the four-lane street between two busy intersections. Jess figured the employees parked in the back. The BPD cruiser following her around this morning had parked in front at the very end of the line of slots.

Dan must have instructed the uniforms not to horn into her space. They were staying back as much as possible.

Little flashes from last night threaded through her mind, distracting her. Somehow she'd just been too weary to care what the cop outside her door had thought or what Lori would think when she picked Jess up this morning. It only mattered that she had needed to be in Dan's arms. When he'd kissed her goodbye this morning she'd almost told him her period was late.

But Lori had arrived and that was that.

'There's a truck,' Lori said, pulling Jess back to the present.

Silver Dodge Ram. Older model. Next to the rear entrance was a picnic table and one of those portable smoking stations.

'Someone's in there,' Jess said. 'Let's go back around front and park. We'll beat on the door until whoever's in there lets us in.' There was a door on the back of the building, but it was steel with no window. Out front she could flash her badge. That usually worked if a person had nothing to hide.

Lori rolled into the parking slot and shifted into Park. 'Who's playing bad cop?' she asked as she opened her door.

Jess pushed her sunglasses up her nose. 'You have to ask?' She emerged from the car and shoved the door shut with her hip. 'Why don't you go around and keep an eye on that back door, just in case.'

'On my way.' Lori headed around the hood of the Mustang. She jerked to a stop. 'Wait! I saw someone behind the counter.' Lori bounded up to the front entrance.

Jess was right on her heels. At the door she peered through the glass, on which a sign boasted an opening time of eight a.m.

Jess rapped on the door. 'Birmingham PD,' she called out. 'Sir, we need to speak with you.'

An older man shuffled to the door, peering at Jess with a frown furrowing his face. 'We open at eight,' he said through the glass.

Judging by his age – seventy, at least – this was likely the surviving brother who had been a part of this company during the Man in the Moon abductions. And apparently he had no desire to open his doors one minute before that posted time. She flashed her badge. 'Sir, I need to speak with you *now*.'

He stared at the badge a long moment, then nodded. 'Give me just a minute.'

Jess managed to keep her smile in place until he'd backed away and turned to do whatever it was he felt necessary before admitting her into his store.

'I guess he has to get the key,' she grumbled.

'I hope I'm not so ornery when I get that old.' Lori set her hands on her hips and leaned closer to the glass to see if he was coming back yet.

'I can't say anything,' Jess admitted. 'I think I was born

that ornery.' She jerked her head toward the police cruiser. 'Have one of our friends go on around and watch that back door just in case Mr Atkins decides he doesn't want to talk this morning.'

Lori hustled over to give the order. Jess heaved a big breath. Maybe at least this guy could offer something new. The more rocks they turned over the greater the likelihood they would uncover new leads.

A flash of black and a deep roar snagged Jess's attention, had her bracing for trouble. A vehicle wheeled into the parking slot next to Lori's Mustang.

Not an Infiniti. *Dodge Charger*.

She managed to relax enough to get a decent breath. 'What in the world does he want?' she muttered as Lori joined her at the door once more.

Buddy Corlew climbed out of the beefy hot rod and gave them a nod. 'Morning, ladies.'

'Corlew.' Jess folded her arms over her chest. If he was here trying to grovel for information he could forget it. Whatever grudge he had with Dan he could settle with Dan. She was trying to solve a case. Besides, she already had enough friends who wanted to play games.

Lori drew down her sunglasses and surveyed his car. 'That Charger could use a good wash, Corlew.'

It was dusty as hell. Made Jess think of gravel roads like the one that led to the creek they'd visited yesterday. Had he been tracking her movements? Fishing for a lead?

If he thought following her around would make her want to be on his team he could forget it. And she damned sure wasn't allowing him to join hers.

She had no problem with his help on a case, but she wasn't dealing with any hidden agendas, and Corlew had a huge agenda. He was not going to draw her into this grudge match he had going with Dan and the BPD.

He grinned at Lori. 'I've got two sweet little college girls who take care of that for me every Sunday afternoon. Gives 'em a chance to work on their tans while picking up a few extra bucks.'

'If they're doing anything more than washing your car,' Lori reminded him, 'it's probably illegal.'

He laughed. 'Why don't you come on over this Sunday and you can see for yourself. I can always use another set of good hands.'

Jess rolled her eyes. 'What do you want, Corlew?'

'Your boy rang me up at seven this morning wanting to discuss my work on this case.'

Good for Harper. He and Cook were interviewing all the cops – the ones still alive, anyway – who'd worked the Man in the Moon investigation. 'Why aren't you talking to Harper instead of horning into my business?'

She glanced beyond the glass to see if the old man she presumed to be Mr Atkins was anywhere in sight. What in the world was he doing? Maybe he was senile as well as ornery. Or maybe he'd had to take a pee and that was taking awhile.

'I owe you an apology, Jess.'

Now that got her attention. 'I'm afraid to ask what for?'

'I wasn't completely honest with you.' Corlew dragged his sunglasses from his face and shifted them around to the back of his neck.

She hated when guys did that. Especially guys over forty. 'What's new? I've known you better than twenty-five years. I'd be worried if you suddenly started telling me the truth.'

'I misfiled those reports on my interviews with the meter readers from Alabama Power. I was pissed at Black, so I thought I'd give him something to worry about if he ever had a reason to pull that cold case.'

Her instincts went on alert. What was he up to? 'You understand that what you're telling me is a criminal offense. I could arrest you right now.' Except she had other more important stuff to do.

He held his hands out as if he were ready to be cuffed. 'Do what you think you have to. I want to make amends. Whatever it takes.'

What a load of BS. The nerve of this man! Getting even was one thing, but playing with innocent people's lives was something else altogether. No wonder Dan fired him. 'Is there anything I need to know in those reports from the meter reader interviews?'

He wagged his head, dropped his hands to his sides. 'Like I said, Black was right about that. The only thing that was even a gnat's ass off was the guy Bullock. Jerry Bullock. He seemed a little antsy when I talked to him. Like maybe he was worried about getting fired.'

Jess had picked up on Bullock's anxiousness, too. Funny that he'd be nervous all these years later. 'What about the one who got fired the next year, Roger Fowler?'

Corlew frowned in concentration before an oh-yeah expression dawned. 'He was off in Cancun when the little Myers girl went missing. He and the woman he was having the affair with apparently sold off jewelry that had belonged to her husband's mother to pay for the trip. When her husband found out, she blamed it on Fowler, said he stole the jewelry.'

'I appreciate the confession, Corlew, but I'm a little busy just now.' Jess hitched her head toward the Charger. 'We'll talk about this later. Have a nice day.' She peered through the glass to see if the old man was coming yet. No sign of him. Damn. 'Detective Wells, why don't—'

A blast rent the air.

'Gunshot!' Jess warned even as both Lori and Corlew shouted the same.

Jess hunkered down next to the Mustang and pulled her Glock from her bag. Lori dropped between the Mustang and the Charger, weapon in hand and calling into dispatch the code for shots fired.

Corlew, his own weapon drawn, had flattened against the brick building rather than hit the ground. The sound had come from inside. As far as Jess knew there was no one inside except the old man.

Corlew signaled that he was going around back. Jess gave him a nod.

The second uniform from the cruiser, crouched down low, moved up behind her.

Jess leaned to one side in an attempt to see through the doors. No visible movement. Doors still secured.

'Stay down, ma'am,' the officers said. 'Back up is en route.'

Jess ignored him.

An SUV pulled into the parking slot next to the Charger. A man climbed out and looked from the police cruiser to Jess and Lori and then to the front entrance of the store.

'Get down, sir,' Jess ordered. 'Someone inside fired a weapon.' She wasn't waiting any longer. There hadn't been any more gunshots. 'I'm going in,' she said to Lori.

As if her words had just sunk in, the man from the SUV rushed for the front entrance. 'My father's in there!'

'Chief Harris!' the uniform shouted as she lunged forward, blocking the man's path.

Jess couldn't have this guy rushing inside until they determined exactly what had happened in there.

Lori shoved the new arrival against the wall. 'Stay back, sir.'

'Mr Atkins, do you have a key for this door?'

He nodded. Jess held out her hand. Worry in his eyes and hand shaking, he passed her the keys.

'Let me go in,' Lori offered.

Corlew would be at the back entrance by now. Wouldn't matter if it was locked. He had learned the art of breaking and entering as a freshman in high school. Just another reason he'd ended up in the military. He'd probably scared the fire out of the officer she'd sent back there to watch the rear entrance.

'You,' Jess said to the young officer next to her, 'come with me.'

'Chief,' Lori argued.

Jess cut her off with a look.

She hugged the wall and eased toward the front entrance. She peered past the glass. Didn't see a thing. Watching for movement inside, she shoved the key into the lock and gave it a twist. Corlew appeared just as she was shoving the door open. Once she and the uniform were inside, she closed and locked the door. Until they had assessed the situation no one else was getting in.

'What've we got?' she asked Corlew.

'I've got your other uniform maintaining the rear perimeter,' he explained. 'Building's clear. Old man, sixty-five, seventy maybe. Single gunshot to the head. I called it in, backup and a bus are on the way, but he's a goner. Most of the back of his head is decorating the wall.'

'You shouldn't be in here.' She tugged on a pair of gloves from her bag. 'I want a list of anything you misfiled, misplaced, or whatever on my desk ASAP.'

He nodded. 'I won't let you down this time, Jess.'

'We'll see about that. Now go,' she ordered.

Remarkably, he didn't argue. He gave her a two-fingered salute and got out of her way.

She dragged on a pair of shoe covers and ensured the uniform with her, Officer Mitchell, did as well. Corlew had said the old man was beyond help and that the building was clear, but she opted to check for herself. With Mitchell trailing her, she walked the scene. Sure enough, the old guy was done for.

The second of two offices and the larger warehouse fronted by the much smaller retail space were clear. The blare of sirens sounded closer as she returned to the office where the old man had ended his life. A .38 lay on the floor next to his chair where it had fallen after he'd fired that single shot. Blood and brain matter had sprayed over the wall and blinds of the window behind his desk.

'Maybe Coleman was onto something,' Jess said to herself. Behind her Mitchell gagged.

She whipped around to order him out of the room but he was already rushing away, hand over his mouth, jaws bulging.

Once backup was on the scene and the area was secured, Jess escorted the younger Atkins to the picnic table at the rear of the building. She sent the officer around to see about his partner Mitchell. There were official vehicles everywhere. Evidence techs had arrived. Someone from the coroner's office was en route. It was a cluster.

'Mr Atkins, I'm going to have Detective Wells here read you your rights.'

He blinked as if he wasn't sure what was happening. He'd figured out his father was dead before Jess could relay the bad news.

'It's standard procedure,' she assured him. 'We don't want to violate your rights in any way.'

He nodded and then listened as Lori recited those rights.

When he indicated that he understood, Jess asked, 'Would you like an attorney, sir?'

'No. I don't need one.'

Jess sat down on the opposite side of the timeworn picnic table. 'Sir, we came here this morning to talk to your father about—'

'I know why you're here,' he said, defeat in his voice. 'That's why he did this. He knew why you were here, too.' Atkins shook his head. 'It shouldn't have ended this way. I told him we'd get a good lawyer, but I guess he figured there was no point.'

Surprise and anticipation sending her heart into a faster rhythm, Jess looked to Lori, who appeared just as startled as she was. 'Sir, why do you believe we're here?'

'He made a mistake,' Atkins fairly shouted. 'He was a good man.' His voice fell with the last.

More of that heady anticipation pounded in Jess's veins. She couldn't put words in his mouth but she needed him to get to the point. 'What kind of mistake did he make, Mr Atkins?'

'It was a long time ago. Thirty years . . .'

Her heart all but stopped beating. Jesus Christ . . . could BPD have overlooked this lead all those years ago and missed the Man in the Moon? Not that she could fault anyone – hell, she'd overlooked it, too, until Gina Coleman brought it up. The distance these guys were working from the actual crime scenes had made them irrelevant.

'He underwired that whole subdivision,' Atkins was saying to her. 'It was the only way to keep costs down. He and his brothers were just starting out and they were desperate. My father never did anything like that again. I swear.' He stared at Jess, his eyes pleading with her to believe him. 'It was his one mistake in a lifetime of hard work. He had no idea that everything would turn around right after that and business would take off. But it was too late to fix what was done and no one was ever the wiser. Then the fire happened.'

'Fire?' Jess prompted. Clearly he wasn't talking about missing children.

'Two months ago there was a fire in that subdivision. An elderly couple died. Dad got the call yesterday that our company and the work he did there was being investigated.'

'You feel he believed we were here to arrest him?' Oh hell. This had nothing to do with her case.

'What else would he think?' He dropped his head into his hands and started to sob. 'I should've seen this coming.'

Jess didn't bother questioning him further. The dead man inside wasn't involved with the Man in the Moon case. She left the younger Mr Atkins be and joined Lori a few feet away. 'Contact someone for him, please. Wife, someone.'

'Will do.' Lori reached for her cell.

Jess needed to walk off some of this frustration. She should have eaten this morning; she felt weak and shaky. The dead, no matter their condition, rarely did that to her. Maybe she'd go around and sit for a minute in the Mustang.

The puker, Mitchell, was in the BPD cruiser, head down in shame. Poor guy.

Her cell clanged. Probably Dan checking to see if she was okay. Sure hadn't taken long for him to hear about this. One of the uniforms had likely reported to him immediately.

Not Dan. *Harper*.

If he was calling to tell her about Corlew he was a little late.

'What's up?'

'Ma'am, I just got a call from dispatch. We have a missing child, eight-year-old female. Cook and I are en route to the residence now.'

The bottom dropped out of her stomach and she swayed. 'Where?' Just uttering that solitary word seemed to shred her throat as if she'd swallowed glass.

Harper provided a Hoover address.

'We're on our way, Sergeant.' She dropped her phone in her bag and turned to the officer waiting near the cruiser and Mitchell. 'Officer Woodson, let Detective Wells know we have a call.' He stared at Jess as if he didn't understand. 'We have to go. Tell her I'm waiting in the car.'

He nodded. 'Yes, ma'am.'

She watched him rush around the corner of the building. To be that young again. God, she felt old today.

A horn blew and she jumped. She surveyed the street. No traffic on the street. She scanned the official vehicles gathered in front of the crime scene. Who had blown the horn? Confused, she checked both directions again, then assessed the parking lot across the four-lane street.

A single vehicle sat there. The man inside waved at her.

'What the . . . ?'

Black. *Infiniti.*

'Son of a bitch.' Fury whipped through Jess.

She withdrew her weapon where he could see it and started walking his way. At the last second she remembered to check the street to her left for traffic. Clear.

The driver with his dark hair and sunglasses just sat there, revving the engine, daring her to either shoot or to get in his face and demand answers.

'You're pretty cocky sitting all the way over there, aren't you?'

He grinned, pointed his forefinger at her and pretended to shoot.

Outrage blasted her again. 'Mother fu—'

A horn blew. The wind from a passing panel truck almost knocked her off her feet.

She stumbled back. Another horn blasted . . . this one behind her.

'Shit.' She dragged in a breath and blinked. She turned her attention back to the parking lot and the Infiniti was gone.

Standing there in the middle of the traffic that seemed to have come out of nowhere, Jess struggled to catch her breath. What the hell had she been thinking? The guy had baited her and she'd been so fixated on getting to him that she'd almost gotten herself killed.

Carefully checking all lanes before moving, she hurried across the street and into the lot where he'd been parked.

He was long gone.

'How in the world?' He'd disappeared in scarcely more than a blink.

The alley. Beyond the hardware store on this side of the street was an alley just like the one behind the Atkins Electric shop. He'd escaped that way.

Jess turned around to see Lori waiting on the other side of the street.

Oh hell. 'This is not going to go well.'

Paying extra close attention this time, Jess crossed the street once more.

She couldn't recall having seen Lori angry – at least not at her. At the moment she looked beyond furious.

'That truck almost hit you,' she bellowed. 'What the hell were you doing?'

'He was there.' Jess exhaled a big breath. 'The guy who left the flowers. The one who took a bead on me that day on the exit ramp. It was him. He's following me. Taunting me.'

'Let's go. Harper's waiting.' Lori stormed over to her Mustang but not before giving the poor guy Jess had sent to get her the evil eye and warning, 'See what happens when you take your eyes off her?'

Feeling like a total idiot, Jess climbed into the Mustang.

'I was wrong to go off half-cocked like that,' she admitted. She had no explanation, at least not one she wanted to own, for why her brain had gone completely AWOL. 'I got angry and then I got stupid.'

'You did,' Lori agreed as she pointed the Mustang toward Hoover.

Silence lingered, and whether it was the idea of her irrational behavior or the reality that Lori had witnessed it, Jess suddenly wanted to cry. The guy in the Infiniti had accomplished exactly what he'd set out to do. What Spears had told him to do. She'd fallen for his baiting hook, line, and sinker. With no regard for her safety or anyone else's. Her hand went to her belly. God, she felt so stupid and frustrated and tired.

'Just don't do it again.' Lori sent her a look that promised there would be serious consequences if she did.

Jess blinked at the ridiculous tears stinging her eyes. 'Yes, ma'am.'

In a few days, when this case was solved and her period had shown up, they would have a woman-to-woman talk about why she'd allowed her emotions to get the better of her back there.

First things first, though. She had to find the monster who'd taken yet another little girl. The harvest moon was still weeks away. He'd upped his timeline.

That was never a good sign.

Chapter Sixteen

110 Boxwood Drive, Hoover, 10.00 A.M.

The neighborhood was an old one, with the houses a little farther apart than the newer, more compact ones builders pushed these days. The woods and a ravine at the rear of the properties separated the homes from the interstate. The constant hum of traffic, all hours of the day and night, was one Jess suspected she would never get used to.

City life came with noise, but there was noise and there was *noise*. Interstate traffic was *noise*.

She sat on the sofa in the modest living room and waited for the mother, Tammy Higginbotham, to compose herself. She'd insisted she was ready to talk to Jess, but then she'd fallen apart as soon as the first question was posed.

This was the part Jess hated most, but she needed to

get all she could before shock set in and stole the devastated mother's ability to recall the little details that might make all the difference. When Tammy lifted her tear-stained face to Jess and cleared her throat, she attempted a response. 'I kissed her good night about eight thirty.' She made a keening sound that sliced right through Jess's heart. 'Her daddy had already read her a bedtime story.' She tried to smile but failed. 'We do that every night.'

The husband, Norris, hugged his wife closer.

'Janey has never walked in her sleep or sneaked outside to play after the two of you went to bed?' Kids did that sometimes. Jess and Lil used to do it all the time – the sneaking-out part. It was a miracle either one of them survived childhood.

Norris shook his head, his own face red and puffy from the tears he'd shed. 'Not Janey. No sleepwalking. Not that we ever knew about, anyway. She's afraid of the dark. Going outside alone at night? No way.'

'That's why she wanted a puppy,' Tammy said. 'She doesn't like sleeping alone. Since her sister died she's been really terrified of the dark.'

That was another part of this tragic story that tore at Jess's emotions. This couple had lost an older daughter to cancer just last year. How were they supposed to cope with this, too? If the Man in the Moon had taken their daughter, the chances of finding her were slim to none. No parent should have to go through the loss of a child once, let alone *twice*. Jess steeled her determination. She would find this child, by God.

'Would Janey have opened her window to a stranger?'

'Oh no.' The mother's tone and expression were adamant. 'We talked about stranger danger often. Janey knows better.'

'You're certain all the windows in your home were down and *locked* last night?' She'd asked this already and gotten an affirmative, but the window in the child's room was unlocked and in the raised position. Someone had opened it.

The father nodded firmly. 'We haven't opened the windows since May. Too hot not to run the central air day and night.'

That was the truth. It was hot as blazes already, and it wasn't even noon.

Jess went through the routine questions. Had they noticed anyone hanging around the neighborhood? Following or watching them? Had there been any trouble with friends or family or neighbors?

A parade of nos followed.

'Mr and Mrs Higginbotham, I'm going to do all within my power to find your little girl. But I need your help. I need a list of any family or friends, public or contracted workers, delivery people, the mailman, anyone you can think of who came to the house or saw Janey in the past couple of weeks. I need the names of anyone you've exchanged heated words with. Anyone who's upset with either of you for some reason. No matter how irrelevant or insignificant it seems, I want to know.'

They nodded in unison at the tall order. She sighed. Christ almighty, was there any chance at all that he'd left a clue this time?

'Do you think it's *him*?' the mother asked. Her lips trembled.

'We've been watching the news,' her husband added, his voice shaky. 'Last night wasn't the harvest moon. Why would he do this now?'

That was a very good question and Jess had no answer. 'We don't know that your daughter's disappearance is connected to that case.' She couldn't take that hope away from them. Anyone who'd grown up in Birmingham or watched the news recently understood what it meant to have a child taken by this monster. 'My team is going to work hard at learning exactly what happened to Jancy and getting her back home. I want the two of you to try as hard as you can to focus on helping us. As soon as we know anything, you will.'

She left the parents in Lori's capable hands and returned to the child's room. The mother confirmed that everything was just as she'd left it last night when she kissed her daughter good night. Except for the raised window. Nothing was missing other than Janey's favorite doll, nothing moved except the window. A photo of the parents and red-haired, freckle-faced Janey sat on the bedside table. More of that emotion she wasn't supposed to feel on the job nipped at Jess.

She thought of how close she'd come to telling Dan last night that they might be expecting, but she'd chickened out. Her arms went around her middle. If that was the case, she had to be more careful. She'd gotten so caught up in the game Spears had his followers playing she'd almost gotten hit by a truck.

Gotta be smarter than that, Jess.

She shook off the worries and shifted her attention to the rumpled bed covers and the stuffed animals scattered there. Janey wanted a dog.

Instinct nudging Jess, she turned to the nearest tech. 'I'd like you to check for animal hair around the window. Inside, on the stool, and outside.' It was a long shot but she was going for it. The ground was too dry and the lawn too grassy for tracks, human or animal.

The tech nodded, and Jess decided on another walk-through of the single-level home. The parents' bedroom wasn't that far from Janey's, but her door had been closed, and they'd stated they always fell asleep watching the little television perched on their bureau.

If only they hadn't left the television on last night . . . if they'd made a habit of not closing their daughter's door . . .

She imagined those same thoughts had already gone through their minds about a million times.

'Ma'am?'

Jess turned to the rookie who'd lost his breakfast this morning.

'Sergeant Harper needs you in the backyard.'

'Thank you, Mitchell.'

He winced when she called him by name. He probably hoped she would forget his name after witnessing his embarrassing reaction to the Atkins' suicide scene this morning. She'd have to explain to him later that it happened to everyone at least once.

She'd puked her guts out the first time she explored a scene with scrambled body parts.

These days it took a lot to faze her. Yet she fell apart when she saw a dog on the side of the road that had been hit by a car. That was the best reason in the world not to have a pet. You wouldn't end up mourning something you didn't have to lose.

Same went for babies. How the hell was a mother supposed to survive this kind of tragedy?

Don't even go there, Jess.

'I'll show you the way, ma'am,' Mitchell prompted when she just stood there, borrowing trouble exactly the way she'd advised the parents of this missing child not to.

Now who was having an embarrassing moment?

Outside, the humidity was working overtime, making it hard to breathe. At least she didn't have to deal with reporters shouting questions. Roadblocks had been put in place early enough to hold back the inevitable flock. Given a little more time the more resourceful ones like Gina Coleman would cut through a few yards and risk being arrested for trespassing to reach the scene in hopes of getting a shot.

Even now, cops at the roadblocks were being grilled for information. As soon as word got out that a little girl under the age of ten was missing, the media would go nuts with theories. Rumors would be rampant, and speculation would push the boundaries and have the community in turmoil. Jess thought of last night's impromptu visit, and she considered that maybe she should let Gina know how her construction company theory panned out. They were friends now, apparently. Friends did things like that.

But that would have to wait. Between now and the press conference Dan would need something to give the worried citizens on this tragic new development. The disappearance of another child was the dead last thing a department wanted to confirm.

Problem was, Jess had no more information than the police had thirteen or thirty-three years ago. Except another missing child who might or might not be related to the case. Bad for all concerned.

Harper waited near the tree line at the back of the property. 'I wish you had different shoes.' He glanced at her four-inch heels that were already giving her fits in the grass.

Sometimes it was extra difficult being a woman. 'We going into the ravine?'

He nodded.

She'd been afraid of that.

'We got a body,' Harper told her.

Adrenaline fired through her veins, followed immediately by terror. Her knees went a little weak on her. 'Not the child?' She prayed it wasn't that little girl. Damn it all to hell, don't let it be that child.

'No, ma'am,' he said softly, as if he spotted the fear in her eyes. 'Male. Late fifties, early sixties. No ID.'

The terror she'd experienced turned to hope. This could be the break they needed. Her pounding heart ramped up another few beats. 'I need different shoes.'

'Mitchell,' Harper barked, 'give the Chief your boots.'

The young officer looked startled then jerked as if someone had kicked him in the seat of the pants. After an uncertain glance at Jess he asked, 'My boots?'

'That's what I said,' Harper confirmed. 'Make it fast.'

Mitchell's head yanked up and down. 'Yes, sir.'

While Jess slipped off her heels Mitchell tugged off first one police-issue boot then the other. She pulled on the boots and laced them up tight. As an afterthought she grabbed her shoes and handed them to the patient officer standing in his sock feet. 'Keep an eye on these for me, please.'

He nodded and Jess joined Harper, the too-big boots clomping with every step. She decided not to ask how the boots looked with the taupe dress she'd thought made her look thinner.

She'd spent no less than fifteen minutes in front of the mirror trying to determine if her abdomen looked swollen.

Just went to show how the lack of sleep and wine affected an overworked cop. Not to mention trying to hide all of the above from Dan, who'd spent the night.

She kicked the static out of her head. They had a body. Maybe a lead.

Harper pointed into the ravine. 'There's a flashlight near the body that he may have been carrying. No weapon and no sign of the little girl.'

Jess could just make out a wide back and a blue shirt. Could this be the monster that had taken as many as twenty little girls? 'Let's get down there and have a closer look, Sergeant.'

Harper assisted her down the steep incline. Thankfully the overgrown bushes provided the occasional handhold. Officer Chad Cook waited near the body. Jess's pulse was racing. She wanted this to be him . . . but why break his pattern?

Stay calm. She had a job to do, and letting her emotions run wild wouldn't get it done.

'I let the coroner's office know we needed someone down here,' Harper said. 'Evidence techs will start processing as soon as you've had a look.'

'Any visible signs of injury?' They were almost to the body now, and her pulse was still racing in spite of her best efforts to maintain her composure.

'Looks like he got a hell of a knock to the back of his skull, which may or may not have happened before the fall.'

As they reached the victim's position, Cook spoke up. 'Morning, ma'am.'

He was right to leave off the good. There was nothing good about this one. Unless this guy was going to lead them to little Janey Higginbotham.

'Cook.' She gave him a nod before crouching down to have a closer look at the victim. He lay facedown in the weeds. There was something vaguely familiar about him. She inspected the back of his skull with a gloved hand. If he had survived that kind of damage it wasn't for long.

'Let's turn him over, Sergeant.'

Cook and Harper wrestled with rolling the victim onto his back. Rigor mortis was well under way. He'd probably been dead at least eight or ten hours.

When he was on his back, Jess gasped. Renewed anticipation started to simmer inside her. 'It's Bullock.' She turned to Harper. 'One of Cagle's meter readers.'

'We were supposed to be talking to Corlew today about his missing reports on that crew,' Harper mentioned.

Jess nodded, still reeling a little at the possibility of

what this meant. 'If Corlew gives you any trouble, you let me know. I spoke to him this morning.'

At Harper's raised eyebrows, she added, 'Don't ask.'

To Cook she said, 'Find Lori and get a warrant for Bullock's home. We're looking for anything related to the Man in the Moon case or an attraction to young children.'

'Yes, ma'am.'

To Harper, she said, 'I want a search team out here looking for that little girl.' She considered the man who'd seemed a little nervous when she interviewed him yesterday. Corlew claimed he acted the same way when he'd interviewed him more than a decade ago. 'If Bullock took her, she may be out here somewhere and there could be a dog with her.'

But Jess had a feeling Bullock had died in this ravine all alone.

Right where the Man in the Moon had left him. That was where she and Corlew, whether he knew it or not, were in full agreement. The Man in the Moon was smart, meticulous with the details, and obviously capable of considerable restraint. Bullock was too nervous, too twitchy, to pull off this kind of elaborate string of heinous acts.

The Man in the Moon was, in her opinion, a sociopath. Talking to the cops or anyone else wouldn't make him nervous. He manipulated, violated, and exploited other humans for his own entertainment. Being interviewed by a mere cop would hardly make him nervous.

What Bullock may have been guilty of was withholding information. Maybe for fear of losing his job . . . or his life.

'I want this guy checked from head to toe,' she said, more to herself than to Harper. 'I want to know everything he touched from the moment he set foot on this property.'

'Unless she's unconscious or asleep or just too far away to hear,' Harper offered, 'I think the child would be calling out for help if she's injured, or already back home if she wasn't.'

Jess nodded. 'I don't believe she's here, but we need to be certain.'

The search for that little girl was priority one. Harper had ensured an Amber Alert had been issued the moment he got on the scene and confirmed the situation. Before leaving, Jess snapped a pic of a photo of Janey holding her favorite doll. Since that was the one item she'd taken with her besides the pink-and-white polka-dot pajamas she'd been wearing, Jess needed to be able to identify the doll.

After ensuring Lori was up to speed, Jess left her in charge of the scene. There was one more thing she needed to do and it could not wait.

'I need to see Fergus Cagle.' Jess exchanged the boots for her shoes and thanked Mitchell. 'Surely Cagle would have some inkling there was a problem with a man he'd worked with for more than thirty years. Why cover for him?'

'You think this Bullock is our guy?' Harper led the way to his vehicle as they talked.

'I do not, but he's the first lead in this case in thirty-three years. I'll take what I can get.'

Sixth Avenue North, 12:15 P.M.

'I'm sorry, Chief Harris,' Ruthie Jeffreys, the secretary said. 'Mr Cagle hasn't been in the office this morning. He's in the field.'

'In the field?' Jess needed to see him . . . to talk to him. Her instincts were screaming at her that Bullock's death was the avenue to a major break in this case.

'Yes,' the secretary confirmed. 'Sometimes he checks on his team and how their routes are going. Issues come up where customers believe their reading was wrong.' She shrugged as if she didn't see why Jess didn't get that. 'It's not unusual for him to spend an entire day in the field.'

'What about Mr Bullock?' Jess asked, just to see what the lady would say. 'Is he on his usual route today?'

Ruthie shook her head. 'No, he's out sick. Someone else is taking care of his route.'

'He's sick?' Jess repeated. 'Did he call in?'

'Mr Cagle said he had a call from him early this morning. Jerry has one of those stomach bugs or something.'

Actually what he had was a fractured skull and rigor mortis. Jess would have to wait for time of death but she would bet her favorite pair of shoes Cagle hadn't gotten a call this morning. 'And what about Mr Gifford and Mr Kennamer?'

'Both are on their usual routes,' Ruthie confirmed.

'I need Mr Cagle's cell number, please.' Jess had the routes for the other two. It wouldn't be too difficult to find them. Besides, it was Cagle she wanted to talk to.

When Ruthie hesitated, Jess tacked on, 'This is police business.'

'Well, all right then.' She wrote the number down and passed it to Jess.

'If Mr Cagle calls in, please be sure to let him know I'm trying to reach him.'

'I'll tell him,' she promised.

With Harper leading the way, Jess hurried out of the building, barely able to keep her mouth shut until they were outside. As soon as she was in Harper's SUV with the door closed she let loose. 'We have to find Cagle.'

'You think he's our perp?' Harper started the engine.

'What I think is that we have a missing child and a dead guy at the scene – a dead guy who worked as a meter reader for better than three decades. No one else had carte blanche for getting so close to each victim's home every damned month of the year.'

The coincidence was just too big. Cagle claimed to

have heard from the victim this A.M., and that was most likely impossible. Cagle had dogs. There were pictures in his office. He loved them that much . . . which meant he knew how to handle a dog like Samson, the Myerses' Lab. He had the means and he had the opportunity. All they had to do was find the motive.

Jess struggled to restrain her anticipation and no small amount of excitement at the idea that she had him. She didn't have squat in the way of evidence, not unless they got something from this morning's crime scene, but she was certain as she could be without it.

The jangling sound in her bag had her fishing for her cell. She stared at the number. Not one she knew, but it was local. Wouldn't be Gina Coleman. Jess had already sent her a text to let her know her lead didn't pan out, but there was a story to be told about Atkins Electric. Giving Gina the scoop was the least she could do. 'Harris.'

'Jess Harris?'

Worry insinuated its way between the barely restrained sense of victory and desperate urgency thumping inside her. She was onto something here. She didn't need any distractions. 'This is Jess Harris.'

What if her sister was back in the hospital? Her heart jolted and immediately she felt guilty for having thought she was too busy.

'This is Elise Van Valkenburg at the Second Life store.'

For a moment she hadn't a clue what the woman was

talking about and then it hit her. 'Did my credit card get declined?' Jesus. Talk about humiliating. These were people Sylvia Baron and Gina Coleman knew, for heaven's sake. Irritation kicked aside the mortification. It sure took them long enough to let her know. She'd bought her sofa and a few other small items at the Second Life thrift store more than a week ago.

'No . . . I was calling about something you left in our storeroom.'

Storeroom? She hadn't gone into their storeroom. 'I'm sorry, but I'm pretty sure I didn't leave anything.'

'It has your name on it.'

Jess wanted to reach through the phone and shake the woman. 'Well, what is it?'

An impatient sigh sounded in her ear. 'It's a blanket all bundled up and . . . oh . . . my . . . *God*.'

'Mrs Van Valkenburg?' What the devil was going on with this woman?

'Mrs Harris, this blanket of yours is full of *bones*.'

Chapter Seventeen

Birmingham Police Department, 12.30 P.M.

Dan thanked the search team commander and ended the call. He collapsed in his chair and rubbed his eyes with the pads of his fingers. With the manpower being utilized on this case it was incomprehensible to admit they had nothing.

'I take it he didn't have good news?' Harold Black surmised.

'No hits on the Amber Alert and no sign of her in the wooded ravine that borders her neighborhood.' Jesus Christ, they had to find this kid. 'Sorry for the interruption.' Dan cleared his throat, worked at keeping his cool. 'You're here to give me an update.' He doubted any of it was good news but a man could hope.

Harold slid his eyeglasses into place and studied his notes. 'I have a conference call with Special Agent Gant at three. I'm hoping we have some news on the Spears investigation.'

Every muscle in Dan's body tightened as he thought of Spears. 'Maybe we'll get really lucky and Spears's rotting corpse has turned up.'

'We can always hope,' Harold agreed. 'I wanted to update you on the Allen case.'

Ted Allen. Captain Allen, head of the Gang Task Force, had been missing almost two weeks now. Until yesterday there was nothing. No credit card activity. No calls to his family. The last time his cell phone had pinged a tower was near Jess's apartment. That he and Jess had been locked in battle over the Lopez case didn't lend itself to the idea that he'd driven by hoping for a friendly visit.

Whatever the hell Allen had been doing, it hadn't been in the line of duty.

Until he showed up or they found his body the only hope for figuring out his mysterious disappearance was if someone came forward with information. Except that his cell phone suddenly turned up yesterday – mixed in with Dan's trash.

'The cell phone held traces of material picked up on the street that had come from your city trash receptacle.'

'You said the blood on the phone was confirmed as Allen's.'

Harold nodded. 'It was.'

Dan felt his temper rising at the idea of where this was

going. As the chief of police he understood it was the right and only thing to do. But that didn't make it feel right. He scrubbed a hand over his jaw. 'Now the investigation turns to how his cell phone got into my trash, right?'

Harold nodded again. 'You understand this in no way means we believe such a ludicrous scenario. Yet we have to follow proper protocol.'

'Of course.' Dan forced a smile. 'Do what you have to do, Harold. I have nothing to hide.'

Harold made a face. 'Certainly not.'

A rap on his door was a welcome reprieve. Tara, his receptionist, poked her head in. 'Chief, there's a delivery for you on my desk.'

On her desk? Tension rippled through him. 'What kind of package?'

He was on his feet and halfway across the room before she could get out an answer: 'A padded envelope from . . . Eric Spears. At least that's the name on the return address.'

Spears? A fist of fear slammed into Dan's gut. He and Harold exchanged a look.

As they rushed down the hall, Dan deliberated about two seconds on calling in the bomb squad, but since the package had passed through the X-ray machine in the lobby he wasn't going to waste the time.

Spears wanted to taunt him, not kill him . . . at least not yet.

At Tara's desk, Dan started to open the package, but Harold stopped him and handed him a pair of gloves. The seconds it took to drag on the gloves had his frustration level skyrocketing. He opened the flap and looked inside. Photos. A stack of glossy four-by-sixes.

His heart stumbled as he shuffled through the stack. They were all of Jess. Leaving her place over on Conroy. Entering the BPD lobby downstairs. Some included Dan. The two of them together this past weekend. Jess leaving the coroner's office . . . at the creek where the flowers had been left from a supposed secret admirer.

At a restaurant he didn't recognize with Detective Wells and Corlew. That one gave him pause. What the hell was Corlew doing there?

'He's getting closer, Dan.' Harold pointed to the FedEx label. 'This was sent from the Twentieth Street location.'

Fury twisted in Dan's gut. 'We need someone over there now. See if the clerks can ID the sender. Maybe there's video surveillance.'

'I'll check out the FedEx store myself,' Black assured him. To Tara he said, 'Call forensics and have them send over a tech to get this to the lab for analysis.'

Tara reached for the phone on her desk.

'You should call Agent Gant,' Black suggested. 'I'm heading to FedEx.'

Dan already had his cell phone in hand. 'Call me as soon as you know anything.' The tightness in his chest made it harder and harder to breathe. He put through the call as he walked back to his office but got Gant's voice mail. Dan left a message.

After he'd closed the door of his office, he leaned against it. One of the photos was of Jess climbing the stairs to her apartment. *How is he getting this close with twenty-four-hour surveillance on her apartment?*

He pushed off the door and stalked to his desk. Probably a rooftop across the street. With the right high-powered lens he might not even need to be that close. Dan shook his head. Their suspicions that Spears had more than one of his so-called followers right here in Birmingham watching her had just been confirmed, as far as he was concerned.

His cell vibrated. Dan tensed, hoped it was Gant.

Jess.

A surge of fear thudded in his chest. 'Everything okay?' If his greeting didn't tip her off that everything was *not* okay on his end, he wasn't sure what would. He had to get a handle on his emotions.

But damn it, he was only human.

'There's been another delivery.'

Her voice was thin. Why the hell was this bastard taunting her? 'Where?' That he managed the one word without his voice trembling was a flat out miracle.

'At the Second Life thrift store. Harper and I just pulled up.'

'I'm on my way.'

'Don't bother coming here,' Jess argued. 'We won't be at the scene long. I'll let you know when we're en route to the coroner's office. I've called Sylvia, and she and one of her assistants are en route.'

'All right.' He forced air into his lungs. 'I'll see you there.'

He dropped his cell back on his desk as Tara announced via the intercom that Agent Gant was returning his call.

'Thanks, Tara.'

Dan stabbed the blinking light. Before he shared this latest development, he wanted whatever updates the FBI had. 'Gant, tell me you're about to make me happy.'

'What I have is bad news.'

Defeat tugging at him, Dan lowered into his chair. 'Let's hear it.'

'The chatter on the Net about Jess stopped abruptly. That's a bad thing considering we were so damned close to tracking down the source. Now that won't happen unless a new thread surfaces.'

Dan bit back a string of curses. 'Still nothing on where he is?'

'Zilch. We've taken control of his company, SpearNet. We've got forensic experts in there digging through electronic files and every piece of hardware in the place.'

That could take a lifetime or two. Defeat tugged at

Dan. He could not let this guy get to Jess. There had to be a way to stop him or to distract him.

'Worse than any of that,' Gant went on, 'we just got IDs on two of the three women in the photos. One is from Mobile, the other from Somerville. Both moved to Alabama just this summer to start college this fall. That's why they weren't in your DMV database.'

'Why am I just hearing about this?' And why wasn't this good news?

'We didn't want to put out the word until we had the women in protective custody. That's where the worse news comes in. Both are missing. It seems each one was recently notified of winning a weekend getaway. No one has seen either woman since last Friday, and no one we talked to had the slightest idea where they were going. We're hoping someone will help us identify the third woman before she goes missing as well.'

'So we can assume that Spears has at least two of them already.' More of that red-hot fury roared through Dan. He needed to stop that son of a bitch.

'I think that's the only rational assumption. Either he has them or one of his followers does. We've got agents tearing their apartments apart piece by piece in hopes of finding some trace of evidence we can use. We're dissecting their e-mails, Facebook, Twitter. We're trying to cover every avenue. We've added their vehicles to the BOLOs on the two women we've identified. If nothing else, maybe we can determine where their vehicles were last seen.'

Dan explained the delivery he'd just received. 'I don't see how one man manages to maintain this kind of proximity to her. There has to be more than one here, we just haven't gotten a visual on him yet.' As terrifying as the perp in the Infiniti was, as least they had pinpointed him.

'I wouldn't admit this to just anyone, Burnett, but frankly we just don't know what we're dealing with here. If Spears has created some elaborate network, this dark-haired man may be only the tip of the iceberg.'

'That's what keeps me awake at night, Gant.'

The call hadn't given Dan any new hope that this situation with Spears was headed in the right direction. Not at all. What he'd gotten was more reason to be concerned about Jess's safety.

A whole hell of a lot more worried.

He checked the time. The mayor and the citizens of Birmingham were expecting him to pass along comforting words in today's press conference but he didn't see how that was possible. They had nothing in the way of evidence and now another child was missing.

He'd scrubbed both hands over his face. Damn it all to hell. He had wanted to keep Jess out of the news as much as possible, but with that little girl's disappearance he had an obligation to broaden the scope of the press conference. The community needed to see that Jess was involved. She had earned a place in the hearts of the citizens.

But his own heart was ice-cold with fear.

He closed his eyes and fought to keep the emotions at bay.

Tara interrupted his plunge into despair to let him know the forensic tech had arrived and bagged the FedEx envelope. He thanked her and checked the time. Jess should be calling him soon and he'd head to the coroner's office.

His cell vibrated. Harold Black calling.

Another spike of tension speared him. 'What'd you find out?'

'If you're not sitting down,' Harold said, 'I'd suggest you take a seat, Dan.'

The frustration that had started simmering when Dan received that package reached a boil. 'You have an ID on the sender?'

'The clerk here at the FedEx store positively identified the man who shipped that package to you. She was so certain that I made the manager pull the security video so I could see for myself.'

Couldn't be the dark-haired man. They didn't even have an artist's rendering on the guy. Jess hadn't gotten enough facial details with him wearing those damned sunglasses.

'The man who sent you that package was Eric Spears,

Dan. I . . . saw him on the video. He was right here in this store, only a few blocks from where you are right now.'

Son of a bitch.

Jefferson County Coroner's Office, 1.50 P.M.

Sierra Campbell. Eight years old. Silky black hair and sparkly blue eyes. Abducted fifteen years ago. From the looks of her small, delicate bones, she had died not long after that.

How did they stop this evil? Jess and her team were doing everything possible. Dan shifted his gaze to her at the other end of the exam table, where she waited next to Sylvia.

One day, if he was lucky, he and Jess would be married and have children. How could they protect their children from monsters like this? Maybe Jess was the smart one. He got the impression she wasn't exactly looking forward to motherhood. Maybe she was right. Maybe people who had witnessed the horrors they had shouldn't have children.

'I don't know how you do it, Harris.' Sylvia lifted her hands and bowed her head in mock worship. 'Somehow you manage to keep everyone who's anyone talking about you. You make the news more often than our esteemed mayor.'

'That's me,' Jess tossed right back at her. 'Every serial killer's pin-up girl.'

'As soon as Elise Van Valkenburg from the Second Life store informed you,' Sylvia said, 'she called Carrie Bradley and half the other brookies she schmoozes with on a regular basis. You're going to have your own fan club.' She made a harrumphing sound she would never dream of making in front of the Mountain Brook friends she'd just mentioned. 'Frankly, I'm a tad jealous.'

Dan wanted to tell her to cut the crap, this wasn't the time. She needed to get on with it, but he kept his mouth shut. The state of mind he was in, the less he said the better.

Jess pointed to the blanket that was child-sized, about three feet by three feet. 'You were saying something about glitter and tinsel.'

'First,' Sylvia reminded her, 'let's not forget about the note.' She glanced at Dan. 'This guy has it bad for Harris.'

More of the frustration and worry already chipping away at his self-control rushed in, swinging a sledge-hammer this time. He hadn't heard there was another note. He'd just as soon not have heard Sylvia's comment-ary on it.

Why the hell wasn't forensics doing this? *Stop. Calm down.* He knew the answer to that one. Sylvia promised to drop everything for this case and get something to Jess immediately. Then the evidence could be turned over to forensics for a final analysis.

'Tell me about the note,' he prompted in a reasonably calm voice.

Sylvia started to speak but Jess cut her off. 'Same as before, he circled words in the newspaper articles. He said, "I couldn't help myself. Find me, Jess. I need you."'

Jesus Christ. 'If we don't find this guy . . .' Dan didn't want to say the rest out loud.

'We will,' Jess insisted with far more confidence than he could dredge up at the moment. 'Then the brookies will really have something to talk about.'

In spite of present circumstances her comment sent a blast of relief through him. Jess wasn't having any trouble holding her own with anyone. Not even his mother, the quintessential brookie. How his mother's issues with Jess could cross his mind right now was beyond bizarre. He was losing it. Pure and simple.

'There's a lot more I need to do,' Sylvia noted, 'but I did find significant trace elements, including dog hair, mostly attached to the blanket.'

'Dog hair?' Jess said. 'Any ideas on the breed?'

'Too long for a Lab. Don't hold me to it yet, but something like a Golden Retriever or a Cocker Spaniel. Not the reddish color, more golden or beige. He got sloppy this time. There are some blood smears on the blanket.'

Jess's face paled. 'New or old?'

Sylvia winced. 'New.'

Dan bit back a scathing curse. If this bastard had already hurt Janey Higginbotham . . .

'We're running out of time,' Jess said, her face pale. 'A little girl goes missing and we're almost a month away from the harvest moon. This forking over of the remains he's obviously kept as souvenirs is telling enough, but this latest move is careless and way out of character. He wants us to find him, but something is prompting this new erratic behavior.'

'He wants *you* to find him,' Dan argued.

Jess looked at him, and he wanted to tell her right then and there this bastard wasn't the only trouble she had just now. Spears was here. God Almighty, how was he ever going to protect her?

'This –' Sylvia tapped one of the slides she'd placed in a tray on the exam table, forcing their attention back to her '– is glitter. It's not new. Red and green.' She moved to the next slide. 'The fragments of silver tinsel-type fiber makes me think the blanket was stuck in a box of Christmas decorations.'

'What about the remains?' Dan's gut clenched. They were talking about a little girl. A little girl, Sierra Campbell, who had lost her life to this madman.

'Clean like the others,' Sylvia explained. 'Nothing I've seen so far that indicates manner of death. As I told you before,' she said to Jess, 'there's other testing we can do, but the bones aren't telling us much from the out-side. Since this set was just delivered, there's a lot I don't know except that the condition, from a visible and structural standpoint, is solid. No fractures, or anything like that.'

'Why is he going in reverse chronological order?' Jess braced her gloved hands on the exam table. 'What the hell is he trying to tell me that I'm missing?'

'I can't answer that one, but before you run off to inform the parents,' Sylvia said, 'I'll need to compare dental records. I haven't had time to do that yet.'

As if her assistant had been standing by for his cue, he rushed in and carefully placed the skull next to the rest of the bones. 'The images are on your iPad, Dr Baron.'

Sylvia compared the current X-rays of the skull to the fifteen-year-old X-rays she'd digitized for this case.

Dan watched Jess gingerly touch the bones, as if touching them would give her the answers she sought. Or maybe it was her way of promising the little girl she would find her killer.

'Okay.' Sylvia turned to face them. 'This is Sierra Campbell.'

'I'll let Chief Black know.' Dan stepped aside to make the call. When Black answered, Dan cut to the chase. 'It's Sierra Campbell. Sylvia Baron just confirmed.' Harold thanked him and Dan put his phone away. One question kept hammering in his brain. *How many more would fall prey to this monster if they didn't get this guy soon?*

If he had changed his MO and was no longer constrained by the moon's phases, there was no telling what he would do next.

Dan joined Jess and Sylvia at another exam table, where the sheet was drawn back to reveal Jerry Bullock, the possible homicide victim from this morning's abduction scene.

'Mr Bullock was struck with a blunt object. Judging by the impressions I'd say a tire iron. The blow was rendered before he fell into the ravine. I'll know more when I've had a chance to do the autopsy, but I can tell you without reservation that the fall didn't kill him, the blow to the head did. As it stands now, I would call manner of death homicide. Estimated time of death is somewhere between nine and midnight last night.'

'Thank you, Dr Baron.' Jess turned to Dan. 'Sergeant Harper's waiting. I should get back out there and track down Fergus Cagle, Bullock's supervisor. Based on the estimated time of death, Mr Cagle needs to explain how he got a call from Bullock this morning as he told his secretary.'

'I'll walk you out,' Dan offered. 'There's an update we need to discuss. Good work, Sylvia.'

She shot him a look. 'Have you ever known me to do anything else?'

'You have a point,' he acquiesced.

Jess waited until they were in the corridor headed for the lobby before she slowed down long enough to give him her attention. 'You mentioned an update.'

He wished they could go somewhere and talk about this. She wasn't going to want to hear his thoughts on what this development meant, and the county coroner's office wasn't the place for a battle.

'I got a FedEx delivery from Spears just before you called. A whole stack of photos – all of you.'

She shrugged, seemingly unfazed. 'I don't know why you're surprised at that. He has that dark-haired man and God knows who else watching me.'

'There's more.'

Uncertainty and dread, maybe a little fear, flared in her eyes before she could banish the reaction. 'Has he taken one of the women?'

This was the part he dreaded telling her the most. She wasn't concerned for her own safety. 'Gant believes he has. They've learned the identities of two of the women, but their whereabouts are unaccounted for.' He explained the vacation connection. 'Still nothing on the third woman, but Gant suspects Spears has already lured her into his trap in that same manner.'

'We're too late.' Jess looked away. 'He'll kill one or all of them, Dan. After he tortures them in unspeakable ways.'

This was where the next bit of news could be as good for the missing women as it was bad for Jess. 'It's possible he hasn't done anything just yet except set and trigger the trap for luring in his targets.'

A frown marred her brow. 'How can anyone know that? He doesn't waste time. If he's lured them to a certain location, he may have killed them right away. He's changing his MO just like the Man in the Moon. When that occurs anything could happen.' She moved her head side to side in disgust. 'God, this makes me sick.' She rubbed at her temples.

Dan wished like hell he could spare her the rest. 'There's a possibility he's not in the same location as the women.'

'Dan,' she said, pointing all her anguish and frustration at him, 'you are confusing the hell out of me. What is it you're trying to tell me?'

'I'm trying to tell you it's more important than ever that you listen to me when I say you are not safe on the streets.' A choked laugh squeezed out of him. 'Hell, I don't know if you're safe anywhere. But I have to somehow get it across to you that we've been warned, Jess. The storm is coming, I need you to take cover.'

She held up her hands. 'I have a sociopath delivering the remains of dead children to me. Now, he's taken another child – a live one. I do not have time to listen to this.'

'He's here, Jess.'

She dropped her hands to her sides. This time there was no mistaking the fear in her eyes. 'How can you be sure when Gant with all his resources can't even speculate where Spears is?'

'The clerk at the FedEx store that shipped that package to me positively identified him. Harold looked at the security video. It was him, Jess. Unless he has another fan who got made over to look like him the way Matthew Reed did, Eric Spears is here.'

Maybe it was the shock in her brown eyes or the way her body began to tremble, but he said to hell with the rules she reminded him of so often and he took her in his arms. He held her tight against his chest while she cried softly. He knew the tears weren't about any fear she felt at the threat Spears represented to her – though he wished they were.

Dan knew her tears were for those women . . . the ones he had lured into his trap.

And for the little girl out there waiting for Jess to find her.

Chapter Eighteen

Sixth Avenue, 2.45 P.M.

Jess had already called Fergus Cagle three times and gotten his voice mail. Certainly his phone could have died on him. It had happened to her a time or two. He could have damaged it in the field. She'd endured one of those uh-ohs as well. Or, the man could just be avoiding her because he had taken Janey Higginbotham and he knew Jess was on to him.

Whatever the reason, she intended to find him and she would save that little girl. She had studied the remains of a child the last time she ever wanted to. She closed her eyes a moment and imagined that Dan's arms were still around her. He'd known exactly what she needed, no matter that they'd been right there in public for all to see.

No getting distracted, Jess. If she stayed on task with this investigation she wouldn't have the time or opportunity to think about the other. She couldn't think about it. Not right now. It was difficult enough to look at all those pictures of those precious little girls and not wonder if she was pregnant and what hers and Dan's child might look like.

Jess and Harper entered Cagle's department at Alabama Power to see Ruthie was still at her desk. Thank God for small favors. 'Hello again, Ms Jeffreys.'

The secretary had a stack of notes and messages on her desk that had apparently accumulated since Jess was here a few hours ago.

'Chief Harris.' She couldn't quite follow through with the smile she attempted, leaving a sort of lopsided expression. 'I'm sorry, but Mr Cagle hasn't been in the office and he hasn't called so I couldn't give him your message.' She waved her hand over her desk. 'As you can see, there are a lot of people who need to speak to him.' Her face pinched. 'And we just heard that Mr Bullock is dead.'

'Murdered,' Jess clarified. She should be ashamed of herself for adding insult to injury, but she needed this lady to understand how important it was that she speak with Cagle.

Ruthie's hand went to her throat. 'Oh no. What happened?'

'I'm afraid we can't discuss an ongoing investigation, but I hope you can see that it's imperative that I speak with Mr Cagle. The sooner the better.'

Defeat slumped the secretary's shoulders. 'I don't know what else to do. I can't reach him. No one can.'

As far as Jess was concerned, the secretary's inability to get in touch with Cagle confirmed a problem. The man was either dead or hiding something. 'There is a way you can help me, Ms Jeffreys. I need Mr Cagle's home address and I need his daughter's phone number and address.' She'd tried getting the daughter's number already. Obviously she was no longer a Cagle. Jess had no idea what her first or last name was or even how old she was.

'I can give you Mr Cagle's home address, but I don't have any contact information for his daughter. Mr Cagle's very private. Frankly, I don't even know her name, and I've worked with him for five years, ever since he moved up to assistant supervisor and then supervisor. He never talks about his family.'

The whole scenario just got stranger and stranger.

'His address will at least get me started in the right direction. I'll need phone numbers and addresses on Kennamer and Gifford as well.' The addresses for all three would be in the case file somewhere, but they could have moved in the past dozen or so years – unless that was part of what Corlew had misplaced. Idiot.

With the information in hand, Jess hurried out of the building. She had to find this man. Harper kept time with her determined strides.

The instant they were outside, she turned to him. 'We

need a warrant for Cagle's home.' Her nerves were taut and her instincts were shouting at her. 'I don't want to wait. That little girl could be there, and we have no idea how long he waits before he makes the kill. If we can't get a speedy warrant, we're going in without one.'

'You're that certain it's him.'

'It's him. He has at least one Golden Retriever. He had opportunity. And his nervous coworker is dead.'

'We could be wrong,' Harper suggested.

'We could be,' Jess agreed. 'But the chances that he got a call from Bullock this morning are pretty slim. The guy was dead. Which can only mean one thing – Cagle lied. And now he's disappeared.'

'You think Bullock was on to him. Followed him to the Higginbotham home. Cagle caught him and bopped him on the head?'

'That's the direction I'm leaning in, but for all we know the two could have been partners. Maybe Bullock decided he didn't want to go there again.'

'What about Kennamer and Gifford?'

Jess had pondered the concept the whole group was involved, but that would be way out of the ordinary. Serial killers at times worked in pairs as partners. Typically one was dominant. But the idea that three or more would gang up together was way outside the norm. Not to mention the possibility of screwups escalated with the number of people involved. It was highly unlikely that

271

they would have gotten away with snatching little girls for twenty years under those circumstances.

The concept that Spears was here and working with several others or with so-called followers filtered through her mind. She would not let him distract her right now. Finding this little girl was top priority. The Bureau was working the Spears case. *This* was Jess's case.

'Have Lori locate Kennamer and Gifford and question each man again. Tell her to push. If either one has the slightest suspicion about Cagle I want to know. Cook can finish up the search at Bullocks's house. You and I are going after Cagle.'

Her cell warned she had an incoming call. *Lily calling.* Jess answered as she walked to Harper's SUV. 'Hey, sis.'

'Jess, I'm on my way to Dr Collins's office. His nurse said he needed me to come in right away. He wants you to be there, too. I'm terrified, Jess.'

Oh hell. 'Where's Blake?'

'Blake isn't home yet. Please tell me you'll be there. I can't do this alone.'

For two decades Jess had rarely been home. She'd missed the births of both her sister's children. She'd missed birthdays, anniversaries, Christmases, and every damned thing else. She wasn't letting her sister down now.

'I'll be there.'

Jess shoved her phone back into her bag. She worked at slowing the pounding in her chest as she turned to Harper. 'Okay, you get the warrant started. I can't imagine a judge in town denying our request, but don't let that slow you down. I want you in Cagle's house as soon as possible.' She had no idea how long this visit with Dr Collins would take and they didn't have the time to spare. 'I have to get to my sister's doctor's office. I'll catch up with you as soon as I'm out of there.'

Harper shook his head. 'Sorry, ma'am, but I have orders.'

Well, damn. Fear and frustration warred inside her, but there just wasn't time to argue. Besides, he was right. Spears was here. And she was mad as hell . . . and scared to death at the same time. Her family was here . . . her friends . . . Dan. And she could be pregnant. Shit. She blinked fast to hold back a rush of tears.

'All right, Sergeant. Let's go.' She gave him the address for Dr Collins's office. 'I'll call Lori on the way.'

'I'm on the warrant,' Harper assured her.

Jess made the call to Lori and then she closed her eyes and said a prayer for her sister. Then she prayed her instincts wouldn't fail her. That little girl was counting on her.

It has to be Cagle.

She prayed for the women Spears had targeted and lured into a trap.

Last, she prayed for the ability and strength to find both these monsters and end their reigns of terror.

Twentieth Street South, 3.30 P.M.

Jess held tightly to her sister's hand as Dr Collins made a production of taking the seat behind his desk and reviewing his notes before he began. Jess wanted to shake him and tell him to get the hell on with it! Her sister had waited long enough to know what was going on inside her body. Knowing this old coot, he was just doing this to get back at Jess. She'd given him a hard time since she was eighteen.

That's what he got for being a judgmental old fart.

'Ladies.' He looked up over his glasses, his expression difficult to decipher. 'We have found the culprit causing all these issues. Wilson's disease.'

Jess exchanged a look with Lily. Both repeated the terrible-sounding disorder.

'You will immediately start an oral treatment, Lily, and we'll need to do screenings from time to time but –' a smile spread across his chubby-cheeked face '– you're going to be fine.'

Happiness bloomed big inside Jess. She hugged Lil even as tears filled her eyes. This was the first thing she'd had to get excited about in weeks.

Okay, maybe there was one other thing, but she wasn't sure excited was the way she would describe how she felt as each day passed with no period.

But this – this was excellent news! 'You're going to be fine,' Jess echoed.

Lil nodded. 'I can't believe it!'

When they'd gathered their composure once more, Lil asked, 'What is Wilson's disease?'

Jess would like to know the answer to that as well.

'It's the strangest thing,' Collins reported, 'and most difficult to diagnose. Wilson's disease is an autosomal recessive inherited disorder of hepatic copper metabolism. To put it plainly, the anomalies you've been suffering are caused by the accumulation of copper in organs and tissues. You end up with all these strange symptoms that tend to send your doctor looking for answers in a whole different direction from the actual cause. Copper is a necessary element to our health and well-being, but not when it isn't properly metabolized and starts to build up.'

'So I take medicine,' Lil clarified.

'We'll be starting you on that regimen right away. You're one of the lucky ones, Lil, you have very little liver damage. It really could have been so much worse. As long as we keep an eye on your numbers and you take your medicine, you'll be fine.'

Jess and Lily hugged again.

Lil drew back first. 'I have to call Blake!'

'There's just one other thing,' Collins said.

The room went instantly silent.

'This is an inherited disorder. You'll need to be tested, Jess. The children too, Lil.'

Well, that wasn't so bad. Wait. The idea that she could be pregnant and this could affect more than herself almost made Jess flinch.

No going there today. She had too many other worries at the moment.

'I'll make the appointments,' Lil offered, 'because Jess has a killer to catch and she needs to go.'

Jess thanked her sister and gave her another round of hugs. Though she wasn't sure he deserved it, she gave Dr Collins one as well. Then she really did have to go. Lil was right. She had a killer to catch.

Harper was waiting in the lobby. 'I'm guessing by those tear-stained cheeks and that smile the report was a good one.'

Jess couldn't help herself. She hugged him too. 'It was, Sergeant. It really, really was.'

Before she could ask, he said, 'The warrant has been inked. Detective Wells spoke to Kennamer and to Gifford, and both were happy to cooperate. Kennamer and his wife were at their daughter's house last night, and Gifford and his wife were at a church function. The daughter and the minister confirmed their whereabouts. Cook is finished at the Bullock residence. He's picking up the warrant and meeting us at Cagle's house. I've requested a forensic team to roll as well. Lori should be there by the time we get there.'

The man had been on the ball. Her whole team was the best. Jess was damned lucky to have their support.

As they rushed across the parking lot, she felt that surge of adrenaline she got when she knew she was getting close.

The Man in the Moon wanted her to find them . . . she was coming.

'Hold on, Janey.'

Warrior River Road, Hueytown, 4.30 P.M.

Cagle's home was an older farm-style house standing on a good-sized chunk of land. Neighboring homes were spread apart with mostly woods in between. The Ford truck registered to him was nowhere to be seen. Since there was no garage, just a barn in the distance, it seemed reasonable that he was MIA.

Jess dragged on a vest and waited for Harper to don his. In addition to her team and the surveillance detail, Burnett had sent along two detectives from Black's division, Detectives Roark and Dotson. She was grateful. They needed all the help they could get just now.

At least two dogs were going crazy inside Cagle's house.

'I didn't consider the dogs,' Jess muttered, as they walked toward the front of the house. She couldn't help looking back over her shoulder as she moved away from the protection of the vehicle.

Spears was here, and as much as she wanted to pretend she could ignore that fact and concentrate solely on this investigation, she would only be lying to herself.

'We need to get in there now.' She shook her head. 'But those dogs don't sound too welcoming.'

'I can handle the dogs,' Cook announced as they approached the front porch. 'There's a pen out back. I'll go in and calm 'em down, then take them one at a time to the pen.'

'I don't want you getting injured, either.' Damn it. Why hadn't she thought about the dogs?

'Chief,' Cook pressed. 'I love dogs. Dogs love me. I can do this. Trust me.'

'I don't want any dogs being shot, either,' Jess warned. 'If you get in there and get into trouble . . .'

'I have pepper spray,' Lori offered.

Cook held up his hands. 'That will not happen. I swear.'

'I'll go around back.' Harper called to Mitchell and his partner to follow him. 'We'll cover the back and any side doors.'

Jess needed a second to think about Cook's offer. 'Detective Roark, you and your partner take the barn and any other outbuildings.'

The team dispersed, with Cook waiting impatiently for her answer.

'All right, but don't do anything I'll regret,' she reminded him.

'No prob, ma'am.'

As Cook prepared to enter through the front door, Jess and Lori braced to cover him from whatever was on the other side besides the very excited dogs.

Cook elbowed the old glass in the door, shattering it, and reached carefully inside to release the locks, all the while talking to the dogs.

Jess found it quite strange that a man she suspected of being a heinous killer didn't have better locks. Maybe he figured the dogs would do the trick. Thieves didn't generally like to deal with ferocious animals, and these sounded reasonably ferocious.

Two large Golden Retrievers growled and bared their teeth, but Cook somehow managed to sweet-talk them into allowing him closer and then petting them. As much as she appreciated his ability to make that happen, he needed to get on with it. Every second that ticked by was one more that little girl might not have.

Cook removed his belt and used it as a leash. He exited the house, closing the door behind him, and led the first dog around to the pen in the backyard.

Jess and Lori shrugged at each other. 'The man has skills,' Lori acknowledged.

'He does, indeed.'

When the second dog was out of the house and on its way to the pen, Jess followed Lori inside. Harper and Mitchell were already coming through the back door. Mitchell's partner would keep an eye on the yard just in case Cagle or someone decided to join the party.

In the foyer, a staircase divided the front of the house in half. 'Take the second floor,' she said to Harper and Mitchell. She and Lori spread out to cover the downstairs rooms. The furnishings were older, comfortable-looking pieces. Only one framed photo, maybe an eleven-by-sixteen, on the wall.

Jess scrutinized the thirtyish woman and two children in the photo. 'Well, hello, daughter. And grandchildren.' Cagle had mentioned a daughter and grandchildren, and here they were. If only she knew their names.

A cell phone lay on the table next to the sofa. 'Well, now we know why he's not answering his cell.' She scanned the call lists, all deleted, except the ones Jess had made. Contacts, deleted. 'I thought you wanted me to find you,' she grumbled.

The team's first priority was to ensure there was no one in the house who was in trouble or who presented a danger. Living room, dining room, and kitchen were clear. Powder room was as well. Harper and Cook reported the same for the four bedrooms and two baths upstairs.

'Listen up, folks,' Jess announced. 'At this point our priority is finding a name and address or a phone number for the daughter.' Since none of Cagle's coworkers had a clue where he was, maybe the daughter would.

The more tedious part of the search began.

Damn it. She had hoped for more glaring evidence rather than another in-depth search. While her team took the rooms apart piece by piece, she walked through again trying to spot anything she might have missed.

A closet under the stairs snagged her attention. She opened the door and something rushed past her.

Jess stumbled back, almost lost her balance.

A cat . . . long white hair with black spots. . .

'You son of a bitch,' Jess muttered. *Spot*. The cat Emma James had drawn in her pictures.

Fury roaring through her like a tornado, Jess moved back to the closet. She found nothing but winter coats and boots. She started to close the door, but after a second thought she parted the coats and had another look. One of the foster homes she'd lived in as a kid had a closet under the stairs like this and the door to the basement had been in that closet.

'Ah-ha.' An access door lay hidden behind the coats.

Not a full-size door. Maybe two feet by four feet. But

plenty large enough to climb through. Anticipation had her feeling for a way to open or remove the panel. Could be nothing more than a way to access plumbing or electrical features, but she had to be sure.

She felt a tiny lever behind the frame around the panel. Jess pressed the lever and the panel opened into the space behind it. A narrow set of stairs disappeared into the darkness below. 'And what have we here?'

Lori joined her. 'A basement? Awesome. Let me get a flashlight.'

'No need.' A big old-fashioned flashlight sat on the floor of the closet.

'I'll go first.' Lori elbowed her way into the closet.

Jess was never going to get used to everyone jumping in to protect her. But right now all she wanted to do was get down those stairs, so she acquiesced and followed her detective into the darkness.

The steps were narrow and steep. In the basement Lori searched overhead with the beam of the flashlight until she found a light fixture. Just a bare bulb, but it would do. She pulled the string and the basement filled with light.

An open box was the first thing to catch Jess's eyes. Inside the box were Christmas decorations. Red and green glittery balls and silver tinsel.

'This is it.' She turned to Lori. 'This is where he kept the last set of remains.'

Lori called Harper. 'We need one of those forensic

techs in the basement. And anyone else who isn't otherwise occupied.'

As quickly as possible Jess and Lori went through the remaining boxes. Nothing relevant. One entire box was filled with old framed photographs. In most of the photos someone had been cut out of the picture. Jess decided it was Cagle's wife who'd been erased. Several were labeled on the back with a girl's name and a date. Judging by the dates, this Lucy was his daughter. The photos abruptly stopped when the girl was about nine or ten.

In the larger framed photo in the living room the daughter was much older. Late thirties, judging by the dates on these photos, but it was definitely this little girl all grown up.

Roark showed up to let her know they'd found nothing in the barn or the tool shed.

Jess checked the time. Five forty-five. She had to get to that press conference.

'Hold on, ma'am.'

She turned to see what Harper had found.

'These bricks are loose.' He was tugging at the wall behind the stack of boxes.

As Jess moved closer she noted that the mortar around the bricks on that wall was different, maybe a little newer than that of the surrounding walls. Her heart started to race.

Cook joined Harper and bricks began to fall. Jess

dropped her bag to the floor and rushed to help, anticipation roaring in her ears.

When the bricks stopped crashing to the floor and the dust settled, Jess stood before the opening and tried to assimilate what she saw. 'Oh my God.'

It wasn't until the words echoed in the silence that she realized she'd spoken aloud.

Beyond the brick wall that had served merely as a divider was another room . . . filled with dolls and toy furniture . . . even a tricycle. Everything a little girl would want.

'We're going to need more evidence techs,' Lori murmured.

Jess climbed through the opening they had made and stood in the middle of the space – the playroom. She reached up and pulled the string that turned on the bare bulb overhead. The meager light chased away the dark shadows.

Jess started to tremble.

Most of the brick walls had been coated over with concrete. Those portions were covered in drawings of animals and stick-figure little girls lined up in a long row like old-fashioned paper dolls. All done in sidewalk chalk. Names . . . little girls' names were everywhere. Dorie Myers . . . Emma James . . . Sierra Campbell . . . and so many others. Jess's head spun and tears crowded into her throat as she tried to take it all in.

Good God, how long had he held each child before her time was up? Her heart thundered so hard she could barely hear herself think.

Dust was thick on every surface . . . including the floor. No one had been in here in more than a decade.

What on earth had awakened this monster?

Jess stared at the dolls on the toy bed and in the little carriage. If not here, where would he have taken Janey Higginbotham?

Chapter Nineteen

Jess left Lori and Roark in charge of the scene. Cook was tasked with trying to track down Lucy Cagle. A grown and probably married Lucy Cagle, married name unknown. Not an easy task this late in the day on a Friday. But they needed to find her. Her father might be hiding out with her.

Or she and her children could be in danger.

Jess had called Dan with the news. Lori had sent Cagle's DMV photo to every news outlet in Birmingham. Wherever he was they were going to find him.

'We won't make it to the press conference on time,' Harper said, as they sped down the country road.

'Do the best you can, Sergeant. I need to be there in case Cagle is watching the news. I want him to know I did what he asked. I found him.'

* * *

Linn Park, 6.50 P.M.

Harper kept Jess close at his side as they slipped up behind the podium, where Dan had just introduced Deputy Chiefs Black and Hogan. Dan caught a glimpse of Jess and smiled. That smile made her quiver when her entire body was as tense as a newly tuned guitar string.

'Ladies and gentlemen, I don't have to introduce this lady to you. Deputy Chief Harris is lead on the investigation that has our entire community frozen in fear.'

Jess stepped up to the mic and made it short and sweet. 'We are closing in on the Man in the Moon. We have a suspect and hope to make an arrest within the next twenty-four hours. His name is Fergus Cagle and his face will be on every news channel. If you see this man, we need to know. He is potentially armed and he is absolutely dangerous.' She stared straight into the crowd as she made this statement. 'This decades-old nightmare is coming to an end.'

Questions were shouted at her but she stepped back, turning the podium back over to the city's chief of police.

Dan's voice drew her attention back to the podium. He looked as handsome as ever in spite of the nightmare they'd been through the last few days. Sometimes just looking at him unsettled her – in a good way. Not to mention the concept that this Dan and the Dan she'd known in high school and college were one and the same. She was so very proud of him, even if she didn't always show it. Ten years ago, when they'd run into each other, he'd been working for the mayor and was just about to move to the police department as a liaison to the mayor's office, the Bureau, and other organizations.

He had certainly climbed his way to the top, and he'd done so based on an outstanding job, not whom he knew. Daniel Burnett was the real thing. A genuinely good man.

Something else she remembered about running into him on Christmas Eve ten years ago – they'd ended up back at his place having mind-blowing sex. God, she must have been out of her mind. Actually she'd been celebrating a much anticipated promotion. Dan wasn't so much celebrating as he appeared to be grateful and relieved to have his second divorce behind him.

He'd also been sporting much longer hair and two weeks' beard growth. She almost hadn't recognized him when she bumped into him that evening at Publix. He'd laughed and told her that he was playing Joseph in a big church production his mother was coordinating. Jess had gotten a good laugh out of that as well.

Dear old Katherine. She'd always had her son wrapped around her little finger.

Jess's hand went to her belly. Good Lord, the thought of that woman being the grandmother to her children was terrifying.

Stop, Jess. No borrowing trouble . . . yet.

There was a little girl out there who needed her. And all those parents who just wanted to bring their little children home for a proper burial. Damn the Man in the Moon.

Damn you, Fergus Cagle.

Moving along the fringes of the audience, she scanned the crowd. Harper was right next to her doing the same. She doubted Cagle would show up here, but it wasn't unheard of.

Deputy Chief Black stepped to the podium and gave an update on the search for the three women in the photos Spears had sent. Jess noticed that he didn't mention their names or anything about the bait Spears had used to lure them to wherever the hell he wanted them. Black relayed only that two had been identified and that every effort was being made to identify the third young woman.

Reporters fired questions at both Dan and Black about Cagle and the missing Higginbotham child. The Man in the Moon case was uppermost on their minds. It hit squarely home, and everyone wanted it solved.

Jess had him. Sierra Campbell's blanket could be connected to the box of Christmas decorations. To top it off, they had that playroom in the basement . . . all those little girls had left their names and drawings on the walls. Sick bastard.

She had him all right, and she was going to get him, preferably alive.

The families of the rest of his victims deserved to know where their children were.

Jess tried to take a deep breath, but the crush of the crowd was becoming a little uncomfortable. She didn't usually feel claustrophobic, but today it was getting to her. She leaned toward Harper. 'Let's move away from the crowd to some place with a better view.'

He gave her a nod and started cutting a path. She followed close behind him. Someone tapped her on the left shoulder. She twisted to see who had touched her and she came face-to-face with the dark-haired man and his snazzy sunglasses.

She reached into her bag for her weapon.

He pivoted and made his own path through the crowd.

Jess went after him, her hand jammed into her bag, fingers around the Glock.

Keeping up with him was impossible, but she kept his head and shoulders in view. She wanted to call out to him, order him to stop, but she couldn't draw attention or her weapon in this crowd.

Harper moved up beside her. 'Where are you going?' he called out above the applause that had started.

'It's him – the dark-haired man. Navy suit jacket. Dark glasses. Up ahead.' As if he'd known she was talking about him, he glanced back.

Harper spotted him and started slicing through the crowd. Jess slowed down, had to catch her breath.

'Keep going,' she muttered. Dredging up a second wind, she burst forward again. She didn't want the guy to get away this time. She cut around to the left in hopes of intersecting with what appeared to be his destination. Harper was closing in on him.

A body slammed hard into her.

She cried out . . . went down on her hands and knees.

Her bag hit the ground, the contents scattering.

Hands and knees stinging, she shoved her Glock back into her bag and gathered her things, muttering one blistering curse after the other.

A hand grasped her elbow and helped her to her feet. She turned to thank whoever had decided to be a gentleman but he was already walking away, moving effortlessly through the mob of bodies. The back of his blond head was all she could see . . .

. . . and still she somehow knew.

No.

The world seemed to lapse into slow motion as the blond man stopped. He looked back over his shoulder as if he'd felt her watching him.

He smiled and the ground beneath her feet shifted.

Spears.

She grabbed her bag, jammed her hand inside for her weapon.

But he was gone.

'Are you all right, Chief?'

Jess turned to face her detective.

'I looked back and didn't see you.' Harper shrugged. 'I had to come back for you.'

Which meant the dark-haired man had gotten away, just as Spears had gotten away.

She blinked once, twice, struggling to wrap her brain around what just happened. 'I think I need to sit down, Sergeant.'

He grabbed her when she would have hit the ground. 'Come on, Chief, let's get you out of this heat.'

Dunbrooke Drive, 9.20 P.M.

Jess was neck deep in hot water and it felt amazing.

It wasn't her tub, it was Dan's. He'd insisted she come home with him and the fact of the matter was she didn't want to be alone tonight any more than she had last night. Maybe she never wanted to be alone again.

Spears had gotten that close to her.

He'd touched her just like he had when she'd interviewed him. Back when she was still Special Agent Jess Harris.

What the hell was he trying to prove? In a park filled with cops and reporters at a press conference?

More important, why hadn't he done what she would have expected him to do?

He could have killed her.

Jess's body trembled in spite of the delicious heat of the water. Eric Spears could have plunged a knife deep into her back or used a hypodermic needle filled with the drug ketamine, which he used on all his victims. He could have shot her with a silenced weapon during one of the many outbursts of applause. He could have taken her with him by force.

But he hadn't done any of those things. Instead, he'd helped her to her feet and he'd walked away unnoticed, but he'd wanted her to know it was him.

Mostly, she suspected, so she would punish herself for not going after him or shooting him. She wouldn't have been able to catch him even if she hadn't gone into shock.

She'd frozen.

Eric Spears was here.

Why?

If the Bureau was right and he already had at least two of those women in his lair, why was he here? He never took a victim and then ignored her. Could those women be here with him?

She closed her eyes and tried to block him out. She'd beaten herself up for not shooting him in the back as he walked away or screaming for him to stop so other cops could have done something. But the risk that Spears might have started shooting into the crowd had been too great.

His friend the dark-haired man had been in that crowd, too. God knows what he would have done.

There was nothing she could have done . . . and for now, she couldn't let him distract her.

Right now, her job was to focus on finding Cagle and that little girl.

Cook was unsuccessful in his search for the daughter. He swore he was going to work on it all night if he had to. But he was young, and Jess doubted he would make it past his first invitation to hit a club. It was Friday night.

Since Cagle had basically vanished and his coworkers, Kennamer and Gifford, confirmed Ruthie Jeffreys's assertion that Cagle was intensely private, Jess's only hope for getting a lead on his whereabouts was finding his daughter. With his face plastered everywhere it was possible someone would spot him and call it in, but that wasn't something Jess intended to wait for.

Apparently his daughter didn't live in the area or she would surely have seen her father's face on the news and called. Unless she couldn't call.

A soft rap on the door came before, 'You doing okay in there?'

Dan had been understandably irate when he learned that both the dark-haired man, who remained unidentified, and Spears had been in this evening's crowd. He'd been even more irritated that Jess had gone after the dark-haired man in the first place and that Harper had left her side to go after him as well.

And no sign of Cagle.

'You still alive?'

Jess cleared her throat. 'I'm fine, thank you.'

'I thought you might like a glass of wine.'

Jess tensed, that pounding started in her chest. Still no period. A responsible person would avoid alcohol just in case. She did a mental harrumph. A responsible person wouldn't be in this predicament.

'No thanks. I need a clear head to ponder this case some more tonight.'

'Dinner's ready whenever you are.'

'Thanks.' Eating had been the last thing on their minds when the press conference ended. By the time they'd gotten here she'd just wanted a bath. Her lips lifted into a weary smile. Leave it to Dan to take care of her.

Her heart rate slowed to a more normal pace. Most likely because the mention of dinner had her stomach rumbling. She washed her hair and scrubbed her body. The idea of Spears touching her creeped her out. Once she was out of the tub and had dried off, she surveyed her reflection. Blow-drying was too labor intensive and she was just too tired. She towel-dried her hair and left it at that.

Her knees were skinned but good. The heels of her hands not so much.

She stared at her nude body in the big mirror. What the hell would she do if her period never came? Eventually she'd have to go to the doctor.

Anyone but Collins. He was far too judgmental and narrow-minded when it came to the needs of women.

The smart thing would be to pick up a test and just get it over with. As soon as she found Janey Higginbotham she would do that. Then all this wondering and worrying would be behind her.

With Dan's robe cinched around her, she opened the bathroom door and followed the wonderful smells to the kitchen. Whatever he had prepared, had delivered, or poured out of a can had her mouth watering.

'Wow,' she said, as she entered his kitchen, 'smells good.'

'This is a test.'

He placed a plate in front of her. On the plate was a bed of noodles with some kind of gravy-like sauce and meat chunks, maybe beef. Asparagus spears were piled next to it.

'You said I never use my kitchen and you were more right than I wanted to admit. I decided to do something about that. From now on, I plan on preparing dinner at home for the two of us as often as possible.'

Jess bit her lip and wondered if he'd mind making it for three a whole lot sooner than maybe even he had anticipated. She swallowed at the massive lump in her throat. 'You cooked this . . . ?' she ventured, her voice a little high-pitched. 'From scratch? No boxes? No cans? No lessons from Gina?'

'I did.'

Oh Lord.

'Try it.' He was like a kid about to get his first star from his favorite teacher.

'I'm not eating unless you're eating.' Good move. If it tasted terrible she'd see it on his face.

He grumbled something unintelligible as he prepared his own plate. She patted the stool next to her.

When he'd settled there, she picked up her fork. 'Bon appetit.' But then she waited until he stuck a forkful in his mouth. He chewed, made a pleasant little sound. Well, all right then. She took a big bite. The sauce or gravy was really quite tasty. The meat – beef – was a little chewy. The noodles were not overcooked, and the asparagus was still the tiniest bit crisp and lightly seasoned.

'It's good,' she said between chews.

The relief on his face was priceless.

That face was reason enough to eat every single bite even if it killed her.

She hadn't realized how hungry she was until she dug in. She finished off the plate and had to resist licking it clean. A yawn escaped her before she could stop it. 'Sorry. I'm just exhausted. I may call it a night and do my pondering with my eyes closed.'

She did some of her best analysis with her eyes closed. Somehow the details that often hid from her came to the surface in that place between asleep and awake.

'You should let me take care of those scratches first.'

'Just show me where the Band-Aids and the Neosporin are and I can handle it.' It wasn't that she didn't want him to touch her . . . she did. She wanted way more than that, but she didn't trust herself not to tell him she might be pregnant. She'd almost told him last night and the night before that. The rules had gone out the window this week.

Guilt pricked her, but if she told him he'd only worry and hover some more. He did too much of that already. She needed to stay on top of this case, and arguing with him about whether it was safe or not was just a distraction she didn't need.

'How's Lily?' he asked, as he cleared the plates.

She'd totally forgotten to tell him the latest news. 'She's good. We found out this afternoon she has something called Wilson's disease. Totally treatable. The little bit of damage that was done to her liver will reverse with proper treatment. It's something to do with the way her body doesn't metabolize copper.'

'So she'll be okay?'

Jess nodded. 'It's a hereditary condition. The kids and I have to be tested to make sure we don't have it. Untreated, it can do serious damage.'

Worry lined his brow. 'Have you had any symptoms?'

Not unless a missing period was one of them. 'Nope. But neither did Lil until recently. I'll get the test just to be sure.'

'Harold called while you were in the tub. Nothing new on the search for the Higginbotham girl or the APBs on Cagle and Spears.'

Jess shook her head in frustration. 'We need to find Cagle's daughter.' Without a married name or address it was like looking for a needle in a haystack. 'Kennamer and Gifford,' Jess went on, 'know nothing about Cagle's daughter. If he owns other property where he might be hiding out, they hadn't heard about it.' She heaved a weary breath. 'It's like he just went back to the moon.'

'Maybe he got desperate and scared and decided to run,' Dan offered. 'But if that's the case, then why did he start this and urge you to find him?'

'Unless we find him alive we may never know.' She chewed her lip. 'That's why he couldn't resist,' she said, the note he'd sent with Sierra Campbell suddenly connecting. 'Whatever his reason for sending these gifts to me, he started the process and the temptation got to him.' Her hand went to her throat. 'He said he couldn't help himself. Now he's out there with that little girl and he's lost control.' She closed her eyes and tried to slow the new rush of fear and frustration.

Don't let him kill that little girl, she prayed.

'Time for you to go to bed.'

Before she could protest Dan scooped her into his arms. She tried not to melt against him, but she had no strength to resist. She loved the way he smelled. Loved the feel of his strong arms around her as he carried her to the guest room. He set her on the bed and disappeared.

She needed to brush her teeth and borrow a nightshirt, but she was just too tired to care. The thought was scarcely finished when he returned with everything she needed, including Neosporin and Band-Aids.

He patched her up, his fingers gentle but swift on her skin. As tired as she was, she found herself smiling at him as he knelt before her. Sometimes it felt good to be taken care of.

When he was done he kissed the top of her head, said good night, and started to leave. Jess caught him by the hand and pulled him back to her.

'I need your arms around me tonight.'

He didn't ask any questions, just swept her into his arms once more and carried her to his bed. He laid her gently there and undressed before crawling in next to her. The feel of his strong arms around her were a healing balm to the pain and misery of the monsters she had faced today.

But even his strong arms couldn't keep the images of Fergus Cagle's basement from following her to sleep.

Chapter Twenty

11.55 P.M.

He had prayed.

Over and over he had prayed for the urges to stop . . . for the need to be taken from him. In twenty years it had not. The Lord had turned away from him, leaving him to drown in the evil he could not escape.

How could a man escape himself?

After years of trying to calm the urge with the sweetness of so many little girls, his girl had come home to him.

His sweet *Lucy*. And the Lord had shown him favor once more.

Tears streamed down his cheeks. His life had been whole again. The urge had subsided. No more searching for treasures to replace the one he had lost.

She was home.

But now he would lose all that made him whole . . . again.

This was *her* fault.

Fury pelted him.

If Jess Harris had stayed away this would not have happened.

Now everyone would know the truth.

He was a bad, bad man. Just like that bitch of a wife who'd left him had said.

I don't want you touching my children! You're a bad man, Fergus. I saw you looking at her the way no father should look at his daughter.

He should have killed that bitch. Then his Lucy would never have been taken from him.

God help him now she knew what a bad, bad, bad man he was.

They all knew.

He couldn't protect them.

All those precious treasures he had collected and cherished even in death were lost to him . . . and now the most perfect one of all would leave him again. She would take her children – his grandchildren – with her. They would all hate and despise him.

He was a monster.

His body burned and ached from the obedience belt and the slashes he had made to his thighs with his pocket knife. He had cut himself and pummeled himself in an attempt to stop the urges and he had failed.

Fergus held the gun to his head and struggled to pull the trigger.

'Do it!' he screamed.

His hand shook with the effort of jamming the gun into his temple. His finger refused to curl and tighten against the trigger.

He couldn't do it. He'd tried so many times and failed.

Instead of slamming that tire iron into Bullock's skull he should have begged the man to slam it into his, then he wouldn't have to do the rest.

Dear God, he prayed, *strike me dead here and now.*

But God had forsaken him for good this time.

He had to finish this. His hand fell into his lap, the gun useless. Everything was lost to him. Now his sole purpose must be protecting his daughter and his precious grand-children.

Fergus wiped the tears from his face and readied the gun for the final act he must stage before stuffing it back into his waistband. He knew what he had to do. It was the only way out.

He checked on his Lucy and his precious grandchildren. They stared at him, unable to speak or move, but he smiled, his lips trembling. They would be fine. They didn't know it yet. Their memories of him would be ruined, but there was no help for that.

No one could know the rest.

The truth would go to hell with him.

The truth was supposed to set him free. But it wouldn't. It would cost him everything.

He closed the door and moved on to the kitchen. This old place had a root cellar and that worked well enough. It wasn't much to look at, like his basement at home, but it served the purpose. In the small kitchen he grabbed the lantern and a storybook.

On the back porch he reached down and pulled open the door that was built into the wood floor. The hinges complained. Down the few steps and into the dank, dark place where the child he had collected whimpered and sobbed.

He lit the lantern. The little girl drew into the corner, her little body shivering with fear. He'd tried to feed her but she refused to eat.

Not much he could do about that. Children were obstinate at times.

'I'm going to read you a story, Lucy.'

She cried harder as if she didn't want to hear the story. She'd told him that Lucy wasn't her name and he'd explained that he always called his treasures Lucy. He couldn't change now after all these years. He was too old to change.

He read the story: 'Cinderella.' One of Lucy's favorites. His, too. He liked that the true beauty of Cinderella was revealed once the rags and fireplace soot and ash were gone. True beauty was often buried deep beneath the surface.

True beauty was often greatly misunderstood.

By the time he finished the story the treasure had fallen asleep. Her calm, even breathing told him that she wasn't pretending in hopes he'd go away.

It was good that she was asleep. Tomorrow was a big day. She would need all her strength for what was to come.

Tomorrow she was going to the burying tree to meet Jess Harris.

Then it would be done and they could all live happily ever after.

Chapter Twenty-One

Southpointe Circle,
Saturday, August 21, 8.15 A.M.

Lori parked in front of Sherry's house. Chet wouldn't like that she had come here to confront his ex, but it was time they settled this thing between them – woman to woman. Sherry had a new husband. She had no right to begrudge Chet his own happiness. She certainly had no right to use Chester as a pawn.

Palms sweating and pulse thumping hard, Lori walked right up and pressed the doorbell.

She could hear voices inside and tiny feet running. Chester stuck his face to the sidelight and Lori smiled at him. He waved and did that little-boy shimmy he did when he was excited. He started shouting for his mom and then he disappeared.

Lori imagined Sherry was ordering him to his room, maybe off to the den with his stepfather.

Finally the door opened and Sherry looked from Lori to the street. 'Where's Chet?'

So much for hello. 'He's at work already. I'm headed that way myself. I thought if you had a moment we could talk. You know Chet's birthday is tomorrow.'

Instantly going on the defensive, Sherry folded her arms over her robe-clad chest. 'I know when his birthday is. Sundays are his day with Chester so there shouldn't be an issue. What do you want to talk about? I thought you were embroiled in some big case.'

'We are.' Lori struggled to hang onto her patience. 'I don't have a lot of time, so if you have a moment . . .'

'You don't look like you're headed to work.' She surveyed Lori's jeans, Magic City tee, and sneakers with something akin to disdain.

'It's Saturday,' Lori defended. 'We opted for casual day.'

'If you have something to say, we can talk out here.'

Lori stepped back as the woman joined her on the stoop. 'That works.' What else could she say?

'What is it you want to talk about? If you're annoyed about the other night, that's tough. My son comes first. If he has a fever he's not leaving the house.'

'I understand.' Lori wasn't a mother, but the concept of keeping a sick child home was simply good common sense – if the child was actually sick. 'That makes perfect sense. I would do the same thing.'

Sherry stared at her for a long, awkward moment. 'Why are you here then?'

Lori had known the woman didn't like her, but she hadn't expected her to be so blatant about it. She'd actually seemed pretty nice the first few times they'd met. Had the idea that Lori and Chet were getting serious somehow started her thinking she'd made a mistake leaving him?

Well, Lori had news for her. *Too late, baby.*

'It feels like you and I are getting off on the wrong foot.' Lori had gone over what she intended to say a dozen times and somehow it still felt wrong and stupid. 'I really want our friendship to work.' She prompted a smile she hoped passed for the real thing. 'I'd like you to feel free to talk about anything related to Chester with me. I adore him but I am not trying to play the part of his mother. That belongs solely to you.'

There. She'd gotten it all out without screwing up or sounding pushy.

More of that awkward staring and no responding. What was this woman's problem?

'I think Chester likes me and I'm very pleased about that,' Lori added. Was Sherry not going to say anything? 'Is . . . that an issue for you?'

'Chester is my son. Why would how he feels about Chet's newest girlfriend matter to me?'

Wow. Talk about cutting deep. Stay cool. No cat fighting allowed. 'I think I'm a little more than just his newest girlfriend. We're fully committed to each other and we're planning our future together.'

'Great. Anything else you want to enlighten me about? I'd like to enjoy a quiet Saturday morning with my family.'

The woman was really trying hard to piss her off. 'So we don't have a problem? You're not upset with Chester liking me or anything related to my relationship with Chet?'

'Look, Lori.' The icy tone in Sherry's voice warned the claws were fully extended now. 'I couldn't care less where your relationship with Chet is going. Who he chooses to spend his time with is irrelevant to me. But Chester is our son. Chester may get a little attached to you but you'll never be his mother. Why would I have a problem with a non-issue?'

Well, shit. 'I told you I'm not trying to be his mother. I just want you *not* to feel threatened by the idea that he likes me.'

'Nothing about you threatens me.'

'Really? That's not the way it looks from here.' Lori couldn't help herself. She looked the woman up and down and let her own slender figure speak for itself. Sherry was a little short and frumpy – that was a place Lori would never have gone if the woman hadn't pushed her there.

Sherry's face reddened with her own fresh burst of anger. 'So you and Chet are talking about your future, are you?'

'Yes, we are. We may buy a house later this year.' So there!

Sherry held up her left hand and wiggled her finger. 'I don't see a ring yet.'

'That's only because I've been holding back,' Lori confessed with a big dramatic sigh. 'But any reservations I had are behind me now. I'm absolutely ready for the next step. Kids, the white picket fence, the works.'

Maybe she'd overstated her confidence and readiness in a couple of areas, but what the hell.

'Kids?' Sherry echoed. 'You and Chet want to have kids?'

'Chet loves Chester and he wants more children. We'll be taking that step in time. Of course our children will never lessen Chester's place in our lives. So don't even try to throw that up. We would never hurt Chester.'

'I'm confident you won't.' Sherry gloated as if she knew something Lori didn't.

'What does that mean?'

'He hasn't told you, has he?'

Lori's composure started to slip. 'Chet and I have no secrets.'

'Really? Did he tell you about the vasectomy he had

after Chester was born? Sounds to me as if he might have kept that one tiny little detail from you.'

'What're you talking about?' The woman was grasping at straws. Trying to make this about something Chet had done wrong rather than what she was doing.

Sherry made a scissoring motion with her fingers. 'Snip, snip. A vasectomy. He's shooting blanks. How does that play into your future plans for that white picket fence and kids?'

Lori did an about-face and walked as calmly as the waves of anger battering her would allow. She climbed into her Mustang and drove away.

This case was too important for her to be caught up in this kind of ridiculous pettiness.

Sherry had to be lying . . . Chet wouldn't keep something like that from her.

Lori trusted him completely. She shared everything with him – her deepest, darkest secrets. He knew opening up like that had been really difficult for her.

He wouldn't have kept secrets of his own.

Yet, on a level she was far from ready to acknowledge, she knew he had.

Chapter Twenty-Two

Jess tacked the crime scene photos from Cagle's basement across the bottom of the case board. She studied the faces of the little girls who had spent time in that playroom.

She'd gone back there this morning and read every word, studied every drawing the girls had made. It was clear he had kept the girls for months, perhaps the better part of the year between harvest moons.

Lastly, she tacked a photo of Cagle on the board. 'Where the hell are you?'

Harper and Detective Roark, still on loan from Crimes Against Persons, were knocking on doors. Talking to Cagle's neighbors again as well as his superiors at Alabama Power. How could no one know this man on a personal level?

'I got her!'

312

Jess turned to Lori, held her breath. 'The daughter?' She and Cook had been searching databases – some official, some not – and social networks.

'Lucy Cagle, born on September 20, forty years ago, in Cooper Green Mercy Hospital.'

But God only knew where the woman lived now. She could be anywhere.

'Hmm. That's interesting,' Lori went on.

'Tell me it's an address,' Jess said, hoping against hope.

'The night Lucy was born was a harvest moon.'

And the pieces began to fall into place.

'Shut the front door,' Cook piped up.

Certain that meant the young man had something with his search of social networks, Jess walked over to his desk. Lori was already moving around to Harper's chair, since his desk was next to Cook's.

Cook had his screen open to Facebook. 'Meet Lucy Cagle Neely. Birthday September 20.' He held up his arms in victory like a boxer who'd just defeated his opponent.

'She has a son named Dennis.' Lori pointed to the boy's image in Lucy's friends box.

Cook clicked the son's image. 'Sophomore at Hoover High School. One sister, Brittany, who goes to the middle school. Go Buccaneers.'

Jess resisted the urge to tap her foot. She needed an address. *Now.* 'Lori, check for Lucy Neely in the DMV database. Locate me a home address. Cook, see if you can drum up a phone number for any of the three.'

With anticipation burning in her veins, Jess returned to the case board and studied the images of the little girls there. 'I will find you. *All* of you,' she promised.

'Here we go!' Lori was on her feet reaching for her purse. 'You aren't going to believe this, but the daughter lives on the same street as the Higginbothams.'

Dear God, he'd gone hunting on his own daughter's street.

120 Boxwood Drive, Hoover, 12.45 P.M.

Two more BPD cruisers were at the scene by the time Jess and her posse showed up. She had new uniforms following her around today. Yesterday had apparently been too much for poor Officer Mitchell and his partner.

'Forensics is five minutes out,' Lori advised, as they emerged from her car. 'I ordered a bus, just in case.'

Jess closed the door, vest on and weapon in hand. 'Good thinking.' The daughter or her children could be injured. Having paramedics en route was a good move.

The neighborhood was quiet, thankfully with no one on the streets. With school about to start next week, families were enjoying the final weekend of freedom from the hectic schedule coming.

That was another thing about kids. When they

were infants and toddlers, life pretty much revolved around the parents' work schedule. But once school started, life changed for at least eighteen or so years. Car pools, homework, teachers' meetings, volunteer activities, sports . . . her stomach roiled at the idea.

She might never be ready to be a parent.

Some people just weren't made out of the right stuff. She hadn't gotten that juggling gene working mothers required. She had no patience. What kid wanted a mother who had no time or patience for him or her?

That was exactly why her body needed to cooperate. As well as solving this case today, she wanted her period.

Once the uniforms were in place, Jess waited on one side of the front door. Lori assumed a position on the other side. Jess gave her a nod and she pounded on the door.

The silence inside the house didn't jibe with the concept that two teenagers lived here.

Another firm round of knocking. 'Ms Neely, this is Detective Wells of the Birmingham Police Department. We need to speak with you, ma'am.'

One last knock and they were going in. No need to wait for the warrant. With Cagle missing and what they'd found in his home, exigent circumstances permitted entry without an inked warrant.

Two of the officers stepped up and took care of the door with the 'big key.' The battering ram made quick work of getting into the house.

Uniforms poured in and spread out in the house. Jess was scarcely in the door when reports of 'Clear!' started to fill the air.

No one was home.

Lori cancelled the bus.

Jess wandered through the bedrooms and noticed the beds were unmade. With the rest of the house in such perfect order, it seemed strange that even the mother's bed was tousled as if she'd been roused from sleep.

A framed photo of Lucy with a man Jess suspected was the woman's husband and her two children stood on the bedside table. She surveyed the pictures of the daughter, in various dance costumes, that lined the walls of her bedroom.

'Where are you?'

'Chief!'

Jess took one last look around and went in search of Lori.

'It's one of those charging centers.' She pointed to the dock where two cell phones waited on the kitchen counter.

'There's one missing.' With gloved hands, Jess checked the pink phone. 'This is the daughter's.'

'This one belongs to Lucy.' Lori turned the screen to Jess so she could see the phone's wallpaper image – a photo of the kids.

'Definitely the mother's,' Jess agreed.

316

'She has twelve missed calls and three voice mails. All from a contact listed as *hubster*.'

Jess moved closer to Lori as she attempted to play the voice mails from the husband. Thankfully there was no password required. A woman after her own heart. Jess hated passwords and codes. She could never remember what she'd selected.

The time and date stamp indicated the first message was left Thursday evening. A male voice filled the air. 'Hey, baby, the first day of negotiations went well. I am pumped! Call me when you get home.'

The next came Friday morning. 'Hey, where are you? You didn't call me back last night. Today's going to be a long one. I don't know when I'll get to call again. Text me or something. Love you. Hug the kids.'

The third had come at eleven last night. 'Seriously, Lucy. What's going on? You're not answering your phone. The kids aren't answering theirs. I need to hear from you. Love you. Hug the kids.'

The cell phone rang.

Jess jumped. Lori did the same.

'It's the husband.' Lori looked to her for the go-ahead.

'Put it on speaker. Maybe he has some idea where Cagle would go and where his family is.'

Lori tapped the screen a couple of times.

'Lucy, Jesus Christ, you had me worried sick. Why haven't you answered my calls?'

Informing a family member in this manner was never Jess's first choice but they were desperate. There was no time to waste. 'Mr Neely?'

A moment of silence. 'Who is this? Where's my wife?'

'Mr Neely, this is Deputy Chief Jess Harris of the Birmingham Police Department.'

'Oh my God. What's happened? Where's my wife? Are my children okay?'

'Mr Neely, we don't know where your family is. I'm in your home and there is no indication of foul play. But we need to find them. What I need is for you to stay calm and listen very carefully to my questions. Can you do that for me, sir?'

Stifled sobs echoed across the line. 'Yes.' The word was too high-pitched and permeated with anguish.

'Where are you, sir?'

'I'm . . .' He gained control. 'I'm in Los Angeles. My company is merging with one here and I've . . . what's happened to my wife . . . the kids? What's going on?'

'Sir, I can't answer those questions just yet but we are doing everything we can to find your family, so please work with me. Okay?'

'I'm sorry.' He cleared his throat. 'What do you need me to do?'

'When was the last time you spoke with your wife?'

'Thursday morning. She wished me luck.'

'Are you acquainted with your wife's father?'

'Fergus? Yes. I even tried to call him and he's not answering. Is he all right?'

'Does your father-in-law have any property other than the farm where he lives? A place he vacations or just a little getaway?'

'I don't understand,' Neely protested. 'What's going on down there?'

Obviously the Man in the Moon wasn't big news in LA. 'Sir, you have to trust me. I can't help your family if you don't help me.'

'Okay.' He moaned a tormented sound that tore at Jess's heart. 'Please, ask me whatever you need to.'

'Does Mr Cagle own any properties besides his home place that you're aware of?'

'I don't believe so.'

'When did you first meet your father-in-law?'

Neely explained that his wife's mother had taken her away from Alabama when she was only seven years old. She never allowed Lucy to see her father for reasons Lucy still didn't know. But after she passed, Lucy wanted to find her father. By then the kids had been born and she had no other family. After their reunion, Neely's company agreed to relocate him to Birmingham. That was thirteen years ago.

The same year the children of Birmingham stopped disappearing during the harvest moon.

'Mr Neely' – this was where things would get hairy – 'have you ever heard of the Man in the Moon case?'

'I heard something about that just before I left. Lucy and I talked about it. Neither of us could imagine what kind of person commits such despicable acts.' He drew in a big breath as adrenaline obviously fired through him, sending his fear to the back burner. 'It makes you wonder why no one was paying attention. It's like all those mass shootings. If people would just pay attention to their families and friends and neighbors, a lot of these tragedies might never happen. Seems like the world is blind to . . .' Silence thickened across the line. 'Why do you ask me about that case?'

The fear in his voice was unmistakable. The adrenaline rush was fading. The naïveté in his philosophy was unfortunately commonplace. Thing was, sometimes the face of evil looked as normal as your own reflection.

'Mr Neely, we believe Fergus Cagle is the man who took all those children.'

'That's impossible. No. He . . . he's a doting grand-father. There has to be a mistake.'

'We found the room in his basement of his home where he kept the children, Mr Neely. There is no mistake. Now a coworker of his is dead and Mr Cagle is missing. Along with your family and another little girl, seven-year-old Janey Higginbotham.'

'The little girl down the street? Oh my God!'

'Mr Neely, we need to find your father-in-law. We need to find him now.'

A moment or two more was needed for the husband to gather his wits once again. 'He never takes a vacation. The kids usually go to his farm for a weekend and he takes them shopping, but never out of town for more than the day. He's always been funny about staying close to home. Dear God . . . this can't be happening.'

Before she lost him to the shock of this news, Jess pressed the question. 'Think hard, Mr Neely. Have you ever heard him speak of a getaway he hoped to visit one day?'

'No. Nothing comes to mind. Nothing at all . . . wait. He works with a man who has a cabin on the lake or a river. He mentioned he liked the idea of a place like that, but he never did anything about it as far as I know.'

'Can you remember this man's name?' The pressure was pounding in Jess's skull. She needed some place to start. If he could just give her something.

'Bulton or Bullot . . . something like that.'

'Bullock?' Goose bumps spilled over Jess's skin. 'Jerry Bullock?'

'That's it! Bullock.'

Jess nodded for Lori to take over as she fished for her cell and put through a call to Cook. 'We need the location of all properties listed to Jerry Bullock. Cagle may have taken his hostages to a place near the water that belongs to Bullock.'

It was a long shot, but it was all they had.

'I'm on it,' Cook assured her.

'Also,' Jess added before letting him go, 'see if you can get the phone company to triangulate a number.' She went back to the charging dock and checked the little pink phone. She gave Cook the number listed for the brother. 'His cell phone isn't in the house. I'm hoping maybe he has it on him.'

The fact that he hadn't answered the father's calls or tried to text him back suggested the phone was either not with him or inoperable. But it was worth a shot.

'I'll call as soon as I have anything.'

Before she could put it away her cell clanged. *Harper*. She hoped he had something more concrete than the news here. 'Harris.'

'Ma'am, I just got a call from dispatch. Fergus Cagle's truck was found on the side of the road on Oak Mountain Lake Road. Detective Roark and I are headed that way.'

Jess got a beep that she had another incoming call. *Cook*. 'Keep me posted, Sergeant.' She tapped the screen to take Cook's call. 'Harris.'

'Bullock has a little house on about ten acres right on the lake, practically in the park. I'm texting you the address so you can GPS it. I'll meet you there.'

'What park?' The wheels in her head were turning and Jess wasn't liking where it was taking her.

'Oak Mountain State Park. The only properties out

there are mansions and a few holdovers from back in the day. Looks like Bullock inherited one of the holdovers. The land alone is worth a fortune.'

As he spoke, Jess checked the address. 'The place is on John Findlay Drive as in f-i-n-d?'

'That's it.'

Find me.

He'd already told her where he would be . . . she just hadn't figured out the clue. Bullock's address was near where Cagle's truck had been found . . . he had to be there.

Adrenaline set a fire in her blood. 'We're heading that way now,' she told Cook before ending the call. To Lori she said, 'We're going to need more backup for this one.'

If Cagle was there, she wanted SWAT standing by just in case. She couldn't risk finding him at this remote location and having to wait for backup to arrive.

Time was their enemy.

John Findlay III Drive, outside Oak Mountain State Park, 3.30 P.M.

The rustic board and batten-style cabin sat on the south side of the lake. The location was just opposite a small peninsula that jutted out from the small slice of land that intersected the lake from north to south. Bullock's cabin didn't appear to have any luxuries, but it had a killer view from a big screened-in back porch.

Harper had checked Cagle's truck. He'd left the key in the ignition. There was gas in the tank, and the engine started with no problem. For whatever reason he had abandoned it on the other side of the lake, only a couple of miles from the cabin.

For the past fifteen minutes while they waited for SWAT to get into position, there had been no movement or sound in or around the cabin.

Jess hoped Lucy and her kids were unharmed. She prayed little Janey Higginbotham was as well.

Dan waited next to her. She'd called him while Lori notified SWAT. Jess was glad he'd gotten here in time. *He should be a part of this.*

The team commander's order to move in came across the wireless communications mics they wore. Jess couldn't breathe as she held her position waiting for the all-clear sign. She, Dan, Lori, Harper, and Cook were standing by, vests on and weapons in hand.

'Come on, come on,' she muttered. She hated the waiting part.

'Take it easy,' Dan urged. 'We'll be going in soon.'

Not soon enough to suit her.

'Clear, move in,' came over the communication link. 'We have three bound hostages inside. No visible injuries.'

Thank God. Jess was on her feet and moving forward.

She tried not to think about the fact that only three people were inside. There were four missing: little Janey, Lucy, and her two kids.

Someone was absent . . . besides Cagle.

Lucy Neely and her two children were bound and gagged in the cabin's one bedroom. As soon as they were free and the hugging and sobbing had subsided, Jess introduced herself and pushed for answers.

'Ms. Neely, where is your father?'

She shook her head. 'Not in front of my children.'

'Detective Wells, would you and Officer Cook take the kids out front so they can call their father and let him know they're safe?' Paramedics were standing by to check everyone over.

'Yes, ma'am.' Lori motioned for the kids to follow her. 'Your dad's waiting to hear from you,' she told them as she ushered them into the hall.

Once the kids were out of the room, Jess asked, 'Did he have the little girl with him? Janey Higginbotham?'

Lucy nodded and her tears started anew. 'He kept repeating that he was a bad, bad man but that he hadn't wanted to do this.' She frowned in confusion or exasperation. 'He said it was because of you. He called your name over and over.'

A quaking she couldn't quite suppress started deep inside her. Jess would need to analyze that part of his motive more thoroughly, but not right now. He had that little girl. Her heart hurt with the idea of what might happen next. 'He gave you no indication of where he was going?'

'He said he was going to find you since you hadn't found him.'

Jesus Christ. More of that anxiety and apprehension heaped onto her chest. This made no sense. 'He didn't say anything else?'

'No. He just kept apologizing over and over. Is he really the Man in the Moon?' Her face scrunched up and the tears started anew.

'I'm afraid so, Lucy.'

'I can't believe it.' She wiped her eyes. 'My mother always told me I could never see him again, but I thought it was because she hated him.'

Jess couldn't explain Lucy's mother's reasons, since she had taken her away before the first little girl disappeared. What Jess did know was that sometimes killers like Cagle started out just daydreaming about hurting others. Sometimes they abused those they felt they could control. Or they harmed animals to relieve their urges. There were many things Cagle's wife may have witnessed that prompted her to get away from him.

Too bad his wife hadn't told someone who perhaps could have stopped Cagle before twenty little girls had to die.

'You talked to my husband?' Lucy asked, struggling to regain her composure.

'I did,' Jess assured her. 'He's been worried sick, but he's on his way home.'

Lucy nodded, relief in her expression. 'Is it all right if I use the bathroom? I already wet my pants one time too many. He wouldn't release us for anything.' Her lips trembled. 'I can't believe he did this.'

'Sure.' Jess tried to give her a reassuring smile but her lips weren't cooperating. 'I'll just wait outside the door.'

Each second that passed had Jess's tension winding tighter and tighter. Where the hell would he go from here?

'Chief.'

She looked up to see Harper striding toward her.

'You're going to want to have a look at the root cellar. Chief Burnett's waiting for you on the porch out back.'

Lucy stepped out of the bathroom.

'Sergeant, escort Mrs Neely to Detective Wells and the children. Her husband will want to hear her voice as well.' To Lucy she promised, 'We'll talk more later.'

'Just go through the kitchen,' Harper told Jess. He smiled for Lucy. 'This way, Mrs Neely.'

Evidence techs were already starting their routine as Jess moved through the kitchen. On the porch a portion of the floor was hinged and opened like a trap door. It stood open now, and narrow steps led down into a musty-smelling cellar. Dan stood partway down the steps. He offered her his hand to assist her in following him.

327

The cellar was dank but at least there was a light. She held tight to Dan's hand as she descended into the small space.

He pointed to a doll in the corner. 'Is that Janey's?'

Jess pulled up the picture she'd snapped on her phone and then crouched down to inspect the doll more closely. Long dark hair, blue eyes. Red overall dress and pink tee. That was the doll. That icky feeling she'd been experiencing in the pit of her stomach lately started its ritual. Combine that with the worry pumping through her veins, and she felt queasy as hell. 'That's it.'

Dan swore.

'The upside is there's no blood.' She studied the hard-packed dirt floor and the few items in the obviously rarely used cellar, a storybook, a short stool – the kind used for milking cows. Shelves had been built along one dirt wall but they were empty. 'No signs of a struggle.'

'But he's not here.' Dan threaded his fingers through his hair. 'He's out there. God knows where. With that little girl.'

Jess wished she could take the doll with her just so she'd have it when she found Janey. Because she was going to find that little girl. But there were tests that needed to be conducted. Tests that would help link a serial killer who had proven his penchant for utter ruthlessness to a missing little girl.

As Jess reached the porch once more, her cell shimmied in her back pocket. She dragged it out and frowned at the name on the screen. George Louis.

Why in the world would her landlord be calling her?

Oh God, what if her place had burned down or blown up? She was just getting used to the eclectic little apartment.

'Harris.'

'Jess?'

Like many older people, Louis shouted as if he feared she wouldn't be able to hear him.

'Yes, Mr Louis, it's me.'

'I'm sorry to bother you on a Saturday afternoon. I'm sure you're out getting your shopping done or having a late lunch.'

'No bother, Mr Louis. Is something wrong?' *For God's sake, man, get to the point. I have a monster to track down.*

'There's a gentleman here to see you. I told him you weren't home, but he insisted on waiting. I thought I'd better call you.'

The first trickle of cold fear leaked into her veins. 'Where is the man right now, Mr Louis?'

'Why, he's in my living room. I couldn't leave him out in the heat. He has the sweetest little girl with him. She's having cookies and milk.'

The terror blasted her. 'Listen very carefully to me, Mr Louis.'

'Now, now, you need to stop calling me that. We agreed that you'd call me George.'

Jess grabbed Dan by the arm and pulled him close as she spoke. 'I'm sorry. George.' Her gaze locked with Dan's. She could hardly breathe. 'Listen carefully, George.' She prayed he wasn't going to freak out when she told him this part. 'The man in your living room is extremely dangerous.' He started to interrupt but she cut him off. 'Listen to me, George! *Please*. That little girl's life as well as yours depends on what you do next.'

Dan rushed toward the kitchen, ran into Harper in the doorway. They would know what to do. She had to ensure George Louis didn't screw this up.

'You tell the gentleman I'll be there in about forty minutes. Be sure to make him feel at home, George. Be absolutely certain not to do anything that will upset him. Just be a good host. Can you do that for me?'

'I understand. We'll be waiting. I'll make tea.'

9911 Conroy Road, 5.05 P.M.

Dan was fit to be tied.

But he'd just have to get over that. She couldn't wait another minute. She had told Louis forty minutes, and by God she wasn't falling down on that promise.

SWAT was almost in place.

Lori, Harper, Cook, Dan, and her two uniformed followers parked three houses down and had assumed positions around Mr Louis's house.

Jess was still wearing her vest. She had her weapon in her bag and a .32 strapped to her ankle.

She was as prepared as humanly possible.

She knocked on Louis's front door. Her hand shook as soon as she uncurled her finger and she had to remind herself to breathe but otherwise she was pretty steady. The com link was other-worldly silent.

Mr Louis opened the door looking completely unperturbed. She would need to make this up to him if they survived this little tea party.

'You're right on time, Jess. Come in.'

Inside, Fergus Cagle sat in a corner away from any windows. If he was armed, the weapon was concealed.

Janey sat on the floor in front of him. Jess's heart lurched. She was okay. Looked good. *Thank you, Jesus.* The child was playing with what appeared to be exquisite china cups and a teapot. Not toys. The real McCoys. *Thank you, Mr Louis.*

'I'm afraid I didn't have any toys,' Louis lamented. 'Join us. Would you like tea?'

'No, thank you, George.'

'I didn't realize,' he said, noticing the vest she wore, 'you were working today.'

331

'It's all right.' Jess smiled for him then walked over to sit in the chair closest to Cagle. 'Hello, Mr Cagle.'

He didn't look at her.

'Would it be all right if George takes Janey in the kitchen so you and I can talk privately?'

His head turned in her direction, his expression grim, his eyes empty. He looked nothing like the man she had interviewed the day before yesterday. That man was gone. This was the one who'd stolen little girls year after year . . . holding them prisoner in that basement of his. This was the face of evil.

'No.' Cagle glanced at Louis. 'You need to leave.'

Louis looked taken aback.

Jess nodded for him to go on.

He hesitated for a moment, but then he left the room. Cagle said nothing else until he heard the kitchen's back door slam.

'It took you long enough.'

'You didn't leave me anything to go on, Fergus. How was I supposed to find you?' Jess had psyched herself up for this meeting but inside she was trembling.

'This is *your* fault.'

'You keep saying that.' She shifted in her seat. He tensed visibly. Jess held her breath until he relaxed. 'To my knowledge we've never met before you sent me the first package.'

'I didn't have to meet you,' he growled.

Janey looked their way, fear cluttering her little face.

Her chest seizing, Jess wanted to tell her everything was all right, but she didn't dare break the connection with Cagle just now.

'I controlled the urges all those years.' He shook his head. 'Until you showed up. Then I was forced to go to the burying tree and exhume my treasures. I couldn't touch them and continue to resist.' He glowered at Jess. 'You have taken *everything* from me.'

'You can redeem yourself in your family's eyes, Fergus. Just let this little girl go and they'll know you're not that man anymore. Everyone makes mistakes.'

'You don't understand. I can't,' he snarled. He leaned toward her. 'I have to finish this.'

Jess fought the urge to recoil. 'You can let her go,' she urged. 'I'll make sure your daughter knows you did the right thing this time. You changed for her and your grandchildren.'

He laughed. 'You really don't understand. I'm doing *this* for my daughter and her children.'

Before she could attempt to reason with him further, he stood and moved toward Janey. Heart crashing against her sternum, Jess leaned forward, reaching for the .32.

Cagle turned back to her, a nine-millimeter aimed in her direction. 'We have to go outside.'

Shit. Her heart stumbled. This was not going to end well.

'Fergus,' she reasoned quietly, so as not to alarm Janey, 'you're an intelligent man. You must know what's outside.

Why don't we stay in here and work this out?'

Whether this monster lived or died was irrelevant to Jess, except that she needed the location of the other children. She couldn't let all hope of finding them die with him just because SWAT's sharpshooter opted to take out the lowlife scumbag child-killer with the first clear shot he got.

'We have to go outside where *he* can see.'

He? Was he working with someone else? Were there two Men in the Moon rather than one? She needed answers, not a gunfight in Louis's front yard.

'Tell me where the other children are, and then you and I will go outside. There's no reason for her to go with us. Let her stay inside.' Jess avoided using Janey's name so as not to scare her any worse than she already was.

For one long moment Jess was sure he would agree, then he barked, 'Janey, come to me!'

The child looked up at him, tears sliding down her cheeks.

Jess wanted to snatch her up and run – her whole body cried with the need – but he was the one who had the gun out and ready to fire.

Shaking in her little pink-and-white polka-dotted PJs, Janey walked over to Cagle. He picked her up with his free arm and then motioned to the door. 'Let's go.'

'Going outside is a mistake,' Jess repeated, mostly so those listening would be fully aware of their movements.

'Move,' Cagle demanded.

Jess walked to the door, took a breath and opened it. Bracing herself, she stepped out onto the broad, shady porch.

Please, God, protect this little girl. Don't let her die like this.

A loud *thwack* sounded behind her, and suddenly Cagle was on top of Jess.

They went down on the porch.

Janey screamed.

A dozen voices echoed in Jess's earpiece.

The child tumbled from Cagle's arms. The dead weight of the man on top of Jess seemed to indicate he was stunned or unconscious.

'Run, Janey!' Jess shouted. 'Run!'

The child stumbled but she regained her footing and took off like a shot.

A man in full SWAT garb tackled her in the yard and whisked her away.

Cagle moved.

Jess reached for his gun.

He snagged it first.

She tried to reach for the .32, but he pinned her to the porch.

'Don't move, Cagle,' she warned. 'They'll shoot and I'm not ready for you to die.'

'This,' he murmured, 'is for my daughter.'

He shoved the nine-millimeter in her face.

Images of Dan and her sister flashed across her mind as her breath stalled in her lungs.

The pop of an assault rifle sounded a split second before a bullet pierced the center of Cagle's forehead.

He slumped on top of her.

Her heart abruptly thundered back into action and Jess shoved him off. She snatched up the nine-millimeter and jumped to her feet.

She glanced back through the open doorway and Mr Louis stood there, not a hair ruffled, with an ornately carved cast iron andiron in his hand.

Jess swayed and Dan was suddenly next to her, steadying her. Members of her SPU team and SWAT swarmed the place.

Jess started to hand over the nine-millimeter to the nearest cop but something felt wrong. She checked the chamber and then the magazine.

There wasn't a single round in the weapon.

Jess stared at the dead man on the floor . . . he'd committed suicide by cop.

And she still didn't know where the other children were.

Chapter Twenty-Three

Parkridge Drive, Homewood, 9.30 P.M.

Chet unlocked the door and stepped back for Lori to go in first. She'd been a little distant all day, but then they'd been a whole lot busy.

'I can order pizza or something if you're hungry.'

She just shook her head and kept walking. He didn't know when she'd eaten last, but he hadn't since this morning and he was starving.

Down the hall he heard the bedroom door close. Her showers always took longer than his. He could call in a pizza, take his shower, and have a piping hot meal waiting for her when she emerged all soft and warm.

He couldn't wait to celebrate this victory with her. The Man in the Moon was in hell, and the little girl who would have been his next victim was safe and sound. Badly shaken but not a scratch on her.

Chet selected the pizza place down the street from his contact list and placed the order. He had thirty minutes. He shoved a couple of beers in the freezer to get them icy cold and headed for the other bathroom – the one in the hall he and Chester shared so Lori would have her own private sanctuary in the master bedroom's en suite.

The hot water felt amazing. All he could think about was sinking into Lori and celebrating life. They were so lucky. Jesus, he loved that woman.

He opened his eyes and thought about the appointment he had with the urologist next week. As long as he wasn't producing sperm antibodies the odds were really good that reversing the vasectomy would make things right. He would be good to go with only a little downtime.

He intended to make love to Lori as many times as possible before that happened.

Once he had the final verdict he would sit down and tell her everything. He didn't want to tell her until he knew one way or the other what they were facing.

Nearly a year ago, when he'd first laid eyes on her, he hadn't dreamed she would ever be his. Not for a second. He had hoped, but he'd been reasonably sure she was unreachable for a divorced father like him.

But now she was with him and he wanted to keep it that way. Whatever it took, he wanted to keep her happy.

He dried himself off and went to their room for a pair of boxers. The shower was still going in the en suite as he'd expected it would be. Boxers on, he went back to the living room to wait for the pizza. He picked a channel on TV that wasn't showing the breaking story about the Man in the Moon.

The doorbell rang and he grabbed his wallet. That would be the pizza. He paid the delivery guy and headed for the kitchen. The smell of hot, loaded pizza had his gut rumbling. When he heard Lori coming he removed the extra cold beers from the freezer and carried them to the table. Clad only in a towel, she paused at the door and stared at the pizza box.

He smiled. 'It's loaded, the way you like it.'

After a long moment that had him sweating bullets she took a seat and opened the box. She couldn't know what he had to talk to her about but somehow it felt exactly as if she did. She'd been a little distant all day.

'I don't know about you but I'm starving.' He had a long draw from his beer and made a satisfied sound.

She didn't say anything. She ate. She sipped her beer but she didn't even look at him.

The anxiety twisting inside him tightened. 'It's a shame the chief couldn't get that bastard to tell her where the other children were buried before he took that bullet to the brain.'

'I'd like to forget about work for the night.'

She still didn't look at him when she spoke.

Not good.

'Is something wrong?' Tomorrow was his birthday. He'd kind of hoped to start celebrating early. Looked like that wasn't going to happen.

She chugged the rest of her beer, wiped her mouth with the napkin and looked straight at him. 'You betrayed me, Chet.'

What the hell? 'What're you talking about?' Deep inside that one secret he'd kept from her twisted like barbed wire. 'I would never betray you. Never.'

'Really? You were going to just keep lying?'

How could she know? 'I've never lied to you.' And that was the truth.

'I saw Sherry this morning.'

Dread stabbed deep in his gut.

'I wanted her to know that I wasn't trying to take her place with Chester. After the way she acted the other night I wanted to try and clear the air.'

'Whatever trouble she's trying to start, she has no right to try to come between us.' If Sherry had told Lori about the vasectomy he wanted to be mad as hell but mostly he was mad at himself.

'You had no right to keep anything as important as this from me. A vasectomy is a major decision for any relationship. I'm not questioning your reason for doing it in the first place – I'm certain that was Sherry's idea.'

'She said the Pill made her fat. We were falling apart.' The pizza soured on his stomach. 'I was just trying to

340

make her happy. I didn't want our family to fall apart.'

Lori nodded. Her eyes glistened with emotion and he wanted to fall to his knees and beg her to forgive him. 'That's the only reason I'm not hating on you right now, Chet. I can see how she manipulated you. I know how much you love your son, and I'm certain it was an act of desperation. But that doesn't change the fact that you kept it from me.'

'I wish I could go back and do it right.' He shook his head. 'I have no excuse except that I was so afraid of losing you that I didn't want to risk your reaction. You said you weren't interested in having kids in the near future, so I thought I had time to make it right. I saw my doctor this week. I'm going for a test that will let us know if it's feasible to do the reversal. The doc's confident there won't be any problems, since it's only been three years. There's a test before the surgery that'll tell us what the chances of success are. It's outpatient surgery. A few days downtime and then I'll be as good as new.' He took a breath, thankful that he'd gotten it all out.

She shrugged. 'I've always thought I didn't really care about having children. I couldn't see putting my career on the back burner. I still can't. Not really. But whether we have children or not is a decision we need to be able to make together with no secrets.'

'You're right. Not squaring this with you was wrong, and if the doctor discovers I can't give you children, then I understand if you don't want to be with me anymore.'

She stood. 'I think the best thing to do is for me to . . .'

Chet held his breath.

'. . . punish you properly' – she unwrapped her towel and let it fall to the floor – 'just to make sure you never forget that I won't tolerate any secrets between us.'

He pushed back his chair, almost knocking it over in his haste. 'Punish me any way you want, baby.'

She gave him a firm look. 'Take off those boxers and follow me.'

He was pretty sure that was the fastest he'd ever snapped off a pair of boxers.

She took his hand and led him to the bed. Moving like a sleek panther, she crawled onto the bed and stretched out to ensure he had a good view of what a lucky man he was.

'Start with my toes,' she ordered.

Anticipation had his body trembling. She arched an eyebrow at his hesitation.

He knelt at the end of the bed and reached for one smooth foot. He licked the arch before sliding his tongue between and around those red-tipped toes of hers. She closed her eyes, and the soft sounds coming from her throat made him even harder. He gave the other toes the same treatment before moving to her ankles. Taking his time, he moved up those toned calves to her silky thighs. He traced a path up the inside of one thigh and she squirmed. He grinned.

By the time he'd burrowed his face between those lush thighs of hers she had fisted her fingers in the sheets and was crying out his name. He gave her her first climax with his tongue. And then he used his fingers to bring her to another before giving her what she kept screaming for . . . every inch of him.

By the time they collapsed together, he'd lost count of the times she'd come.

'I love you, Lori.'

She pulled his face to hers. 'I know you do, and I love you, Chet Harper.'

She kissed him and they started that sweet, hot dance again.

Chapter Twenty-Four

9911 Conroy Road, 10.00 P.M.

Jess sat in the middle of her living room floor and stared at the faces lining her wall. At least seventeen little girls were unaccounted for.

'The burying tree' – that was what Cagle had called the place he kept his treasures. There were thousands of trees between the ones on his property and the ones at Bullock's cabin. Not to mention that whole damned park around Bullock's cabin. How the hell were they supposed to know which one was Cagle's burying tree?

Budgets were already stretched too thin. No one was going to waste resources looking for remains when there was no comprehension whatsoever of where to start. With Cagle dead there was very little chance they would ever find those children.

That made Jess sad.

We have to go outside where he can see.

Who was *he*? Why had Cagle needed anyone to see? There was no indication whatsoever that he had worked with an accomplice. To the contrary, he had a reputation as a loner. Even people he had worked with for decades didn't know his daughter's name or where she lived.

Jess had put together many of the pieces of the puzzle. Cagle's wife had left him when their daughter was just a child – the daughter she had given him on a harvest moon. What had he done that prompted his wife to fear him? They would probably never know. Whatever she had seen was the beginning. The evil had been there, waiting patiently until something triggered the first act.

Once he'd crossed that line, the urges he obviously attempted to resist became too great to conquer. The torture belt he wore cinched around his waist was loaded with nails that had dug deep into his skin. The marks of vigorous self-punishment were all over his body – any place that would be covered by clothing bore the telltale signs of his struggle. Scars of varying sizes and ages told the tale of how long he had fought his heinous desires. Until his daughter showed up in his life again. She and her children had given him the strength to fight those cravings.

'Why start digging up bones then?' It just didn't make sense.

Thirteen years. His family was happy. He was only a couple years from retirement. He had nothing to gain and everything to lose.

And why use Jess as an excuse to launch back into that abyss of darkness? Or insist that someone had to see? That part nagged at her.

Her cell did its thing and she checked the screen. *Sylvia Baron*.

If Jess were smart she would just let it go to voice mail. Sometimes she wasn't so smart. 'Sylvia, what's up?' It was pretty late for a social call, but with Sylvia she never knew.

'Congratulations, Harris. You pulled it off again. Got the bad guy and made the news as Birmingham's most beloved hero.'

'Thanks.' She didn't feel like a hero. She hadn't found all those little girls.

'Listen, I hope it's okay, but I invited Gina to your party tomorrow.'

'I'm not having a party.' The woman had obviously had too much wine. Something Jess wished she were doing. *Whine, whine*.

'Your detective's birthday party,' she explained with her usual indignant impatience. 'That won't be a problem, will it? She's still a bit down, and I wanted to make sure she felt included.'

'I'm not hosting the party, but I'm sure that's fine.'

She'd have to try and remember to text Lori in the morning.

'Great. I'll see you then. Why don't you wear that red suit of yours? It's very flattering. Very slimming.'

Jess hugged her belly with her free arm. Did she look fat? Already? Maybe she was bloated since her period was late. How nice of Sylvia to point that out.

'See you tomorrow,' Jess said in hopes of ending the call.

'Really, Harris,' Sylvia said before Jess could hang up, 'you did well.'

Jess wasn't sure how to take what sounded like a real compliment. 'Thanks.'

Sylvia said good night and ended the call.

Jess had no idea if the woman could really be counted as a friend, but she was leaning in that direction. Tomorrow she'd probably say or do something to have her leaning in the other direction.

The alarm sounded, warning her that she had company coming up the stairs.

She got up and checked the monitor. *Dan*. He had promised to come straight here as soon as his chief-of-police duties were done. She had been far too exhausted to hang around for the press conference.

She unlocked and opened the door. He smiled, and she felt better already.

She angled her head and tried to see where he had his hands. 'What've you got behind your back there?'

He grinned and held out both hands. Flowers and chocolates!

'The flowers are gorgeous.' She went for the box of chocolates. 'There's a vase under the sink.'

While he filled the vase with water and then arranged the summer mix of blooms, she climbed onto her bed and opened the chocolates. She checked the diagram on the inside of the cover to locate the ones with caramel centers, her favorites.

Dan placed the flowers on the table and she smiled. 'They're really gorgeous, Dan.' She popped another candy in her mouth, closed her eyes, and flat out moaned.

He sat down on the sofa and patted the spot next to him. 'Come sit with me.'

Was he kidding? She patted the bed. 'Come sit with *me.*'

He got up and started her way. She gathered the box of candy, put the lid on top, and set it on her bedside table. After a couple swipes of her tongue the caramel was no longer stuck to her front teeth.

The mattress moved as he climbed on and plopped next to her.

'Did you come to talk about something, or is this our usual Saturday night visit?' Her body was already heating up in anticipation of the latter.

'Wow, that was romantic.'

She laid down on her side facing him. 'Is it not okay to be unromantic sometimes? I mean, we've known each other forever. Do we have to make everything a production?'

She wanted him. She wanted to have sex with him. As in *now*.

'You should take the pictures off your wall.'

She glanced at the makeshift case board she used for homework. 'I don't want to forget them. If I leave them right there, I can't. No matter how many cases I investigate, I won't forget those faces.'

'How about you make a separate case board at work for the ones you need to get back to when you can?'

That wasn't a bad idea. 'That could work.'

'I mentioned your landlord the hero in my press release.'

'I saw that.' Jess had thanked Mr Louis at some point between washing Cagle's blood off her face and his body being carted off by the coroner's office. 'But what he did was very dangerous, and I can't help wondering if we could have taken Cagle alive if dear old George hadn't made that bold move.'

'We had no way of knowing the gun wasn't loaded, Jess. Hindsight is twenty-twenty. You can't second-guess yourself or the SWAT commander's decision. Every move today was the right one.'

She sighed. 'Maybe.'

349

Except she didn't have her period. That was wrong in so many, many ways.

'I think, when the forensics business is done –' Jess bit her lip, summoned her courage to say it '– that we should allow the parents to see Cagle's basement if they want to.'

'I thought about that, too. Their children were there for who knows how long. Maybe it will help with closure, since we can't tell them where this burying tree is.'

'I hate that part.'

He tugged at a strand of her hair, wrapped it in his fingers. 'I know. I do, too.'

She reached up and caressed his jaw. 'Make love to me, Dan.' She needed to feel alive . . . to feel him inside her.

'First you need to check out your *other* present.' Those blue eyes of his twinkled.

'What other present?'

'Look in the chocolate box.'

She grabbed the box, anticipation making her grin. 'You didn't need to get me presents.' She moved aside the top tray of candies, and beneath it, where more rows of chocolates should have been, was a slim velvet box. 'Dan!'

'I got it at that charity auction my mother held a couple weeks ago. It made me think of you.'

She resisted the urge to roll her eyes at the mention of his *mother*. She opened the box and her breath trapped in her chest. 'Oh . . . it's beautiful.' It was a heart-shaped locket on a gold chain. Not a new one. Old, very old. A tiny diamond sat in the center of the locket. On the back the words *you are my heart* were engraved. She batted her eyelids frantically but the damned tears slid down her cheeks anyway. She slugged him on the shoulder. 'Thank you.'

He brushed at her cheeks with his fingertips. 'You had a locket like this when we first met.'

She nodded. 'It wasn't so fancy. Plain old gold colored, no diamond. Lil gave it to me. I don't know what happened to it.'

'And it didn't have this.' He took the locket from her and opened it.

Inside the locket was one of those silly pictures of them done in the old mall photo booths. The air fled her lungs and for a moment she couldn't speak. 'You kept that old picture all these years?' God, they were so young.

'Of course.'

'Help me put it on.'

The mattress shifted as he got onto his knees. He fastened the delicate chain and she pressed the cool metal of the locket against her skin. 'I love it. This is the best present anyone ever gave me.'

He shoved the box of chocolates aside and pushed her down onto the bed. 'You're the only present I've ever wanted.'

She smiled, swearing silently at herself for crying some more. 'I love you, Dan.'

The look of joy in his eyes had her trembling like a virgin. Tenderly, he opened her robe and kissed his way down her body. She responded instantly. When he lingered near her belly button a new rush of tears stung her eyes.

He dragged the robe off her and then she slowly helped him undress. Once they were both naked, she kissed him all over, paying special attention to the scar left by Eric Spears's knife.

When their bodies were entwined fully she stopped thinking and let the wondrous sensations fill her up, making her whole again.

Chapter Twenty-Five

Sunday, August 22, 08.00 A.M.

The alarm sounded and Jess sat up in bed. She stared at the clock. Eight o'clock, but it wasn't the alarm clock that had awakened her.

Someone was coming to her door.

God, she hoped it wasn't Mr Louis with breakfast.

She snatched up her robe and cinched the belt tight. She stared at the monitor and she had to close her eyes and look again.

Wanda Newsom.

What the hell would her aunt be doing here? Dan had picked up those damned useless notes on the family's medical history. Notes that told Jess and Lil absolutely nothing.

'Who's out there?' Dan, braced on his elbows without

a stitch of cover over him and looking far too good, yawned. 'Do I need to get dressed?'

'It's Wanda.'

'Your aunt?'

The knock she'd expected came, echoing through the room.

'Just stay put,' Jess ordered.

'Yes, ma'am.'

She released the locks and slipped out the door, closing it behind her.

Wanda looked a bit startled, or maybe she just hadn't expected to have to back up suddenly.

Jess wasn't going to waste time exchanging social pleasantries with the woman. She didn't deserve the necessary energy. 'Is something wrong?'

Wanda held her purse close to her chest, as if she feared Jess might try to snatch it from her. She was dressed up, for Wanda anyway. Conservative was the theme. Evidently she was on her way to church. Hoorah for her. Too bad she hadn't thought about that back when she had two little girls to raise instead of only worrying about where her next score of drugs would come from.

'Your sister called and told me she was going to be all right. She said there was a test I needed to get.'

Jess was going to give Lil what for. They were not obliged to tell this woman anything. Jess gave herself a mental kick in the butt. That wasn't fair. No matter that

Wanda had let them down when they needed her most, she had a right to know about any possible health issues. 'Lil's going to be fine. Yes.'

'I hate to bother you so early but I was afraid I might not catch you if I didn't come this morning.' She smiled – it looked forced. 'I see you on the news. I know you're very busy.'

Jess folded her arms over her chest. 'Well, you got me. So what's up?'

Wanda looked away for a moment and Jess rolled her eyes. She had no patience for this woman's theatrics. None whatsoever. She should f'ing get on with it.

'I lied to you, Jessie Lee.'

Well, duh! 'If you're hoping for forgiveness, Wanda, I'm the wrong person to talk to. Try your priest.' What was with all these people from her past suddenly confessing? First Corlew and now Wanda.

Pain etched its way across the older woman's face.

Harsh, maybe, but that was how Jess felt.

'I don't blame you for hating me. I know what I did.'

Jess met her gaze then. 'I don't hate you, Wanda. I just don't like you very much.' *Keep your cool, Jess.* 'What is it you came here for?'

'Your mother and I were close at one time. As close as you and Lil.'

Jess didn't see how that was possible, but whatever.

'I fell apart after my Johnny was killed in the war. I did

a lot of things I shouldn't have. Helen tried to help me but I pushed her away. So she stopped coming around. Mostly to protect you girls. You were more important to her than anything else in the world.'

Jess didn't want to listen but somehow she couldn't stop. The train had crashed and she couldn't look away from the devastation.

'When you were about seven – Lil was nine, I think – your mother came to see me. It had been a year or so since we'd seen each other.'

Jess said nothing, just let her talk.

'Lil was in school but you'd been to the doctor for shots that day.' Her gaze was distant, as if she were looking back. 'You were running around the house getting into everything.' A faint smile lifted the corners of her mouth. 'It took awhile with keeping you from climbing the curtains, but your mother finally admitted the fears that had been tormenting her.'

If this was some attempt on Wanda's part to draw Jess back into her life, she could forget it. Jess held her tongue. Whatever her aunt's motives, anything she could learn about their parents she wanted to know.

'I didn't really ever intend to tell this to you girls. There wasn't any point I could see. After they died . . . who was it going to benefit? Just something to add to the bad memories of loss.'

'What is it my mother confessed to you?' She needed

to get to the point. Jess was hungry and she needed to pee.

'Your mother would be very proud of both of you. But these past couple of weeks, all these terrible cases you've been working on have got me to thinking that maybe you need to know what your mother told me. It's been weighing on my heart, and I can't hold it in any longer. I believe the Lord wants me to tell you now.'

Jess signaled for her to get on with it.

'Your mother was worried about your father. She said he was involved with people . . . bad people. She couldn't or wouldn't tell me anything specific, but she made me promise that if anything ever happened to her or you kids that I would go to the police and tell them that her husband had connections to bad people and that at times she feared for her life as well as those of her children.'

'Are you talking criminal connections?' This made no sense.

'I don't know. That's all she told me. And that was the last time I saw her. If I tried to call after that she wouldn't talk to me. If I went over there she wouldn't come to the door. Finally, I refused to leave, and she told me through the door that it wasn't safe for me to be there and that my being there put her in danger. He didn't want her to talk to me or see me. That's what she said.'

'That makes no sense.' Outrage filled Jess. 'I remember my father and my mother. I don't recall anything even remotely resembling what you're telling me in any of the memories I have of them.' How dare this woman try to ruin what few memories she had of her parents!

'I knew you wouldn't believe me.' Wanda's chin hitched up a notch. 'But I did what your mother said. When they were killed in that accident I went to the police. Nothing ever came of it. That's the way it is when you live on the wrong side of town. No one cares. But I gave my statement and I signed it. It must be on file there somewhere.'

If there was any investigation into her parents' deaths the file would be God only knew where. 'I don't know what to say to all this except my father was a salesman. He traveled a lot, but when he was home he laughed and played with Lil and me.'

'Whatever you remember, your mother was terrified of the evil your father was involved with. And for some reason evil seems to gravitate toward you. If you don't care what happened to your parents or how it relates to your life, think of your sister. What touches you touches her.'

Jess's jaw dropped. What the hell?

That was apparently all Wanda had to say since she hurried down the stairs and rushed to her car and drove away.

Jess's first thought was to toss out the whole conversation as the ramblings of a demented old woman who'd damaged her brain with alcohol and drugs.

But, if there was one speck of truth to what she said, Jess needed to know.

Had the woman just tried to tell Jess that she was a magnet for evil?

If so, she was behind the curve. Jess already knew that. Didn't matter anyway. At least she hadn't likened Jess to a coonhound the way Dan's mother had.

Jess went back inside and locked the doors. Dan had brewed two cups of coffee. He passed a cup to her. It smelled amazing, but the best part was that he served her in the buff. 'What would you like for breakfast? I can run out and get something,' he offered.

It just wasn't fair that he looked that good after all these years.

Oh well, she might as well take advantage of her good fortune.

'Then you'd have to put your clothes on,' she reminded him.

'You don't want me to put my clothes on?'

'Maybe in a couple of hours.'

Pablo's Restaurante and Cantina,
John Hawkins Parkway, 2.30 P.M.

By the time a final toast was offered in honor of Chet Harper, Jess was stuffed and ready to go home for a siesta.

Lori had done an amazing job pulling off this surprise birthday party.

Jess wrapped her arm around Dan's as they joined the others in the Old World-style courtyard. Didn't matter that the party was full of cops; she had decided that life was too short to play that game anymore. She and Dan were in a relationship. The world might as well get used to it.

Sylvia Baron, margarita in hand, strolled up to them. She looked amazing as always in a formfitting jade dress that hit just the right number of inches above the knee.

'I suppose you two celebrated last night?'

'I was too exhausted,' Jess tossed back. The woman was seriously nosy. 'I crashed early.' No need for her to know she'd crashed into Dan's naked body.

Reality swooped in on the heels of that thought. After they left here she had to somehow find a way to get her hands on a pregnancy test. Tomorrow she would be a week late. She had no more excuses for putting off the test.

'They've set the date for moving Nina,' Sylvia was telling Dan. 'The middle of September. I was hoping for sooner but that didn't work out.'

'Keep me posted on her progress,' Dan said. 'I'm hoping for the best.'

They were all hoping the new clinic in New York would be able to help Sylvia's sister.

While Dan and Sylvia discussed the Baron family annual Labor Day barbecue, Jess mingled some more. She spotted Gina Coleman chatting with a couple of cops Jess didn't know, both female. She waved to Jess and then made a path for her.

'Sorry that Atkins Electric lead didn't pan out.'

'Hey.' Jess held up both hands. 'You did the right thing. I was grateful for any and all leads on that case.'

Gina nodded. 'You did a great job, Jess. The public loves you. You should let me do a feature on you soon.'

Jess mustered up a smile. 'We'll see.'

Another guest dragged Gina away but Jess was thankful for the reprieve. Too bad she didn't think to suggest Lori invite Clint Hayes. With the crazy week they'd had, Jess hadn't gotten to interview him. Lori had scheduled an interview for tomorrow. Jess looked forward to meeting him. She had to fill the vacancy on her team soon. The last few days were proof positive.

Her stomach burned and she pressed her hand there. Maybe she shouldn't have indulged in that second helping of refried beans. She dug in her bag for the pack of Tums she carried. It was like digging in a box of rocks for just the right pebble. One day she had to get this thing organized. One of these days she had to stop thinking she had to get organized and actually do it.

'Gotcha.' She nabbed the roll and peeled off a couple of antacids and popped them into her mouth. That should put out the fire in her belly. As she dropped the roll back into the bottomless pit that was her bag, she checked her cell out of habit.

She had a text . . . from *Spears*.

Terrified that he was sending her a photo of one of the women, she opened the text. A link. What? Too curious or too stupid to ignore what was probably a virus-laden ploy to get at her yet another way, she clicked the link.

A map appeared and a red dot lit up. The direction boxes read from current location to . . . 'Oh my God.'

The Burying Tree.

Her bag hit the cobblestone.

Dan's attention swung to her and he rushed to her side.

'We have to go,' she told him.

Oak Mountain State Park, 6.45 P.M.

Jess hugged her arms around herself, feeling chilled despite the heat. She had no idea how Spears could have known about this place, unless his dark-haired spy had been watching Cagle as well as Jess.

Even if that were the case, how had either of them known Cagle was the Man in the Moon? Was it possible that Cagle was one of Spears's followers? But what would have been the purpose?

The sun tried valiantly to filter through the trees but

hardly any light made it to the ground beneath the *burying tree*. Spotlights and equipment were scattered around the area cordoned off with crime scene tape. The digging was slow. Great care had to be taken to protect any remains discovered.

'I have something!' Harper shouted from the far side of the massive Live Oak.

What a thing for a guy to do on his birthday, but he had insisted on coming.

He set the shovel aside and got down on his knees to dig by hand. He unearthed a plastic wrapped bundle and Jess's knees went weak.

Dan's arm went around her and steadied her.

'Olivia Chapman,' Harper said, his voice quavering as he read the name from the article in the plastic photo sleeve. Cagle had marked each of his treasures in the same way.

And that was only the first. Night had enveloped them long before the task was anywhere near done. The spotlights gleamed through the darkness, aiding the search. Each precious bundle unearthed was carefully labeled, and the names of little girls echoed in the night until all were found.

Tears slid down Jess's cheeks. She didn't know what was wrong with her; she just couldn't help it.

But they were tears of joy . . . these little girls were going home.

Chapter Twenty-Six

Monday, August 23, 6.00 A.M.

Jess groaned as she scooted out from under Dan's arm.

It was Monday morning and there was something she had to do before Dan woke up.

Pulling on her robe, she grabbed the Walmart bag from the sofa and tiptoed to the bathroom.

When she and Dan left the burying tree last night, around midnight after all seventeen sets of remains had been accounted for, Jess had insisted they stop at a Walmart for deodorant.

The man had followed her in the store and she'd had to send him in search of snacks to get a minute of privacy. Hadn't been too difficult once she'd headed down the feminine products aisle. Dan had been only too happy to go the other way. She had grabbed a pregnancy test and then a box of Tampons and some pads for cover. The nice little officer who followed her around, even when she was with Dan, had turned his head.

The bathroom door clicked shut and she locked it. She hoped he didn't wake up before she was done with this.

With the package in hand she sat down on the toilet to read the instructions. 'Shit.' She needed her glasses.

Praying the door wouldn't squeak too loud this time she hurried over to the bedside table and got her glasses. While she was at it she snagged her phone.

In the bathroom, she read the instructions. Seemed easy enough. All she had to do was pee on the stick and wait three minutes.

To avoid the possibility of him hearing her tearing the package open she turned on the water in the sink.

She stared at the pink and white stick and wondered how something this innocuous looking could hold so much power.

She sniffed. However powerful it was, the stick's whole purpose in life was to get peed on. Ha!

She hefted her robe up out of the way and assumed the position.

'Here goes.'

She peed as instructed and then set the stick aside for the prescribed number of minutes.

Three minutes wasn't that long. She set the timer on her phone.

Then she waited.

Her foot started to tap and she forced it to still.

The idea of what all those families were going through tortured her for a moment. Then her mind moved on to Wanda's visit.

Was she hoping to be accepted back into the fold?

'No way.'

Still, the idea needled at Jess.

There was one way to put that worry to rest. She tapped Corlew's name in her contact list. To make sure Dan didn't hear she turned off the sink and turned on the shower. She dragged the curtain around the claw-foot tub so water didn't go everywhere.

As soon as Corlew grumbled a what-the-hell, she whispered, 'I want to hire you to look into an old case.'

'Jess? Why're you whispering?' He coughed. 'Where are you? Sounds like you're in a car wash.'

'I want you to look into my mother's and father's deaths,' she whispered a little louder. 'Find out exactly what happened.' She moistened her lips. 'And I want to know who my father was. Who he really was.'

'Is something going on, Jessie Lee?' he asked.

She tensed. 'I'm just curious, that's all. You want me to trust you again? For us to be friends?' she reminded him. 'Then you do this for me. Prove you mean what you say.' If he really wanted to make things right, he could do this for her. He was a PI, after all.

'All right. All right. Call me this afternoon and we'll

talk about it. I just went to bed a couple hours ago.'

' 'Kay. Talk to you later.'

'Hey,' he caught her before she ended the call. 'You did good, kid. You might just single-handedly turn the BPD around.'

She was not going there. 'Thanks.'

She ended the call and took a big breath. 'Get it over with.'

She walked to the sink and stared at the stick lying there.

Two vivid pink lines stared back at her.

'Oh . . . my . . . God.'

Her phone slipped from her fingers and bounced on the floor. She reached for the door facing to steady herself. *Positive.*

Dear God, she was pregnant.

The deep rumble of Dan's voice snapped her to attention. She pressed her ear to the door and listened. He was either on the phone or someone was here.

She quickly gathered the packaging, shoved the stick inside, and looked for a place to hide it. For now, she jammed the whole kit and caboodle in the plastic Walmart bag, tied it tight, and then tucked it inside the toilet tank. She grimaced when porcelain rubbed against porcelain as she settled the heavy lid back into place. Then she grabbed her phone, grateful that it had survived.

'Okay.' She stared at her reflection in the mirror over

the sink. 'You can deal with this. Sit down and talk it through.' Dan would probably be ecstatic at the news.

Doubt plagued her. She hoped he would, at any rate.

Jess stripped off her robe and climbed into the tub. Thankfully the water spraying from the shower was still warm. Feeling numb, she went through the necessary motions as quickly as possible. She dried herself, donned the robe, and emerged with her damp hair stacked haphazardly atop her head. She didn't care.

Dan had dressed and was waiting for her.

She frowned. 'You don't want to shower?'

'There's no time.'

Her shoulders slumped. Oh, no. 'What's happened now?'

He closed in on her, took her face in his hands. The anguish in his eyes stabbed right through her heart. 'He chose his victim, Jess. Two of the women were found on the side of the road near a wilderness retreat outside Gatlinburg, Tennessee.'

She wanted to scream. She wanted to throw something. Mainly she just wanted to throw up. 'Are they dead?' The tears burst from her. She couldn't help it.

'No, no, they're okay. They confirmed that the third woman was being held with them but he didn't release her.'

Jess closed her eyes against the images of what she knew he would do to this woman.

'You need to get dressed. We have a conference call with Gant in half an hour.'

Every swear word in her vocabulary bounced around in her head. Jess snapped a bra into place and pulled on underwear. She reached for something to wear without even looking.

Her arm fell back to her side. How could she do this?

How could she make her world safe enough for a baby?

She looked across the room to the man who was on his phone rescheduling meetings and doing what he had to do to protect this city . . . their home. The father of the child she was carrying.

Her hand flattened on her belly.

If Spears learned this news . . . he would use this child to get to her . . . to get to Dan.

No one could know.

Not until Spears was dead.

She thought she'd left the murders – and his obsession – behind . . .

If you can't get enough of

DEBRA WEBB

go to **www.headline.co.uk** to
discover more in her terrifying
FACES OF EVIL series

Read on now for an extract from
OBSESSION, and follow Agent
Jess Harris back to where it all began…

Chapter One

Birmingham, Alabama
Wednesday, July 14, 1.03 P.M.

Special Agent Jess Harris's career was in the toilet along with the breakfast she'd wolfed down and then lost in a truck stop bathroom the other side of Nashville.

God, this wasn't supposed to happen.

Jess couldn't breathe. She told herself to either get out of the car or power down a window, but her body refused to obey a single, simple command.

The scorching ninety-five degrees baking the city's asphalt and concrete had invaded the interior of the car about two seconds after she parked and shut off the engine. That appeared to be of little consequence to whatever reason she still possessed, considering that ten minutes later her fingers were still locked around the steering wheel as if the final hours of her two-day drive had triggered the onset of rigor mortis.

She was *home*. Two weeks' worth of long overdue leave was at her disposal. Her mail was on hold at the post office back in Stafford, Virginia, where absolutely no one would miss her. Still, she hesitated in taking the next step. Changing her mind and driving away was out of the question no matter how desperately she wanted to do exactly that.

Her word was all she had left at this point. The sheer enormity of her current circumstances should have her laughing hysterically but the muscles of her throat had constricted in equal parts disbelief and terror.

Screw this up and there's nothing left.

With a deep breath for courage, she relaxed her death grip, grabbed her bag, and climbed out. A horn honked a warning and she flattened against the dusty fender of her decade-old Audi. Cars and trucks whizzed by, determined to make the Eighteenth Street and First Avenue intersection before the traffic light changed. Exhaust fumes lingered in the humid air, mingling with the heat and the noise of downtown.

She barely recognized the heart of Birmingham. Renovated shops from a bygone era and newer, gleaming buildings stood side by side, their facades softened by carefully placed trees and shrubbery. An elegant park complete with a spectacular fountain welcomed strolling shoppers and relaxing picnickers. Great strides had been taken to transform the gritty streets of the city once recognized as the infamous center of the civil rights movement to a genteel version of a proud Southern town.

What the hell was she doing here?

For twenty-two years she had worked harder than a prized pupil of Henry Higgins himself to alter her speech patterns and to swipe the last damned trace of the South from her voice. A master's degree in psychology from Boston College and seventeen years of relentless dedication to build an admirable career distinguished her résumé.

And for what? To come running back with her tail tucked between her legs and her head hanging low enough to the ground to smell the ugly truth.

Nothing had changed.

All the spritzing fountains and meticulously manicured storefronts couldn't hide the fact that this was still Birmingham the place she'd put in her rearview mirror at eighteen – and the four-hundred-dollar red suit and matching high heels she wore would not conceal her plunge from grace.

He had called and she had promised to come and have a look at his case. It was the first time he'd asked her for anything since they parted ways after college. That he extended any sort of invitation astonished her and provided a much needed self-esteem boost. No one from her hometown had a clue about her current career debacle or the disaster zone that was her personal life. If she had her way, they would never know. The million-dollar question, however, remained: What did she do after this?

The wind from a passing car flapped her skirt around her legs, reminding her that this curbside parking slot was not exactly the place to conduct a cerebral overview of *This Is Your Life*.

Game face in place, her shoulders squared with determination, she strode to the Birmingham Police Department's main entrance. Another bout of hesitation slowed her but she kicked it aside, opened the door, and presented a smile for the security guard. 'Good morning.'

'Good morning to you, too, ma'am,' said the guard, Elroy Carter according to the name tag pinned to his shirt. 'I'll need your ID. You can place your bag here.' He indicated the table next to him.

Jess handed over her official credentials and placed her bag as directed for inspection. Since she'd stopped bothering with earrings years ago and the gold band she still wore for reasons that continued to escape her didn't set off any alarms except in her head, she walked through the metal detector and waited on the other side for her bag.

'Enjoy your visit to the Magic City, Agent Harris.' Another broad smile brightened the big man's face.

Probably retired Birmingham PD, undeniably Southern through and through. He obviously took pride in his work, past and present, and likely carried a wallet full of photos of his grandchildren. The only trait that wouldn't be readily discernible by way of a passing inspection was whether he was an Auburn or an Alabama fan. By September that, too, would be as clear as the rich color of his brown eyes. In Alabama, college football season turned even the closest of friends into fierce rivals.

'Thank you, Mr Carter.'

Extending a please, welcome, and thank you remained a stalwart Southern tradition. On the etiquette scale, the idea of passing a stranger without at least smiling ranked right below blasphemy. Keeping up with your neighbor's or coworker's business wasn't viewed as meddling. Not at all. It was the right thing to do. Concern was, of course, the motive.

Jess would give it twenty-four hours max before speculation about her business became the subject of water-cooler talk. Then the sympathetic glances would begin. Along with the reassuring smiles and the total pretense that everything was fine.

Fine. Fine. Fine.

As much as she wanted to avoid her dirty laundry being aired, the odds of complete circumvention fell along the lines of being hit by falling satellite debris twice in the same day. Once the news hit the AP there would be no stopping or even slowing the media frenzy.

Her life was a mess. She doubted any aspect of her

existence would ever be *fine* again. But that was irrelevant at the moment. She was here to advise on a case – one that wouldn't wait for her to gather up the pieces of her life or for her to lick her wounds.

Jess set those worries aside, steeled herself, and headed for the bank of elevators that would take her to the fourth floor. *To him.*

None of the faces she encountered looked familiar. Not the guard who'd processed her in or either of his colleagues monitoring the lobby and not the woman who joined her in the elevator car to make the trip to Birmingham Police Department's administrative offices.

Once the doors glided closed, the woman attempted a covert inspection, taking note of Jess's Mary Jane pumps with their four-inch heels, the swath of skin separating the hem of her pencil skirt from the tops of her knees and the leather bag that had been her gift to herself on her fortieth birthday. When eye contact inevitably happened, a faint smile flashed, a superficial pleasantry intended to disguise the sizing-up of competition. *If she only knew.*

The car bumped to a stop. The other woman exited first and strolled down the long corridor on the right. Jess's destination waited straight ahead. The office of the chief of police. At the door she conducted a final inventory of her appearance in the glass, straightened her belted jacket, and plucked a blond hair from her lapel. She looked . . . the same. Didn't she? Her hand fell to her side.

Did she look like a failure? Like the woman who had just provided a heinous killer with a get-out-of-jail-free card and who'd lost her husband to geography?

Deep breath. She reached for the door sporting the name Daniel T. Burnett and passed the point of no return.

'Good afternoon, Agent Harris.' The young woman, Tara Morgan according to the nameplate on her desk, smiled. 'Welcome to Birmingham.'

Since Jess hadn't introduced herself, she assumed that the chief had ensured his office personnel, certainly his receptionist, would recognize his anticipated visitor. 'Thank you. I'm here to see Chief Burnett.'

'Yes, ma'am. If you'd like to have a seat, I'll let the chief know you've arrived.'

At last, Tara politely left off. Jess was late by twelve minutes, most of which had been spent fortifying her resolve and gathering her composure to face the final buffeting winds of the emotional hurricane that had descended upon her life. The receptionist offered water or a soft drink. Jess declined. Getting anything, even water, past the massive lump lodged firmly in her throat was unlikely. Keeping it down, an unmitigated no-go.

Jess used the intervening time to evaluate the changes Birmingham's newest chief had made since taking over the office of top cop. From the marble-floored entry to the classic beige carpet and walls, the tranquil lobby looked less like the anteroom to the chief of police and more like

379

the waiting area of a prestigious surgeon's office. Though she hadn't been in this office since career day back in high school, the decorating and furnishings were far too fresh to have seen more than a couple of years' wear.

Law enforcement and political journals rested in a crisp stack atop the table flanked by two plush, upholstered chairs. The fabric resembled a European tapestry and carried the distinct flavor of his mother's taste. It wasn't enough she'd influenced the decorating scheme of the palatial homes belonging to select members of Birmingham's elite simply by hosting a grand soiree and inviting the city's who's who list. Katherine Burnett set the gold standard for keeping up with the Joneses.

Jess wondered if the fine citizens of Birmingham approved of such wasteful use of their tax dollars. Knowing Katherine, she had paid for the renovation herself and spelled it all out on the front page of the Lifestyle section of the *Birmingham News*.

Just another example of how nothing changed around here. Ever. Jess deposited her bag on a chair and stretched her travel-cramped muscles. Eight grueling hours on the road on Tuesday and four this morning had taken its toll. She was exhausted. A flight would have provided far more efficient transportation, but she preferred to have her car while she was here. Made the potential for escape much more feasible.

Actually she'd needed time to think.

'You made it.'

Whether it was the sound of his voice or the idea that he looked better now, in spite of current circumstances, than he had on Christmas Eve ten years ago, she suddenly felt very fragile and unquestionably old. His dark hair was still thick without even a hint of gray. The elegant navy suit he wore brought out the blue in his eyes. But it was his face, leaner than before but no less handsome, that conveyed the most damage to her brittle psyche.

The weight of the past seventy-two hours crashed down on her in one big knee-weakening wallop. The floor shifted beneath her feet and the urge to run into his strong arms or to simply burst into tears made a fleeting but powerful appearance.

But she wasn't that kid anymore. And they . . . they were little more than strangers.

She managed a stiff nod. 'I did.'

Funny how they both avoided calling each other by name. Not funny at all was the idea that five seconds in his presence had the two little words she'd uttered sounding as Southern as the day she'd hit the road after high school graduation.

She cleared her throat. 'And I'm ready to get to work. First, I'd like some time to review the files.'

'Of course.' He offered his hand, then drew it back and gestured awkwardly, as if belatedly realizing that touching was not a good idea. 'Shall we go to my office?'

'Absolutely.' She draped her bag over her shoulder and moved toward him, each step a supreme test of her self-control. Things that hadn't been said and should have battled with the numerous other troubles clashing in her head for priority. *This wasn't the time.*

'Coming all this way to help us figure this out means a great deal to me.'

Still skirting her name. Jess pushed aside the confusion or frustration, maybe both, and the weariness and matched his stride as he led the way. 'I can't make any promises but I'll do what I can.'

He hadn't given her many details over the phone; that he had called at all was proof enough of the gravity of the situation.

He introduced her to his personal secretary, then ushered her into his office and closed the door. Like the lobby, his spacious office smacked of Katherine's touch. Jess placed her bag on the floor next to a chair at the small conference table and surveyed the four case files waiting in grim formation for her inspection. Clipped to the front of each jacket was a photo of a missing girl.

This was why she had come all this way. However much his call gratified her ego, piecing together this puzzle was her ultimate goal. She leaned forward to study the attractive faces. Four young women in the space of two and a half weeks had disappeared, the latest just three days ago. No common threads other than age, no suggestion of foul play, not a hint of evidence left behind. Macy York, Callie Fanning, Reanne Parsons, and Andrea Denton had simply vanished.

'These two are Jefferson County residents.' He tapped the first and second photos; Macy and Callie were both blondes. 'This one's Tuscaloosa.' Reanne, a redhead. 'The latest is from Mountain Brook, my jurisdiction.' The fourth girl, Andrea, was a brunette and his attention idled there an extra moment or two.

Jess lowered herself into a chair. She opened the files, one by one, and reviewed the meager contents. Interviews with family and friends. Photos and reports from the scenes. All but one of the missing, Reanne, were college students.

'No contact with the families? No sightings?'

She looked up, the need to assess his facial expressions as he answered a force of habit. His full attention rested on the files for a time before settling on her. The weight of the public service position he held had scored lines at the corners of his eyes and mouth. Lines that hadn't been there ten years ago. Funny how those same sorts of lines just made her look old, but on him they lent an air of distinction.

He shook his head in response to her question.

'No credit card or cell phone trails?' she went on. 'No goodbye or suicide notes? No ransom demands?'

'Nothing.'

With a fluidity and ease that spoke of confidence as well as physical strength and fitness, he propped one hip on the edge of the table and studied her, those familiar blue eyes searching hers as blatantly as she had assessed his seconds ago. 'Sheriff Roy Griggs – you may remember him – and Chief Bruce Patterson in Tuscaloosa are doing all they can, but there's nowhere to go. The bureau won't budge on the issue of age of consent. All four of these girls are nineteen or older, and with the lack of evidence to indicate foul play there's nothing to investigate, in their opinion. File the report, add the photos to the various databases, and wait. That's what they can do.'

According to the law, the bureau was correct. Unless there was evidence of foul play or vulnerability to a crime, there was no action the bureau or any law enforcement agency could take. He knew this but his cop instincts or his emotions, she hadn't concluded which yet, wouldn't let it go at that. And she did remember Griggs. He had served as Jefferson County sheriff for the past three decades.

'But you think there's a connection that suggests this is not only criminal but perhaps serial.' This wasn't a question. He'd told her as much on the phone, but she needed to hear his conclusion again and to see what his face and eyes had to show about his words.

His call, just hearing his voice, had resurrected

memories and feelings she'd thought long dead and buried. They hadn't spoken since the summer after college graduation until ten years ago when they bumped into each other at the Publix in Hoover. Of all the grocery stores in the Birmingham area how they'd ended up at the same one on the first holiday she'd spent with her family in years still befuddled her. He had been newly divorced from his second wife. Jess had been celebrating a promotion. A volatile combination when merged with the holiday mania and the nostalgia of their explosive history. The last-minute dessert she had hoped to grab at the market before dinner with her sister's family had never made it to the table.

Jess hadn't heard from him since. Not that she could fault his after-frantic-sex lack of propriety; she'd made no attempt at contact either. There had been no random shopping ventures since on her rare visits to Birmingham.

'There has to be a connection.' He surveyed the happy, carefree faces in the photos again. 'Same age group. All attractive. Smart. No records, criminal or otherwise. Their entire futures – bright futures – ahead of them. And no one in their circle of family or friends saw a disappearing act coming.' He tapped the fourth girl's photo. 'I know Andrea Denton personally. There's no way she would just vanish like this. No way.'

Two things registered distinctly as he made this passionate declaration. One, he wasn't wearing a wedding band. Two, he didn't just know number four personally. He knew her intimately on some level.

'Someone took her,' he insisted. 'Someone took them all.' His expression softened a fraction. 'I know your profiling reputation. If anyone can help us find these girls, it's you.'

A genuine smile tugged at the frown Jess had been wearing most waking hours for days now. She had absolutely nothing to smile about but somehow the compliment coming from him roused the reaction. 'That might be a bit of a stretch, Chief.' Sitting here with him staring down at her so intently felt entirely too familiar . . . too personal. She stood, leveling the playing field. 'And even the best can't create something out of nothing and, unfortunately, that's exactly what you appear to have so far.'

'All I'm asking is that you try. These girls,' he gestured to the files, 'deserve whatever we can do.'

He'd get no argument from her there. 'You know the statistics.' If they had in fact been abducted, the chances of finding one or more alive at this stage were minimal at best. The only good thing she could see was that they didn't have a body. *Yet.*

'I do.' He dipped his head in a weary, somber move, emphasizing the grave tone of his voice.

Eventually she would learn the part he was leaving out. No one wanted to admit there was nothing to be done when anyone went missing, particularly a child or young adult. But this urgency and unwavering insistence that foul play was involved went beyond basic human compassion and the desire to get the job done. She could feel his anxiety and worry vibrating with escalating intensity.

'Will your counterparts cooperate?' Kicking a hornet's nest when it came to jurisdiction would compound her already complicated situation. That she could do without. Once the news hit the public domain, there would be trouble enough.

'They'll cooperate. You have my word.'

Jess had known Daniel Burnett her whole life. He believed there was more here than met the eye in these seemingly random disappearances. Unless emotion was somehow slanting his assessment, his instincts rarely missed the mark. More than twenty years ago he had known she was going to part ways with him well before she had recognized that unexpected path herself, and he had known she was his for the taking that cold, blustery evening in that damned Publix. She would lay odds on his instincts every time.

She just hadn't ever been able to count on him when it came to choosing her over his own personal and career goals. As ancient as that history was, the hole it left in her heart had never completely healed. Even knowing that hard truth, she held her breath, waiting for what came next.

'I need your help, Jess.'

Jess. The smooth, deep nuances of his voice whispered over her skin and just like that it was ten years ago all over again.

Only this time, she would make certain they didn't end up in bed together.

Obsession

Debra Webb

EVIL CAN HIDE

In the frantic race to catch a brutal and obsessive serial killer, Jess Harris broke the rules and lost everything. Her reputation in tatters, she has no choice but to return to Birmingham, Alabama, to the hometown and the past she ran away from long ago.

BEHIND MANY MASKS

Dan Burnett, Police Chief of Birmingham, is running out of options. Four young women are missing and, in desperation, he turns to his estranged first love, Special Agent Jess Harris, whose skill and experience offer a glimmer of hope.

DO YOU KNOW WHAT IT LOOKS LIKE?

As Jess and Dan race to find the women, a fifth disappears. And, for Jess, the search becomes all the more terrifying when she receives a startling personal message. Can Jess confront her past to save five futures? Or is it already too late?

Acclaim for Debra Webb:

'*Obsession* is her best work yet. This gritty, edge-of-your-seat, white-knuckle thriller is peopled with tough, credible characters and a brilliant plot that will keep you guessing until the very end. Move over Jack Reacher – Jess Harris is comin' to town' *New York Times* bestselling author Cindy Gerard

978 0 7553 9686 3

headline

THRILLINGLY GOOD BOOKS
FROM CRIMINALLY GOOD WRITERS

CRIMEFILES INTERNATIONAL
THRILLINGLY GOOD BOOKS

CRIME FILES INTERNATIONAL BRINGS YOU THE LATEST RELEASES FROM HEADLINE'S TOP CRIME AND THRILLER AUTHORS.

SIGN UP ONLINE FOR OUR MONTHLY NEWSLETTER AND BE THE FIRST TO KNOW ABOUT OUR COMPETITIONS, NEW BOOKS AND MORE.

VISIT OUR WEBSITE: WWW.CRIMEFILESINTERNATIONAL.COM
LIKE US ON FACEBOOK: FACEBOOK.COM/CRIMEFILESINTERNATIONAL